P9-DGI-360

Need

Carrie Jones

New York • Berlin • London

Published by Bloomsbury U.S.A. Children's Books
175 Fifth Avenue, New York, New York 10010

Library of Congress Cataloging-in-Publication Data
Jones, Carrie.
Need / Carrie Jones.—1st U.S. ed.
p. cm.
Summary: Depressed after the death of her stepfather,
high school junior Zara goes to live with her grandmother in a small Maine town,
where new friends tell Zara the strange man she keeps seeing may be a pixie king,
and that only "were" creatures can stop him from taking souls.
ISBN-13: 978-1-59990-338-5 • ISBN-10: 1-59990-338-5
[1. Grief—Fiction. 2. Supernatural—Fiction. 3. Pixies—Fiction. 4. Metamorphosis—
Fiction. 5. High schools—Fiction. 6. Schools—Fiction. 7. Maine—Fiction.] I. Title.
PZ7.J6817Nee 2010 [Fic]—dc22 2008022353

First U.S. Edition 2009
Book design by Nicole Gastonguay
Typeset by Westchester Book Composition
Printed in the U.S.A. by Quebecor World Fairfield
4 6 8 10 9 7 5 3

All papers used by Bloomsbury U.S.A. are natural, recyclable products
made from wood grown in well-managed forests. The manufacturing processes
conform to the environmental regulations of the country of origin.

To Doug Jones and Emily Ciciotte
and William Rice—yes, you, William—for
doing everything you could to help me succeed.
I need you all.

Need

Phobophobia
fear of phobias

Everybody has fears, right?

I'm into that.

I collect fears like other people collect stamps, which makes me sound like more of a freak than I actually am. But I'm into it. The fears thing. Phobias.

There are all the typical, common phobias. Lots of people are afraid of heights and elevators and spiders. Those are boring. I'm a fan of the good phobias. Stuff like nelophobia, the fear of glass. Or arachibutyrophobia, the fear that you will have peanut butter sticking to the roof of your mouth.

I do not have the fear of peanut butter, of course, but how cool is it that it's named?

It's a lot easier to understand things once you name them. It's the unknown that mostly freaks me out.

I don't know the name of that fear, but I know I've got it, the fear of the unknown.

Mnemophobia
fear of memories

Planes stink because you're stuck staring out at the sky and that makes you think about things—things you might not want to think about, I mean.

Mnemophobia is a real fear. I did not make it up. I swear. You can be afraid of your memories. There's no easy off button for your brain. It would be really, really nice if there were.

So I crush my fingers into my eyelids, trying to make myself stop remembering things. I focus on the present, the now. That's what talk-show people always tell you to do: live for today.

I wrapped a white thread around my finger when my dad died. I keep it there to remind me that I once felt stuff, once had a dad, a life. It's twisted so the knot is against my pinkie. I move it around just as the guy next to me crosses his legs and bumps my thigh with his monster-big shoe.

"Sorry," he says.

"It's okay." My fingers decide to put away all my Amnesty

International Urgent Action papers, which plead with me to write more letters on behalf of tortured monks, missing students.

"No offense, but you okay? You look a little like a zombie."

I manage to turn my head to look at him. He has a beefy nose, jowls, a corporate white man look. My mouth moves. "What?"

He smiles. Coffee breath leaks out of his mouth. "This whole flight you've been on autopilot; writing those letters, saving the world, but you're like a zombie."

Something inside of me tweaks. "My dad just died. My stepdad, really. I call him my dad. He was my dad. He raised me."

The man loses his hearty old-boy smile. "Oh. Sorry."

I feel badly for his awkwardness. "It's okay. I'm just . . ."

There are no words for it. Dead inside. Zombie-esque? That's not even a word. Zombified?

He keeps at me. "So, you going back to school or something? You go to school in Maine?"

I shake my head no, but I can't explain it all to him. I can't explain it all to myself. My mom sent me up here because for four months I haven't been able to smile. For four months I haven't been able to cry or feel or do anything.

"I'm going to my grandmother's to stay," I finally manage.

He nods, coughs, and says, "Oh. That's good. Bad time of year for Maine, though. Winter. Cold as hell."

My grandmother, stepgrandmother officially, is picking me up at the Bangor Airport in Maine, which is probably the smallest airport with the longest runway in the world. Our plane lands and I see sunless skies, which figures. You know things aren't going to be good when even the sky is gray and cold.

I eye my parka, but don't slug it on. It's like giving in too soon.

It's late October, right?

How bad can it be?

Bad.

Cold air rushes in as soon as the flight attendant opens the plane door. I shiver.

"Toto, we aren't in the tropics anymore," the guy next to me says. He hauls a parka out of his carry-on bag. He's a much smarter guy than I gave him credit for. My dad used to say that we should expect the best in people.

People say my dad's heart attacked him, but the truth is his heart failed him. It decided not to beat anymore, not to move the precious blood around in his veins. It seized up and failed.

He died on our kitchen floor next to a water bottle I dropped. That doesn't seem like it should be real, but it is.

Anyway, I slip on the stairs leading out of the plane and onto the tarmac. The man behind me (aka my seat mate) catches me by the arm.

"It's hard to save the world when you can't save yourself," he says, all smartass.

I stumble some more and a knot starts forming in my stomach.

"What?" I ask, even though I got what he said, I just can't believe he said it. It's so mean. He doesn't repeat it.

The wind gusts and my hair smashes against my cheek. I duck low, like it's going to protect me from the wind.

"Got to love Maine," the flight attendant at the bottom of the stairs says.

She's not smiling.

What I'm afraid of, right now, in this very moment, is being helpless as I watch my dad die of a heart attack on our kitchen floor.

But that has already happened, right?

So I will go with my second-biggest fear, fear of the cold. This is cheimaphobia, also known as cheimatophobia or frigophobia or psychophobia. There are lots of words for that one.

I'm not used to the cold. But I will be soon. You have to face your fears. That's what my dad always said. You just have to face them.

So, to face them, I chant them. Each slippery footstep on the tarmac heading to the terminal I whisper another one.

Cheimatophobia.

Frigophobia.

Psychophobia.

Cheimaphobia.

Why is it that naming the fear doesn't make it any better?

My grandmother, Betty, is waiting in the terminal. The moment she sees me, she strides over like a lumberjack and folds me into a big hug with those long arms of hers. She's built just like my dad and I kind of lean into her, happy to be with someone but at the same time wishing she were him.

"Well, aren't you a sight for sore eyes. Hard trip?" she asks, then steers me out into the parking lot and up into her huge black pickup truck. She stashes my suitcase and backpack in the back. We've already shipped up the rest of my Charleston stuff, not that all those T-shirts and camis are going to do me much good in Maine. She comes back around and smiles at me as I struggle to get inside the cab.

"This is a monster, Betty," I say, hauling myself in. I start shivering. I can't help it. All my bones feel broken from the cold. "Your truck is massive."

She smacks the dashboard and laughs. "You better believe it. All the better to haul butt in."

"Haul butt?"

"You want me to say ass? I don't want to affect your tender sensibilities."

Tender sensibilities? I almost laugh, but I can't quite do it. "Is it new?"

"Yep. Your mom see you off?" she asks.

"She cried." My finger runs along the edge of where the window meets the door and stops. "I felt awful when she cried."

I dare to look up into her eyes. They are light amber brown like my dad's. They tilt at the ends, by her temples, slanting up, just the tiniest of bits. They soften a little as I stare into them. Since I don't know my biological father, Grandma Betty is the only grandparent I have. My mom's parents died when she was a teenager. She actually lived here with Betty and her husband, Ben, and my dad, while she finished up high school. Betty was amazing, just taking her in like that, kind of like how she's taken me in.

Betty nods and turns on the car. "She would. It's hard on her, letting you go."

"Then she probably shouldn't have gotten rid of me."

"That's what you think she's doing?"

I shrug and put my hands back in my lap.

"She's just trying to keep you . . ."

"What? Sane?" I laugh but it's hard and bitter and it doesn't sound like something that should come out of me. It sort of echoes in my chest. "She's shoving me off to the land of zero population growth to keep me sane?"

"Little bitter there, sweetheart?"

"Yeah. I know. I'm sorry."

Betty smiles. "Bitter is better than nothing. From what your mom says you've been awful depressed, nothing like your normal stubborn, save-the-world self."

"He died, Betty."

"I know, sweetie. But he would want us to keep living. God, that's a cliché, but it's true."

Betty's pretty decent as far as grandmothers go. She used to head up a life insurance company, but then my grandfather died and she retired. She didn't have anything to do other than play golf or go fishing, so she decided to start some new ventures.

"I'm going to improve myself and then the community," she told my dad. So she started running, and trained until she could compete in the Boston Marathon at the age of sixty-five. That goal achieved, she got a black belt. Then, she decided to become an EMT. So that's what she does now. She's the head EMT for Downeast Ambulance in Bedford, Maine. She doesn't let them pay her, though.

"I have retirement money. I want them to give it to the young guys with families," she explained to my dad back when she first started riding ambulances. "It's only fair."

Grandma Betty is big on fair.

"I'm not sure how fair it is you being stuck with an old coot like me," she says as we drive down Route 1A toward Bedford.

I shrug because I don't want to talk about it.

Grandma Betty notices. "The leaves are beautiful, aren't they?"

That's her way of letting me not talk about it.

"They sure are," I say. We drive past all the trees turning colors. It is a last stand, I know. Soon they'll be naked and dead looking. They're beautiful, but they're barely hanging on to the branches. They'll plunge off soon. Lots already have. They'll rot on the ground, get raked up, burned, trampled on. It's not easy being a leaf in New England.

I shiver again.

"You know we're all just worried about you?"

I shrug; it's all I can bring myself to do.

Betty turns up the heat and it blasts in my face. She laughs. "You look like a model with the fan blowing your hair so you look suitably sexy."

"I wish," I mumble.

"You'll adjust to the cold."

"It's just so different from Charleston, so cold and bleak . . ." I put my head in my hands and then realize how melodramatic that is. "I'm sorry. I'm so whiny."

"You're allowed to whine."

"No, I'm not. I hate whining. I have nothing to whine about, especially not to you. It's just the land in Maine isn't half as lush or alive. It looks like the whole state is getting ready to be buried under snow for winter—a season of death. Even the grass looks likes it's given up."

She laughs and makes a creepy voice, "And the trees. They crowd in on you so that you can't see off in the distance and you can't see what is on the ground, hiding in the ferns or behind the tree trunks, in the bushes."

My hand presses against the cold glass window. I make a hand print.

"It's not a horror movie, Zara." She smiles at me so I know she's kind of sympathetic, but also teasing. This is how Betty is.

"I know."

"Maine is cold compared to Charleston, though. You're going to have to bundle up here."

"Yep."

Cheimaphobia.

"You still chanting phobias?"

"Did I say it out loud?"

"Yep." Her hand leaves the steering wheel and she pats my leg for a second before adjusting the heat again. "I've got a theory about that."

"You do?"

"Yeah, I think you are one of those people who believe that if you can name something, then you can overcome it, conquer it, which is what you're going to have to do about your dad dying. And I know that it hurts, Zara, but—"

"Betty!" There's a tall guy standing on the side of the road, not moving, just staring.

Betty jerks the truck across the double yellow line and then puts us back where we belong.

"Crap!" she yells. "Idiot!"

She's almost panting. My hands clutch my seat belt. She pulls in a couple big breaths and says, "Don't start talking like me or your mom will kill me."

I finally manage to speak. "You saw him?"

"Of course I did. Damn fool standing on the side of the road. It's a good thing I saw him too, or else I'd have run him over."

I stare at her, trying to figure it out. Then I look behind us, but we've gone around a curve, and even if the tall man was still there I wouldn't be able to see him anymore.

"You really saw him?" I ask.

"Of course I did. Why did you ask?"

"You'll think I'm stupid."

"Who says I don't already?" She laughs so I know she's joking.

"You are one mean grandmother."

"I know. So, why did you ask?"

She's not the type to give up, so I try to make it sound like no big deal. "I just keep thinking I see this same guy everywhere, this tall, dark-haired, pale guy. That couldn't be him, though."

"You saw this guy in Charleston?"

I nod. I wish my feet could touch the floor so I wouldn't feel so stupid and little.

She thinks for a split second. "And now you're seeing him here?"

"I know. It's silly and weird."

"It's not silly, honey, but it is most definitely weird." She honks at another truck heading the other way. "John Weaver. He builds houses. Volunteer firefighter, good guy. Zara, honey, I don't mean to scare you, but I want you to stay in the house at night, okay? No fooling around, no going out."

"What?"

"Just humor an old woman."

"Tell me why."

"A boy went missing last week. People are worried that something happened to him."

"He could've just run away."

"Maybe. Maybe not. That's not the whole reason, though. Look, my job is all about saving people, right? And I know you are used to training at night in Charleston, but there aren't that many streetlamps here. I don't want to be scraping my own granddaughter off the Beechland Road, got it?"

"Sure." I stare at the trees and then I start laughing because it's all so ridiculous. "I'm not running much anymore."

"You aren't doing anything much anymore is what I hear."

"Yeah." I pick at the string around my finger. It's part of a rug my dad bought. It used to be white but now it's sort of a dull gray.

I shudder. Grandma Betty and I toss back some tidbits for the rest of the ride, and I try to lecture her about the War on Terror's impact on worldwide human rights issues. My heart's not in it though, so most of the time we're pretty quiet.

I don't mind.

"Almost home," she says. "I bet you're tired."

"A little."

"You look tired. You're pale."

Betty's house is a big Cape with cedar shingles and a front porch. It looks cozy and warm, like a hidden burrow in the cold woods. I know from what my mom told me that there are three bedrooms upstairs and one down. The inside is made of wood and brick with a high ceiling in the kitchen, a woodstove in the living room.

The first thing Betty does when we pull into the driveway is wave her hand at the Subaru parked there.

My mouth drops open. I manage to say, "It still has the sticker in the window."

"It's brand new. The driving's tough in Maine. I wanted you to be safe. And I can't be driving you around everywhere like some sort of damn chauffeur."

"You swore."

"Like a fisherman. Better get used to it," She eyes me. "Like the car?"

I fling my arms around her and she chuckles, patting my back. "Not a big deal, sweetie. It's still in my name, you know. Nothing big."

"Yes, it is." I jump out of the truck and run over to the car, hugging the cold, snow-covered metal until my fingers freeze stiff and Betty hustles me inside.

"I don't deserve this," I say.

"Of course you do."

"No, I don't."

"Don't make me swear at you. Just say thank you and be done with it."

"Thank you and be done with it."

She snorts. "Punk."

"I just . . . I love it, Betty." I throw my arms around her again. The car is the first good thing that's happened in Maine. It is the first good thing that has happened in a long time.

Of course, people in third world countries have to save their entire lives for a car, and here is mine, right there in the driveway, waiting for me. My head whirls.

"I don't deserve this, Betty," I say again, once we're back in her cozy living room. She bends over and starts up a fire in the woodstove, crumpling up paper, stacking kindling.

"Enough with that sort of talk, Zara," she says. Her back cracks when she stands up. It reminds me that she's old. It's hard to remember that. "You deserve lots of things."

"But there are people starving in the world. People who don't have homes. People who—"

She holds up a finger. "You're right. I'm not going to say you aren't right, but just because they go without doesn't mean you have to go without too."

"But . . ."

"And it doesn't mean you can't use what you have to make other people's lives better." She pulls off her hat and runs her hands through her crazy-curly, grayish/orangish hair. "How are you going to do any volunteer work without a car? Or get to school? Huh?"

I shrug.

" 'Cause I'm a busy woman, Zara," she continues. "Although I've changed my schedule so I'm not going on any night calls. We'll have dinner together, be all domestic." She smiles a little and her voice softens. "You're just like him."

She means my dad. My throat closes up but I manage to whisper, "How?"

"Always trying to save the world. Always worried that you have too much when other people have too little," she says. "And always trying to get out of going to school."

She stomps over and gives me a quick hug, followed by a smack on the butt. She's so football coach sometimes.

I call my mom even though I don't really want to.

"I'm here," I say.

"Oh, sweetie. I'm glad you made it safe. How is it?"

"Cold."

"Sounds just like the Maine I remember." She laughs and then pauses. I listen to silence and then she asks, "You still mad at me?"

"Yep."

"It's for your own good."

"Right. Did you know a boy up here went missing last week?"

"What? Put your grandmother on the phone, okay? Zara . . . I love you."

I point at Betty. "She wants to talk to you."

Then I say into the phone. "Love you too."

Betty grabs it from me, covers it with her hand, and says, "Now, go on up to your room and get settled in. It's the second door on the left. You have to get that car registered tomorrow at town hall. And start school. First thing. No sulking around the house."

I nod and trot up toward my bedroom. Pausing on the stairs, I just make out Betty's hushed voice saying, "She sure doesn't look like herself. You were right."

She plods across the room and stares at me eavesdropping. "Are you listening to my conversation with your mother?"

My throat closes up. I manage to nod.

"Up to bed, missy!"

I run up the rest of the stairs and head into my bedroom. With its lace curtains and cozy quilt-covered bed my bedroom doesn't seem so bad either. The walls are pale and not wood. Boxes of my clothes hunker against the wall. I yank off my jeans and hoodie and grab the bathrobe hanging from the back hook of the door. There's a *Z* embroidered into the puffy baby blue cloth. I wrap it around me and for a second I feel almost happy. The warm shower to get off all that airport grime feels amazing, even if there are rubber ducky decals all over the tiles. I towel off and head back to my room. Grandma Betty lets me settle in by myself. I even put up my Amnesty International poster. It's a candle with barbed wire around it, the symbol of the organization. I stare at the flame on it and feel almost—but not quite—cozy. I'm pulling out my International Rights reports when she sticks her head in my bedroom doorway.

"You settling in okay?"

"Yeah. Thanks for having me." I leave the reports in a pile, stand up, and smile at her.

She smiles back and closes one of the shades. "I'm honored to spend time with my only granddaughter."

I walk away to the other window to close the shade, but I want to look out first. I have to wipe away the cold to see out. It's just trees and darkness, darkness and trees. I pull the shade down. "I really don't want to go to school tomorrow."

She comes and stands next to me. "Of course you don't."

"I don't really want to do much of anything."

"I know, but it'll get better." She bumps her hip into me and then drapes an arm around my shoulders, giving me a sideways hug. "You could always pray for a snow day."

I hug her back. "That is an excellent idea. Maybe I could do the snow dance."

She laughs. "Your dad taught you that?"

"Yep. You drop an ice cube into the toilet and dance around chanting 'Snow. Snow. Snow.' "

"Until it melts. That son of mine. I sure do miss him." She settles against me for a second, pats her strong hands on my back. "But I'm glad you're here to keep me company, selfish or not. Now, no worries. You'll be okay, Zara. I'll make sure of that."

"I just don't know if I'm up for the whole school thing." I pull away, cross my arms over my chest.

She kisses the top of my head. "You will be just fine, princess. And if anyone gives you any crap, I'll go jack 'em for you, okay?"

The thought of my ancient life-saving grandmother pummeling someone makes me laugh, even though I know I shouldn't laugh at violence.

"I mean it, Zara. Anyone hassles you, you let me know. Anything scares you or bothers you, you tell me. That's my grandmotherly duty. You let me do it. Okay?"

Outside, the snow keeps trucking down. Shivering, I look up

into her eyes, amber like a wild cat's. The pupils seem to expand a little because she means it. She really means it.

I grab her hand. "Okay."

The howling wakes me up in the middle of the night.

It is a long noise, full of grief.

I shudder and sit up in bed.

Something outside howls again. It's not too far away.

Coyotes?

There's a series of excited yips and another howl. I remember this movie we watched in wildlife biology class about how coyotes act when they have a kill. This sounds sort of like that, but not exactly like coyotes, deeper maybe, like big dogs or wolves.

I pad over to my window, move the curtains back, and look out. Whiteness covers the lawn and my car. The moon glistens off it, making the snow seem as if it's made of crystals or diamonds, gleaming, shining. It's beautiful.

I breathe out. Have I been holding my breath? Why would I hold my breath?

Because I'm thinking of my dad.

My dad grew up here. And he'll never see this snow or this house or the forest or me again. He's locked away from it, locked away from me, from life, a prisoner. I would do anything to set him free.

My hand presses against the cold window frame. Something moves at the edge of the woods, just a shadow really, a darkness that seemed a little darker than the tree trunks and limbs.

I tilt my head and squint. Nothing.

Then it comes, the feeling. Imaginary spiders scurry against my skin.

My hand leaves the window. The curtain swings closed. I tiptoe back to bed, closing the distance between window and bed as quickly as I can without actually running.

"It's nothing."

That's what stinks about lying. It's hard to do it to yourself and actually believe it. It's much better to just chant your phobias, face the truth, and be on your way, but I can't do that. Not yet.

Didaskaleinophobia

fear of going to school

The best thing about crying is that it always knocks me out. I slept really well last night, even with the stupid dogs howling around midnight or so. It's a good thing I'm not cynophobic because I would have freaked all night.

It's quiet now.

The snow muffles the outside world and when my alarm goes off there is no way I want to get up and face it. Grandma Betty's house is just too safe and cozy, especially my bed. Still, I haul my tired butt up to look out the window. Snow covers everything and it's . . . what? The middle of October.

"This is just wrong," I announce and pull the lace curtains all the way open. The strange white light that snow reflects drifts into my room.

It's breakfast and I'm by my lonesome. Grandma Betty left me a huge note in the middle of the table, right by a water mark that looks just like South Carolina. I swallow and touch where Charleston would be. Then I check out the note:

Zara . . . I'm off to the station. A logging truck jackknifed on Route 9. Minor injuries. There is still school. You didn't pray hard enough. Better luck next time. Ha-ha. All juniors have PE so make sure you bring clothes. Drive careful. It's slippery out. Here's a map. It's a pretty straight shot. Do not drive after dark. I'll be home by nightfall. Knock them dead. The keys are right here.

→

She drew an arrow pointing at the keys, next to the note on the table, like I'd miss them.

I scoop them up and dangle them in the air. One catches at the string around my finger. It's getting loose.

The disaster that is my morning begins when I dash down the front steps and skid into the tree. A thin layer of ice is hiding beneath the snow. I don't see it. I wobble and skid, windmilling my arms until I run right into a big pine tree. I hard-hug it to keep from smashing my face into the bark.

"Damn."

Slowly, carefully I edge away. If you don't pick up your feet, you can sort of glide across it like ice skaters do; of course, it's hard to do that in heels.

"One foot in front of the other," I tell myself. "One foot in front of . . . Ack!"

Another wobble, another arm windmill, and I lunge toward the car, slamming my hands down on the hood. I puff out my breath. It makes a cloud in the air. My pretty shoes I'd bought in Charleston? Totally covered with snow. Near my footprints are work-boot prints and tiny specks of gold glitter, like the kind you use in an art project in first grade. Betty must have checked out the car at some point last night. That's right; the sticker on the side is peeled off.

I stop thinking for a second because it's not the boot prints that are interesting.

Not at all.

Near Betty's footprints are huge dog prints. I mean, I think they're dog prints. Cats don't get that big. I tilt my head. I didn't know she had a dog. Maybe that's what I heard howling at midnight. Maybe that's what I saw at the edge of the woods. Or maybe it was some big Cujo rabid dog thing, waiting to pounce on me, with its red, red eyes and shiny jowls, and its monster evil teeth. Total cynophobia.

I smack my hand against my head to stop myself.

"I've been reading too much Stephen King."

But the truth is that I haven't read those Maine horror stories since seventh grade, when my dad forbade me.

What had he said?

"Love Stephen, but he gives Maine a bad rap."

Thinking about my dad makes every breath I take seem like a gulp. I yank my purse up on my shoulder and clamber inside my car. Grandma Betty also left a note on the dashboard.

Turn on defrost. That's the button with the squiggly lines.

I find the button, but my shaking fingers have a hard time turning it on. Cold air cranks out full blast. It's like being kissed by the Abominable Snowman or a Stephen King horror monster from hell that sucks out your soul. Or is that from the Harry Potter books? I don't remember.

The air smashes against my lips. I swear I can feel them chapping.

"Great."

It takes five minutes for the windshields to clear. I use that time to slide back into the house and get my hat, keeping an eye out for rabid dogs. Then I get back in the car, pull out of the driveway, and learn something else about ice. It isn't easy to drive on. You can't go above thirty if you don't want to fishtail into the other lane.

Ice stinks.

By the time I get to school, my knuckles are white from fear *and* frostbite and my heart's beating a million thumps a minute, so I'm not too happy when some jerk in a beautiful red MINI Cooper cuts me off and speeds into the parking lot in front of me. He has chains on his tires. They don't spin. I love MINIs.

"Hey!" I yell as my brakes lock up again.

I inch into a parking space, rest my head on the steering wheel, and let myself exhale. I'd like to pummel that guy in the MINI, which is not a very nonviolent thought. But instead I will be peaceful and good and make my dad proud. I touch the string on my finger, loose, frayed, still there.

"I will not be violent," I chant-mutter. "I will not be violent. I am peaceful and good. I am peaceful and good. I do not want to give anyone the finger."

I switch off the car, thrust myself out the door, and wait.

The MINI Cooper guy jumps out of the car with the grace that only really good jocks have and lands on an ice patch without slipping at all. He has boots on. God, the guys up here wear boots; tan, I'm-a-carpenter boots. It's like I've completely abandoned civilization.

He slams the door, turns around, and finally notices that I exist. How kind of him.

My heart stops. It starts again, but it beats a lot harder when I meet his eyes. I'm frozen there and he strides across the ice like he's moving across gravel or grass. He doesn't slip once. Each step he takes brings him closer to me, and he only stops when I make out the deep brown irises around his pupils, the tiny bit of stubble on his cheeks and chin (not too much but enough that you know he has to shave a lot). I can actually smell the musk of him. He's so close it's like he's invading my territory—no, my personal space. I take a step backward and slip. His hand reaches out and grabs my elbow, balancing me.

"Be careful. It's wicked slippery here," he says, a smile leaking across his face.

I would smile back, but I'm too busy feeling all wiggly inside. I tough up my voice. "Oh. Yeah."

His thick chestnut hair lifts with the wind. He sniffs the air. "You sure you're okay?"

"Yeah." I pull my elbow away but I don't want to. I want his hand to stay there steadying me for hours, basically.

This guy is huge, just super tall, and well muscled, but not professional television wrestler muscles, just a lot of nice long ones. I can tell just from his hands and his neck. I don't know how he fits in the MINI.

He flashes another smile at me. "You're new. Zara, right?"

I grab the hood of the Subaru. "How'd you know that?"

"I know Betty. Your grandmother."

"You know Betty?" I let go of the hood, try to take some steps toward the school, and slip.

"She taught a wilderness first-responder class. She's great." He grabs my arm. "I can't believe she didn't make you wear boots."

"She'd already left."

"You should wear boots."

He walks slowly even though we can hear the bell ringing.

"You don't have to help me," I say. "It's okay. You're going to be late."

"I'm not going to let you fall."

I swallow and look up at him. "Thanks."

He holds open the door. "Any time."

The school is a much happier place than I expected. The hallways smell like pancake syrup and they are bright and filled with student artwork, a total contrast to the outside world, where everything is stark, white and gray, sort of magical. Walking into the school makes me feel like I've entered the real world again. They even have a diversity mural, just like at my school, only in my school it was in the library.

"Thank God," I mutter, and stomp the storm off my shoes, hoping that maybe my toes will warm up to twenty degrees soon. They might fall off, one toe at a time, just leave me until I'm deformed and hobbling. That's happened before.

Not to me, obviously.

"The office is that way," he says, pointing to a room on the right separated by a big window. "You going to be okay?"

"Yeah. Thanks."

He nods and gives a little half smile and waves before he walks away. He strides, really. He's beautiful, even from the back.

I shake my head to stop staring, bustle off to the school's front office, and push open the door. It's a lot lighter than I expect. It slams into the wall with a big thud. My cheeks get all hot and I say, "Sorry."

The good-looking pale girl doing the announcements gives me one of those "Who the hell are you?" looks.

I smile at her and try to channel total sweetness while I say it again. "Sorry."

It doesn't work. She flings her long strawberry blond hair behind her shoulder and lifts her lip in a little snarl. I raise my eyebrows in some sort of movie move. Touché.

My apology works on the school secretary, though. She perks right up and bustles over to the counter. She reminds me of Mrs. Santa Claus, only without the red jumpsuit and the sugar cookies.

"Oh! You must be Zara White! Betty's granddaughter." She pushes her long, thinning hair behind her ears like a little girl. "You look so much like your mother. It's really remarkable. I would have known you anywhere. It's like twins . . . only different hair. You must have your father's hair."

She takes a breath in the middle of her gushing and I take advantage.

I nod, all awkward. "Yep, that's me. Hi. I need to register for classes. Sorry if that makes extra work for you."

Evil Announcement Girl huffs and her nose actually twitches but the secretary smiles and says, "How sweet. She's sorry. Your mother raised you well. I'm so sorry about your stepfather, dear."

A gulp sticks in my throat but the word manages to get out. "Thanks."

"I knew them, you know, your parents . . ."

The secretary pulls off her glasses and squints at me with smiling pity eyes, then she pulls the edge of her shirt sleeves down closer to her wrists and hauls out a folder, plopping it on the counter. Evil Announcement Girl rolls her eyes and turns her back. The secretary lady doesn't even notice. She yanks out a class schedule. "Here you go, sweetie. All your classes. I'm Mrs. Nix."

I take the computer printout with my shaking hand. The whole paper shakes with it. God.

"It'll be okay, dear. First day's the hardest!" She turns to Evil Announcement Girl. "Megan, you want to show Zara to her first class?"

Megan. What an absolutely perfect name for Evil Announcement Girl. Megans always hate me.

This Megan isn't about to break my record.

She turns and glares at me. "I have announcements."

Mrs. Nix smacks her head. "Oh, that's right."

She calls behind her shoulder. "Ian. How about you bring Zara to her homeroom?"

Megan smirks and points at my jeans. "Nice peace signs, hippie freak."

I smile at her and mutter in my head, "Nice shoes made by child slaves in Asia, materialistic Barbie."

After she turns her back on me, I cover my mouth to make sure I don't actually say my come-back out loud. Mrs. Nix bounces on her heels, watching for Ian.

"Here he is," she sings. "Show Zara to her class, dear?"

The boy in the back of the office unfolds his long legs from behind a computer and smiles at me appraisingly. "Sure thing."

He saunters over and stands so close that I have to crane my neck to look up at his long, pale face crowned with out-of-control reddish blond waves. Are all the boys in this town tall? My stepdad wasn't that tall, although I'd always thought he was, especially compared to me.

"Pullman. Easy. Mine too." Ian slings a pack behind his shoulder, smiles at me, and grabs my paper. "You have her locker number, Mrs. Nix?"

Mrs. Nix smacks herself in the head again. If she keeps that up, she'll bruise. "Sure, right here. How could I forget?"

She shakes her head at herself and smiles at me. "Sorry. Age."

"It's okay," I say. "Thanks."

I shoot a look at Megan, amazed by how much she hates me already, and scurry out of the office with the loping Ian picking up speed ahead of me. He notices and slows down.

"Sorry." He blushes. "Long legs."

I smirk. He blushes harder and starts stumbling over his words. "I didn't mean that you were short or anything. I just meant that my legs are . . . well . . . they're long, you know, and . . ."

I touch his arm. "It's okay."

"Really?"

He smiles at me, one of those little boy smiles, like he's just been offered a chocolate chip cookie even though he spilled coffee grounds all over the Persian carpet.

"Really." I take in a deep breath. "You a runner?"

"You could say that." He grabs my elbow. "I won All-State in the 1600 last spring and I was All–New England in the—"

"Bragging competition," someone grumbles as they bump me, jolting me away from Ian, whose hand tightens on my elbow in a way that is way too protective to be normal. MINI Cooper guy waves and says, "Excuse me."

I stare after massive MINI Cooper guy. His shoulders are huge inside his sweater, not that I'm looking or anything. And the sweater looks cashmere, which is pretty hoity-toity for Maine. They must have Big and Tall stores around here, or maybe he ordered it off the Net.

Ian makes a little growling noise. I pretend like I don't hear it but I touch his arm again, trying to calm him down.

"Who is that?"

He shudders and leans down so I can hear him. "That is Nick Colt, otherwise known as bad news."

I laugh. "Otherwise known as bad news?"

"What?" Ian's big eyes turn sad in his banana-long face.

"It's just everyone around here sounds like they're fifty years old: *otherwise known as bad news*."

He puts his hand on my shoulder and steers me through the hall. "Don't people say that where you're from?"

"In Charleston?" I've come across a lot of interesting ways of speaking while traveling with my parents outside the U.S., but Maine still *is* in the United States, last time I checked.

"You're from Charleston." He nods. "No wonder."

"No wonder what?"

He stops outside a door. "Nothing."

"No, really." I hope he doesn't think I'm a hick or a bigot, which is what some people think about anyone who lives south of New York City.

"You just seem different."

"Hollow?"

"What?"

I drag my feet for a second, horrified that I said that out loud. "Nothing. Sorry."

He doesn't seem phased. "So if you need any info about anything, just ask me. I'm on cross-country and basketball, and I'm in key club and I'm the junior class president, and some other clubs too, so if you want to join anything, just let me know. I'll get you in like that." He snaps his fingers. "Sorry. Corny."

"No. It's . . . good. You're a little bit of an overachiever, huh?"

"There's no point in blending in, you know? Got to grab the power where you can." He shakes his head at himself. "That sounds awful. I just mean . . . you've got to do what you can to get ahead, to get into college, that stuff. Well, we're here."

He gives a little lopsided grin as we face a classroom doorway. Beyond it people are shuffling their stuff around, cramming themselves into seats, gossiping about all sorts of things I don't understand. They all have Gap clothes and that sort of almost-designer, mall-casual look, except all the guys wear work boots. There are a few guys wearing flannel and black sweatshirts. And here I am in my holey jeans with peace signs. I take a deep breath. I have no chance of fitting in, transferring in the middle of junior year. It's hopeless.

The ache inside me grows and grows.

Auroraphobia, Northern Lights creep you out.

Autodysomophobia, you are afraid of someone who smells vile.

Automatonophobia, ventriloquist's dummies terrify you.

Automysophobia, being dirty is the end of the world.

Autophobia, you are afraid of yourself.

. . .

The evil Megan girl is not in my homeroom, but she is in my Spanish class. Ian drops me off at the door there too and she eyes us suspiciously. I swear, if she were a cat she'd be hissing.

"It really wouldn't be a big deal for me to come and walk you to your advanced chemistry class," Ian says for the fourth time. "I mean, I don't want you to get lost or anything."

"Okay. Yeah. Thanks. Who *is* that girl?" I nod at Megan.

"Oh, Megan Crowley."

I stand up on my tiptoes and whisper, "I think she hates me."

He laughs and nods while I go back to my flat feet. "Probably."

I wait for more. He just kneads at the top of his shoulder and yells hi to some guy in a soccer shirt who yells hi back to him.

My hands find their way to my hips. "Are you going to tell me why she hates me?"

His attention turns to me. His eyes flash. "Probably doesn't like the way you smell."

"What?" I step back. I thought he was nice, not slap worthy. Not like I go around slapping people, but whatever.

He raises his hands. "Just kidding. Just kidding. You're the competition. Megan hates competition. She has a thing for Nick Colt. She saw you come into school with him. End of story, beginning of competition."

"Right, like *I'm* competition. Mini me." I walk into Spanish class, where Megan whispers snide things as Mrs. Provost, the teacher, introduces me to everyone and finds me a place to sit. The girl next to Megan giggles behind her hand and looks at me. Great.

The last thing I'm paying attention to is Mrs. Provost, who is saying, "Zara, what an unusual name."

She glances at my ripped-up jeans with the peace signs and her eyes shift into another thought. "Nice to have you here. Class, let's begin. All in Spanish."

I stare out the window, zone out, and wish more than anything that I'm back home with my dad and he's alive and my mom's all happy and we're eating eggplant smothered with mozzarella cheese and everything is normal again. But it can't ever be normal again.

Outside, a birch tree bends from the weight of the snow. It'll spring back up once the snow melts, back to its normal, upright self.

Could that happen to me?

The answer is a big fat no.

Megan Crowley turns all the way around in her seat to stare at me. Something evil flashes in her eyes and for a second I think she's not real, not human. She lifts a perfectly manicured fingernail at me and mouths, "I am onto you."

¿Qué? No entiendo.

"What?" I mouth back.

She does it again. "I am onto you."

Mrs. Provost sweeps between us. "Girls, I am so happy that Zara is making friends, but now is not social time. Now is Spanish time. Zara? Why don't you tell us about Charleston?"

"Um . . ." I look around for help. It's just a bunch of pale people staring at me. God, how can Maine be so white? "Um, Charleston is really beautiful and warm. There are these antebellum houses and—"

"In Spanish, *por favor*," Mrs. Provost interrupts. She pulls at her bra strap and lifts it farther up her shoulder.

She wants me to talk about antebellum houses in Spanish?

I hate this place. Megan laughs behind her hand and turns back around. I shiver. It is so cold here.

"Charleston *es caliente y hermosa*," I start again. "*A mi me gusta allí.*"

A thin girl with wild brownish hair waves at me as we leave class. An orange Hello Kitty T-shirt bags off her shoulders. Her nose twitches like a bunny's and she hops up and down to get me to look at her.

"Hey." She waves again, this massive kind of wave, like when you're trying to hail a taxi on a busy street. But this is a hallway, not a street, and it's nowhere near busy.

"Hi."

I put my oh-so-exciting, brand-new Spanish textbook into my pack. Then I snap it shut. In passing I notice that one of the snaps is missing.

"I like your pack. Did you get it at an army-navy store?" She bounces on her toes when she talks like she has way too much energy for her body and just has to do something with it.

"Yep."

"In Bangor?"

"No, Charleston."

She smiles super wide. "Are you Zara White?"

I step back, swinging my pack over one shoulder. "How does everybody know that?"

"Small town." She smiles an apology. "News travels fast. We get all excited when someone new comes. I'm Issie."

"Oh, so you knew I didn't get my bag in Bangor."

"Sort of." She pushes her teeth together and smiles big. She makes big eyes to go with it and then blurts, "I love Bangor, though, so I was hoping. 'Cause I love your bag too. Oh, I am babbling. I hate when I babble. Devyn says it's cute, but I know it's not, it's super annoying. So, is your name really Zara?"

I try to calm my nerves and be friendly. I smile back. "It's really Zara."

"Like Sara but with a *Z*. That is much cooler." She bee-bops her head up and down. "Cool. Cool. Cool. Good to meet you. Where you going next?"

"PE." I smile again. I like PE in Charleston. It's always outside. There are no books involved. You don't have to talk to anyone except to try to annoy them. You can blend in.

She bounces up and down on the back of her feet. Her skirt flits around her legs. It's super long and flowy, like her hair. "Cool. That's in the gym. Of course PE is in the gym. Duh?"

She bonks her forehead with her hand so hard I want to get her an ice pack, but she seems fine and she bounces out, "I'm going there too. I'll show you."

"Oh." I stop in the hall and look around for Ian. I don't see him. I'm not sure if this is a good thing or a bad thing. Suddenly, I feel sort of abandoned.

"Are you looking for Ian?"

I shrug. "Um . . . yeah. I guess so. He's showing me around."

She has been beaming at me but now she frowns.

"What?" I ask.

"He must like you. I'll tell him I've got you from here. He's very overachieving. He'll be your escort all year if you let him." She grabs her phone and sends him a text telling him that she'll take me to PE. "There. All set."

She is efficient, this girl, and I like that. She links her arm in mine and says conspiratorially, "It's hard being new. I was new once too."

"Really? When did you move here?"

"First grade."

I smirk at her and she laughs. "It was still hard. I still remember it. Totally uncool. Everybody looking at me, sniffing me out, because I was the new girl, trying to decide if I was worthy to be in their pack or not. It was awful. Nobody played with me at recess for an entire month. Swinging by yourself is not cool, not every day. Not when everyone else is playing tetherball or tag."

She sounds so sad; I pull her closer to my side. I want to take care of her. "It was a long time ago."

She shrugs and smiles at me. "Yeah. And it didn't last forever, right? But I remember how hard it was."

She lowers her voice to a whisper as we walk by Megan Crowley and her little posse of girls trying to look hip in the high school hallway, which is a ridiculous thing to even try to do, because it *is* a high school hallway. "Megan Crowley hated me too."

"Is it that obvious?" I ask.

Issie nods. "She hates everyone she thinks is a threat."

"Why am I a threat?"

She pulls her arm away from mine and uses it to bash me with her notebook. "Don't even play that game with me."

She giggles again, and pulls open the door to the locker room. I smell baby powder and stinky running shoes and I smile. It smells so familiar. If I close my eyes, I think I could almost pretend I'm home.

But I'm not.

"That Megan girl," I whisper because Megan's flounced into the locker room with her posse, "do you think she's kind of weird?"

"What do you mean?"

"I don't know . . ." I remember the way she didn't seem real for a second. "It's silly. It's nothing."

"Nothing is ever nothing," Issie says, and then she staggers backward. "Oh my God!"

"What? Issie, what is it?" I look around for a spider on the floor or something. Maybe Issie has a spider phobia. Those are pretty common.

Issie turns panicked eyes on me, swallows, and then gushes out her words like they have a life of their own. "We're running today. They're testing our mile. Oh God, this is so uncool. This is yabba-dabba bad."

I almost jump in midair and hug her. "The mile! Great."

"Great? Running a mile? You *are* crazy." She opens a locker and pulls out gym clothes. "Maybe you'll fit in here after all."

I yank my old, gray U2 War concert shirt on. It is excellent to run the mile in, all soft and faded. My dad got it at a concert back in the eighties. "You don't want me to fit in?"

"It's nice to have someone different," she says, gesturing toward Megan's gaggling crew putting on their spaghetti-strap camis. "Someone not like them, you know?"

Megan hoists her hair up into a new ponytail for PE. She adjusts her perfect breasts beneath her perfect cami and gives me a perfect glare.

"I'm not like them, Issie," I say, sticking my finger through a hole at the bottom hem of my T-shirt.

"Cool."

"I just like running."

She hauls on a Snoopy shirt, baby blue and cute. "Why? Why would you like running?"

"It makes me feel safe," I tell her as we tie our shoes. I do not tell her that it makes me feel closer to my dad.

As I stretch, Coach Walsh, the gym teacher, nods and takes my name, then blows the whistle and we all take off around the track for a warm-up lap.

"Bedford's the only high school in northern Maine with an indoor track," he boasts to me once I'm back. "The whole community rallied behind this. Fund-raising and everything."

"Right. That's cool." I stretch out. Again. No one else is even stretching out, except Issie and she's almost falling over every time she bends down and reaches for her toes. It's funny to see someone so cute be so uncoordinated. She has the same color hair as my dad.

Megan scowls at me and I get that feeling, the squiggly feeling. I push my fingers into my eyes.

The gym teacher grabs me by the elbow and barks at me, "You okay? You have low blood pressure or something?"

I run a hand through my hair. Issie stops stretching and stares at me. Everyone seems to be staring at me.

I feel a little ophthalmophobic, which is a very normal phobia, where people are afraid of being stared at.

"Yeah, I'm good," I lie.

Coach Walsh trains steely eyes on me and lets go of my elbow. "Okay, line up then."

We all line up except for this guy in a wheelchair, Devyn. He smiles at me when I line up, introduces himself. He has a movie star smile, just white teeth and charisma, big eyes, dark skin. He'd be perfect looking if he didn't have such a large nose, but the truth is it looks good on him, natural and powerful. He winks at Issie, who blushes.

"You can do it, Is," he says.

She rolls her eyes, twists her lip, and says, "As long as I don't pass out."

"If you pass out, I'll put you in my lap and wheel you across the finish line," he says, and it somehow isn't sleazy because you can tell by his eyes how much he cares about Issie. I instantly like him.

She blushes worse. Her face looks like she's already sprinted a mile.

I bounce on my feet, crazy happy for a chance to run, even if it *is* inside, even if the perfect, plastic, Megan Crowley *is* there, glaring at me. Ian stands next to her with a half smile on his face.

"Think you're a runner or something?" She flips her hair down and then back into a ponytail, which again accentuates her perfect cheekbones. "Nice shirt."

I shrug.

Ian wiggles his eyebrows. "She looks like a runner to me."

His words don't seem real. They seem flat, like he's playing at flirting with me. This is probably a continuing side effect of my dad's death: the feeling that nothing is real. I touch the thread on my finger.

Megan arches a perfect eyebrow. "Maybe she ran in whatever little southern hole she crawled out of, but not up here. We're a different breed of runner up here. Plus, how can anyone possibly run on such short little legs?"

"Don't be mean, Megan," Issie says. "It's so much cooler to be nice."

Megan lashes at her. "Like you know what it is to be cool."

My hands close into fists and I try to think of something to say but all my words seem to be stuck somewhere near my heart. Then another voice comes from behind us, a low growl type of voice, full of deepness. I recognize it right away and the little hairs on my arm arch up into the air.

"Issie's beyond cool," Nick Colt says. He puts a hand on Issie's shoulder. She smiles at him. She's friends with the MINI Cooper guy? Are they dating? Please, God. Do not let them be dating.

He turns to perfect Megan. "You worried, Megan? Think she could be faster than you?"

Nick Colt smiles at her, but there's no warmth in it and it makes me shudder. It's the smile of a predator. Okay, it's the smile of a really incredible-looking predator with a really nice jaw line. I shake my head to get that image out of it. No, he has the smile of a bad driver, someone who makes my body scream, "Danger! Stay away!"

Wow. I am such a liar.

He has the smile of gorgeous. He taunts her a little bit. "She might be faster . . ."

"Yeah, right." Megan arches down to touch her toes. She moves like a cat, graceful, like she's thought about how each muscle will look as she moves. "Like *she'd* worry *me*."

Something like anger rises up from the pit inside me, dark and haughty. I am so not used to feeling that way. I'm not used to feeling anything except numb, but this Megan girl, she just does something to me. The air in the gym cools down, getting fierce, like it's waiting for something to happen, like a fight. I am *really* not about to let something happen. I am *not* about to make the world more full of hate.

My dad used to quote Booker T. Washington to me, along with some other cool people. But it is the Booker T. quote that sticks in my mind right now. Booker T. once said, "I will permit no man to narrow and degrade my soul by making me hate him."

I fake smile, pretend I am a white-girl Booker T., and say in as nice a voice as I can manage, "I'm not trying to worry you, Megan."

She turns her face toward me, her eyes fierce and focused. "Good. You don't."

Issie grabs my elbow and gives me worried eyes. Megan pretends we suddenly don't exist and moves closer to a group of blond girls, the class cutie brigade, I figure. Nick and Ian eye each other, like dogs squaring off, measuring each other up. Ian looks away first, bending to tighten his laces.

Nick smiles at me, a much nicer smile. A real smile? "You've already made friends."

"Good one," I say, shifting my weight between my feet. "Ha-ha. Funny."

Issie perks up and locks her arm in mine. "That's right, Nick. Zara's doing fine. I'm her friend."

He nods. This time his smile seems even warmer, even more real. "Good, Issie. I should have known."

"Known what?" I ask, but nobody answers me. So I try a new tactic and whisper to Is, "Are you dating him?"

Her head jerks up. "Devyn?"

"No. Nick."

She starts laughing. "Nope. No interest there at all."

Devyn lifts his head to stare into Nick's face. He drums his fingers against the armrests of the wheelchair. "You find out anything?"

Nick shakes his head.

The coach comes to the starting line and gives Devyn a

stopwatch and clipboard. "You guys ready? This is serious stuff here. Run all-out. Do your best."

Nick leans toward me and whispers. His breath is warm against the side of my face. "He has a bet with all the other PE teachers in the county. If we don't have the best average time, he has to buy everyone strudel."

"Strudel?"

Nick raises his hands in the air. "I have no idea."

"The PE teachers are into strudel," Issie says. "I'm not sure why. It's so gooey."

"Gooey is good," Nick says.

"Seriously?" I ask him. "You like strudel."

"I like a lot of things that aren't good for me." He smiles slowly at me. My mouth must be hanging open because he starts laughing.

"You made her blush!" Issie says. "Don't blush, Zara. He's just teasing."

Coach Walsh blows the whistle and we take off. A lot of the girls just jog, but Megan Crowley bolts, and I dash after her, hating how cute and long her legs look as she runs with a perfect stride, her feet swinging low and quick. Does Nick notice how perfect she is? Why do I even care? Megan turns her head and flashes a smile at me. It is not a friendly smile. What is wrong with that girl? What is wrong with me?

"Go get her," Issie huffs out. Her form is all off. She's loping and too loose, her arms flapping everywhere. "Don't wait for me."

"But . . ."

"I'm not much of a distance runner, more of a sprinter." She smiles apologetically. "More of a walker, really."

We haven't even gone a quarter of a mile and Issie's face is already red.

"Go. Catch her."

She smiles and waves me away.

Then she adds, "You know you want to."

I pick up my pace, easily catching up to Megan. I flash her my own version of the evil-Megan, super-unfriendly smile and pass her at the quarter-mile mark.

Let me just say that there's nothing better than running fast. There's nothing better than the way your legs feel when you stretch out to sprinting speed and you know that your lungs and heart can sustain it.

My running shoes pound over the red track and I start to catch up to the leading boys.

The gym teacher switches on some really ultra-urban hip-hop music, which almost breaks my stride because it has to be the strangest thing in the world listening to ultra-urban hip-hop in a gym in northern Maine. I swear, Maine is the whitest state in the nation.

We went running the day my dad died, in Charleston. My breath hiccups out of my mouth and I lose my breathing rhythm. Crap.

"Don't think about it. Go faster." I am mumbling to myself. What is wrong with me? Running never makes me nervous. I lap the jogging girls. They're singing, "*Whassup. Whassup with you . . .* "

I lap sweet Issie. Her arms are still all loosey-goosey and she waves at me before she yells, "Watch out. She's catching up."

I just run faster and hit the slowest of the lead boys. I wink and race by him. He smells like onions and he has big, wet circles in the pits of his shirt. He speeds up, but can only stay with me for a tenth of a mile before he drops back. Then it's Nick.

I cruise next to him. He's some sort of running god, because he isn't close to being winded. His stride is long, powerful, and quick.

"Hi."

Why I said this, I do not know. He's cute. Okay. I am a sucker for cute boys and he *was* nice to Issie. Plus, he has good hair and he isn't as pale as most Maine males. He looks like he works in the sun, or at least has seen the sun once, maybe many weeks ago. Plus, life is all supposed to be about making love, not war. My dad listened to John Lennon; I know this stuff.

"You're fast," he says, easy. No huffing. No puffing. No blowing the house down.

"So are you."

We run together, keeping pace. The only one ahead of us is Ian, who is loping around the track as if it's nothing.

Nick shrugs at me while he runs, which is really something, because when I'm running full tilt it's hard for me to speak, let alone break form to shrug.

"You can go faster, can't you?" I huff out.

He just gives a little smile again and then his eyes shift into something cold, like gravestones with just the barest information about a life etched onto them.

"Zara," he whisper-says.

I lean in closer to hear him. "What?"

My voice is not a whisper. It matches the thudding beat of my heart, the bass of the music that blares out of the speakers.

"Awesome job, new girl!" Devyn yells, clapping.

Nick locks his eyes into mine. "You should stay away from Ian."

"Why?"

"I don't know. He's just . . . he's a user."

"A user?"

We thunder past the jogging/singing girls.

"What do you mean, a user?" I ask again.

We flash by some unhealthy boys, including the onion-smell guy.

Nick sniffs the air. "Smells like they might not make it."

Might not make it. Like my dad.

I gulp and turn my head to look at him. He is oblivious. My dad's face flashes into my head, the water bottle on the floor, the way I couldn't do anything to help him. I ache, just ache, and it makes me mad. I start kicking. It's way too early, but I have to get ahead and get away, like I can outrun death somehow, like I can run away from what's real.

Might not make it.

Every muscle rebels but I ignore them and push past Nick, closing the distance between Ian and me in the final lap. I pass people but don't really notice who. Some yell, but I don't really hear them. With every footfall I increase the distance between me and Nick, between me and bad memories.

Might not make it.

Just Run. Run. Run.

I halve the distance between Ian and me. I quarter the distance.

People yell, I think. People holler. My red running shoes blur as they move over the grainy track. My arms pump. Kicking high to catch up, all power, all speed, and I get so close I can smell Ian, cold and icy like my windowpane this morning. He turns and looks at me.

He isn't even concerned. A runner never turns to look back unless he knows he can't be beat.

He smiles kindly—amused, I think—and picks up his pace. No sweat soaks his shirt, no beads on his forehead. Nothing.

God, that's incredible, to be able to run like that.

He crosses the line three strides ahead of me, standing up, smiling.

I stumble across the line and fall to the ground, gasping for air, clutching my cinched-up stomach, and suppressing the urge to vomit, which is what happens sometimes when I run hard.

"You were great." Ian bends over me and reaches a hand out to help me up.

I grab his hand, stagger, and the world dizzies around me. Ian wraps his arm around my waist, steadying me. My dad used to put his arm around me like that and I liked it, liked the comfortable feeling. Some part of me notices that his arm isn't even warm. It's cold. It makes no sense.

"You're amazing," I tell him. "I've never seen anyone that fast."

"I do okay."

"Okay?"

"Lots of training."

My eyes lock with Nick's eyes. He's not winded, but he is sweaty, musky smelling. He glares at me and I'm suddenly super conscious of Ian's arm around me.

"Everyone is an amazing runner here," I pant, bending over again. "I can't believe how good everyone is."

"You were too," Ian says. "You need a little Maine training, that's all."

The gym teacher pounds me on the back. "I want you on the

team. That time! That's a minute better than the girls' Maine state record. I can't believe it."

I nod and smile. My heart lifts and starts to settle. The world loses its blurry edges. Ian still hangs onto my waist. He says something, but I'm too tired to hear it. Nick stands near Devyn, hands on his hips. There's a little sweat on his forehead and he wipes it off with his hand before his eyes sear into mine.

That's all it takes. I'm hooked.

Sitophobia
fear of eating

The PE teacher is tallying up everyone's times and giving them out. Nick's eyes are still locked with mine. He mouths the word again, "User."

I open my own mouth to say something. But before I can he turns his back to me and walks away.

Ian scowls and points at Nick. "He bothering you?"

"I don't know," I answer honestly, pulling away.

Ian's face clenches. "Ignore him, okay? He's a jerk. He's got this cop-complex thing going on."

"Cop complex?"

"Thinks he knows everything. Thinks he's better than everybody else. He isn't. He's just an overgrown thug who can run. He's been a freak ever since Devyn's accident, and then this other kid ran away last week and Nick's all 'there could be a serial killer.' I swear he watches way too many crime shows. It's no wonder his parents took off."

"Took off?"

"Supposedly on some photography work. They do nature movies. I don't know. I like your shirt."

I glance down at my U2 T-shirt. Sweat mars the light gray of it and it seems crumpled, all used up after a hard run. The title of their old album, *War*, has started to flake off. I can't stop thinking about Nick. "He seems so . . . I don't know . . . stressed."

Ian takes me by the shoulders. Maine people are way too intense. I try to back away. His fingers sink in and hold.

"Zara, just ignore him," he repeats. His fingers relax and he flicks some lint off my shoulder. "He's a jerk. Okay?"

Nick stands by Devyn. He taps the wheel on Devyn's chair with his foot. I meet his eyes.

"Okay," I say to Ian.

But I know I'm lying.

I know I don't want to stay away.

The rest of the morning goes fine, as far as the first day in a new school goes. There's a lot of gawking at me and whispering. Issie tries to explain who everyone is, but the names and connections don't stick. I can't remember anything.

"Is the blond guy Jay Dahlberg?" I ask Issie as we charge down the stairs to the cafeteria.

"No, that's Paul Rasku, who makes the pumpkin bombs," Issie explains for the eight hundreth time. "Jay Dahlberg is the skater who made this sound-cannon thing out of a nine-foot-long cardboard tube. It's super cool. He trumpets through it during basketball and soccer games and stuff."

"I give up."

"You'll get it," Issie reassures me.

I can't believe I live here now.

But Issie is terribly sweet. She and Devyn sit with me at lunch, which, having watched enough Disney tween movies, was what I worried about the most. The whole "new girl alone in the lunch room" thing.

I'm pretty content, actually.

I bite into my veggie sandwich and stare at Devyn's happy face. "So, you guys have always lived in Maine?"

Devyn nods. "Yep. But Issie moved up here from Portland."

"In first grade," I remember.

Issie laughs and points at Devyn with her carrot stick. "I already told her."

She yawns a ferocious yawn—I can see down to her tonsils—and stretches her arms over her head.

Devyn reaches over and covers Issie's mouth as she yawns. "I wonder where Nick is?"

I must have made some sort of frightened face because Devyn explains, "Nick's cool. He just has this weird protector thing going on."

I open up my sandwich. The lettuce is limp against the bread. I shut it again and twirl the string on my finger.

"Do you have an Amnesty International chapter here?" I ask, changing the subject. I wipe my mouth and pluck a cucumber out of my sandwich.

"I have *always* wanted an Amnesty chapter. Are you in Amnesty?" Issie pops up. She's been staring at her pizza slice, picking off the pepperoni. Devyn scoops them off her plate and gobbles them down. She smiles at him. "He always does that. He's so into protein. He eats raw meat."

"Like sushi?" I ask.

"Yeah, like sushi . . . ," Issie's voice trails off.

"Some people are afraid of fish. It's called ichthyophobia," I say, and then cover my mouth with my hand. I try not to give people useless phobia information, but Devyn is into it.

"Hey, that's better than ideophobia," he says.

My hands drop down. "You know what ideophobia is?"

Issie answers for him. "Devyn knows everything about phobias and mental conditions."

"My parents are psychiatrists," he explains. "Ideophobia is the fear of ideas."

"Duh, even I could get that one." Issie wiggles her nose at him. "But anyway, about Amnesty. We should start a chapter, shouldn't we, Devyn?"

He nods and wipes the pepperoni grease off his fingers.

Life here could be okay after all, really, if it weren't so cold.

Then Devyn tenses up, a low sound comes from the bottom of his throat, almost like a whimper.

Issie puts her hand on his arm.

"Is?" he says quietly.

She doesn't answer.

When I follow her gaze out the big cafeteria windows, I see what it is that's freaking him out. At the edge of the woods there's a man.

"Crap," I say.

Issie snaps out of it. "You know him?"

She and Devyn both focus their attention on me. I try to shrink myself down even more. I'd like to stare back at them, but I'm too busy watching the man lift his arm and point, point into the cafeteria, at us, at me.

"He's pointing at me," Devyn says, almost curling up into

himself. Fear changes his voice into something frozen and brittle. Issie grabs at him. "He's pointing at me, Is. Oh God . . ."

"No. He's pointing at me," I say, muscles tensing. "Jesus. Who the hell is that?"

A dog hurtles across the snowy field toward the guy. At the same time, I jump up and start toward the fire-exit door, smashing past people carrying green lunch trays and Cokes, flying by Megan and her little posse all drinking water. I push the big metal handle of the door open. An alarm sounds. Like I care.

"Miss! Miss!" Some random teacher hauls me back inside, whirling me around and spitting in my face as he talks. "What do you think you're doing?"

Issie and Devyn's mouths are hanging wide open.

"I, um, I was feeling a little claustrophobic," I lie. "I get lightheaded."

"Mr. Marr . . . she has sugar issues," Issie interrupts.

"That's not her only issue," Megan snarks at her table. People laugh. I ignore them because the man outside has gone, vanished into the woods or something. The dog is gone too.

Issie keeps going, keeps explaining. "Her grandmother told me. Her grandmother is Betty. You know Betty. She works for Downeast Ambulance."

I flash her a thank-you look.

Mr. Marr's got the comb-over thing that some bald men try to pull off. It flaps in the wind. He slams the door shut. "Well, you better go get some sugar then, miss."

Issie brings me back to the table. Once I sit down, pretend to take some sugar via a caffeinated cola beverage, and Mr. Marr no longer stares, she goes, "Why did you do that?"

I shrug. "He's been following me."

"He's been following you?" Devyn says. "The man outside? Are you sure?"

"I know it sounds weird." I'm all flustered, folding my napkin into smaller and smaller squares. "I swear it's true, though. I saw him in Charleston. I saw him at the airport. And now he's here. Something is seriously going on. It is not normal. This . . . this is not normal."

Devyn shakes his head. "That can't be good."

"What do you mean?"

The bell rings. Issie stands up, but Devyn doesn't push away from the table. "Let me do a little research on that, okay? Then we'll talk."

I stand up. "What? Do you think he's a serial killer or some kind of stalker or something?"

Devyn nods slowly.

"It makes no sense. I don't know why he'd be where I am. You don't think this is connected to that boy who went missing, do you?" I stare at the top of his head. His hair swirls around like a whirlpool. But it's his eyes that get me. It's like he's holding something back. "You thought he was pointing at you."

A muscle twitches in his cheek. His head turns away, just a little bit. "I guess I was wrong."

"You were scared."

He faces me again. His eyes flash like he's recognizing something. "So were you."

I spend the rest of the day looking out windows, searching for the man. Every class I stare into the woods, watch snow fall off tree limbs, but I don't see him. I'm so psyched out that just getting up from a chair makes my heart beat fast, like I've been running. So when someone's hand clomps down on my shoulder in the hall right when I'm putting stuff in my locker, I whirl around and scream.

The coach jumps back. His yellow-tinted glasses slip on his nose. "Zara? It's Zara, right?"

"Uh-huh."

"You jumpy? Did I scare you?" He says things bullet-fast, which does not seem like the Maine way.

"Sorry."

His hand waves away my words. "Whatever. Listen. I know there's not much time left in the season, but I thought you might want to join."

I rub my elbow. "Join?"

"Cross-country."

People meander by. They stare at us. Face after face that I don't recognize. "Yeah, I'll join. That would be great."

"Don't smile too big." He laughs and points at my mouth. "Bugs'll get in there."

I clamp my jaws shut as he coach-punches me in the shoulder.

"Just kidding." He laughs again. "See you tomorrow, kid."

"Cool!" I manage to say once he's halfway down the hall, his buzz-cut head almost lost in a mass of fully haired Mainers. I yell, "Thanks!"

He sticks his arm up in the air and gives me a thumbs-up right when my cell phone rings. I check out the display, momentarily psyched that someone's already calling me. It's my mom.

"Everything going okay?" she asks.

I stare into my bland gray locker, totally unlike everyone else's locker. Those are all decorated. Issie's is full of Hello Kitty stuff.

"Yep."

"Good."

Someone in the hall yells for Megan.

"Make friends yet?"

I grab some books, not paying attention to what I really need. "Yep."

Silence on the phone.

Then she says, "You were always good at making friends, so outgoing."

I jostle the books around. One falls open. The pages bend. I yank it back up.

"I'm doing cross-country," I say. "It's almost over. And then track."

"Indoor?"

"Of course."

More silence.

"I miss you," she finally says.

Issie comes up next to me. I smile at Issie and say into the phone, "Then you shouldn't have sent me away."

I click it off and guilt pulls my stomach into all sorts of weird shapes.

"It was my mom," I tell Issie as she walks me out to my Subaru. She pretty much bounces the entire way.

"She must miss you."

"I guess."

"You mad at her for sending you up here into the Arctic?" she asks as she pushes the school's big glass front door open. A wind blasts us, blowing snow off the roof and into our faces.

"A little." I decide to be honest. "I miss Charleston. It's so busy and there's a lot of people and flowers and here it's so . . ."

"Cold?"

I nod. A rabbit pokes up her gray head and looks at us. She sits at the edge of the parking lot, watching. Her nose twitches.

"Oh, a bunny." I sigh. The little girl in me really likes bunnies. "I've always wanted a bunny."

Issie cocks her head. "Really? A bunny?"

The bunny twitches her whiskers again and surveys the parking lot. The only thing that moves is her eyes.

I blush. "I know it's dumb, but they're so furry and cute and cuddly. I don't know."

"You're just like me!" she says. "I knew it."

"Just like you?"

"A bunny lover." She smiles and hugs me. "There are people who like cute, furry things and people who eat cute, furry things."

I pat her back, probably awkwardly.

"I am so glad you're here," she says, finally letting go. She must think about this and then she revises it. "I mean, it's cold and everything, but we have bunnies, although maybe you have bunnies in Charleston . . ."

I bite my lip, feeling like I'd revealed way too much about myself. I even have bunny pajamas, but I'm not about to tell Issie or anybody else about that, or about my old stuffed bunny, Edgar, and how he sleeps next to my pillow every night.

"Do you want to come over?" Issie asks. The wind blows her fuzzy hair off her forehead and then into her mouth. She spits it out and keeps smiling.

"Hair is not tasty," she says. "You look super cold."

"Ah . . ." I unlock the car, pressing my hand against my stomach. "I think I need to go get my car registered at the town office, I'm sorry."

I am. Really. Disappointing Issie is like telling a four-year-old that ice cream cones have been banned. If it has to be done, you don't want to be the one to do it.

She stands still. Her face crumples. She tries again.

"Oh, okay. I have a really cute cat, Muffin. You'd love her, I know."

I nod. "That's a cute name for a cat."

"It's not really original," she says and then she hugs herself. "How about just for a minute? There's a lot of stuff about town I should tell you. And Devyn wants to talk to you about the guy you saw. We'll just swing around front and pick him up. I always bring him home. Thank God. He hated riding the special-ed bus."

"That would be cool," I say, unlocking my car door. "You don't think he's still out here, do you?"

"Devyn?"

"No. The guy."

"Oh, I'm sure he's long gone," she smiles. "Right? Okay. Just follow me, okay?"

She waves and bounces away and I start smiling, really smiling. I can feel it all the way to my heart, even though I can't actually see the smile. I haven't smiled that big for a really long time, but Issie is just so cute and lovable that maybe Maine will be okay after all.

Giant snowflakes drift down from the sky. I tilt my head back as they fall. They are really beautiful when they fall soft and gentle. I stick out my tongue and catch one. It melts in a second.

I catch another.

And another.

. . .

The roads aren't too terribly icy and I manage to follow Issie's little Volkswagen to her house without skidding, slamming on the brakes, or anything like that.

The whole time I'm driving I'm thinking: *This is where my dad grew up. These are the roads he drove. These are the roads he won't ever drive again.* Then I swerve to avoid a pothole.

Issie is hauling out Devyn's wheelchair while I park and check out the house.

"Your house is cute," I say.

"It's very shingled Cape." She grimaces. "Very Maine. Charleston houses aren't like this, are they?"

"Not really," I say, and lock the car. It makes a comfortable beeping noise.

"You don't have to lock it," Devyn says. He's standing up beside his chair. I must make some sort of funny look. "Yeah, I can stand."

"I'm sorry. I'm such a jerk. I was staring, wasn't I? God, that's awful. I'm awful." I can feel my face go all red as Devyn plops himself into the wheelchair.

"I'll forgive you this time." He smiles. He unlocks some gadget thing on the side and starts wheeling toward the front door.

"Devyn may eventually walk again," Issie brags, opening the big red door. "He's got the doctors all astonished. He wasn't ever supposed to stand after the accident. He's a good healer."

Devyn gets this pained, embarrassed look so I don't ask about the accident. He changes the subject. "Issie's parents work late."

"At the bank," Issie explains. She flops on the couch, pats the cushion next to her, then lunges back up. "Oh. I should offer you something to eat. Are you guys hungry?"

"I'm good," I say, taking in the room, the coziness of it. It's almost like a timber frame house, I would guess.

"Starving," Devyn says.

Issie bounds into the kitchen and comes back with a tub of Breyers ice cream. She plops it on Devyn's lap and gives him a spoon. "You are always hungry."

He flips off the top and digs in. "Too true."

We watch him eat. Issie falls back on the couch, but she's so hyper she starts twitching her foot. The silence is big.

"So . . . ," I say. "You guys were going to tell me about the man outside the cafeteria. Have you ever seen him before?"

Devyn swallows. "I'm not sure. He creeped me out, which is not manly, I know."

"You are totally manly," Is announces in a way that makes both Devyn and me blush. She stops twitching. "Devyn looked up some stuff. You are probably going to have a hard time believing this."

I wait. "Uh-huh . . ."

"You want to tell her?" Issie asks.

Devyn sticks the spoon in the ice cream carton. It stands up straight. He toughs out the words, "We think he's a pixie."

I wait more.

Issie rushes in. "Okay. I know it sounds weird, but hear us out, okay?"

I wonder for a second if everyone in Bedford, Maine, is insane or just Devyn and Issie, and possibly me. I decide to play along. "Okay."

"Okay," Issie continues. "Okay . . . um . . ."

"You said you saw him at the airport in Charleston," Devyn starts.

"On the runway." I pull my legs up under me and settle into the couch. "And then I saw him here."

I shudder, remembering.

"That's so weird," Issie says, tapping her fingers against her leg.

"I know it's weird." I nod. I take a pillow from the couch. It's dark green and has felt leaves on it. I hug it. "I thought I was imagining it. But you guys saw him today, right?"

They nod.

I ask the question. "You think he's a pixie?"

They nod again.

The spoon falls over in the ice cream.

"Aren't pixies little winged things that dance around flower gardens?" I ask.

"Not exactly." Devyn grabs the spoon like it'll steady him somehow.

"Why do you think he's a pixie?" I finally say, trying to take it all in.

"He gets from place to place really fast and he leaves gold dust where he walks," Issie says. "Totally pixie ruler behavior. At least, um, according to the Web site Devyn found."

"Gold dust? Like Tinker Bell?" I stand up. It's too much. "Is this a joke? Some initiation prank, like let's torment the new girl?"

"We would *never* do that to you. That would be so mean." Issie frowns, all crushed.

Devyn's voice raises an octave. "I told you not to tell her the dust part. It sounds stupid."

"I know it sounds stupid." Issie stands up with me. "But it's true."

"Right. It's true," I say. I jingle my car keys, itching to leave, but still wanting to hear this for some stupid reason.

Issie's practically pleading. "But the Web site said so."

"Well, we're not sure it's true, Is. It's a working theory," Devyn says. His eyes look pained. "I know it seems ridiculous, Zara. I mean, *I* think it's kind of ridiculous, but I've been all over the Web and I can't find anything else that would explain this guy."

"And why is he following me?"

"That's a good question," Devyn says. "When did you first see him?"

I do not want to think about it. I have been actively not thinking about this for four months, but Is and Devyn stare up at me with these wide-open, trusting eyes and I just plunge ahead, ignore the ache in me. "After my dad died."

Issie and Devyn look confused.

"You saw him when your dad died?" Issie says.

Then I remember. This morning there were little glitter sparkles by my car. Dust. Pixie dust. No, it can't be that. But maybe it's something else—a calling card, some sort of serial killer hallmark.

"What?" Devyn asks, wheeling closer. His chair hits a copy of *People*. "What did you just figure out?"

"How do you know she figured something out?" Issie asks.

"She has a look."

I close my eyes. I open them. "I'm not sure if I believe the whole pixie thing . . ."

"But?" Issie straightens herself up, waiting.

"But," I continue, "I am pretty positive that the man I saw when my dad died is the same one at the high school. I am pretty damn sure, actually, and I want to find out who the hell he is."

Issie tries again. "What if he's a pixie?"

I almost laugh. "I don't think he's actually a pixie. Maybe a stalker or something."

Issie's eyes light up. "You mean he read the Web site and he's modeling his behavior?"

"Yeah. I don't know. But if he's just some normal psycho how can he get everywhere so quickly? It makes no sense. It might just be a big coincidence."

"You don't believe that. You're just trying to fool yourself, to not be scared," Issie says.

I swallow. She's right. I am.

"What about the dust?" Devyn urges. "There's not a lot of it, but it's there. I saw it."

"I don't know about the dust. Maybe he plants it, like some sort of creepy calling card," I say, checking my watch. "I'm sorry. I have to go get the car registered before they close."

It's true, but I'm really trying to leave because I just want a second to myself, a second to figure this out.

When I get to the door, Issie puts her hand on my wrist, gently. "You'll be careful, right?"

I nod.

"You don't believe us?" Devyn asks, pivoting the chair so he can look at me.

"I don't know," I say. "I don't know. The whole pixie thing is weird, but I mean, it's also weird that I'm here in Maine."

"And that he followed you," Devyn adds.

"That's not just weird," Issie says. "It's creepy. Really creepy."

Amaxophobia

fear of riding in a car

This is a fear I've never had. Until now.

"I am amaxophobic!" I announce to the steering wheel. I half hug it to make the point.

The steering wheel does not hug back.

There should be a rule that says you can't get too settled into things because something bad will happen. Oh, I think there is. It's called Murphy's law, and it's about expecting things to go wrong.

I've only driven about three miles from Issie's when the Subaru tires make this horrible noise. The whole car just slides off to the right. The car angles itself toward the woods.

"Stop!" I yell. I slam the brakes. The car slows. It stops at a forty-five-degree angle in the breakdown lane.

"Okay. Stay calm," I tell the steering wheel. "No need to panic."

The wheel does not panic.

"This is my karmic payback for not figuring out the whole psycho-stalker thing sooner, right?"

I try to move the car back onto the road and its tires skid. Smoke flies up from beneath them.

"Okay, little car, you are protesting roads. They are death traps for animals. They are environmentally unsound impervious surfaces that cause runoff. I understand this. But could we protest in the summer?"

I try to back up again.

One of my tires falls into the gutter thing on the side of the road.

My whole body shakes. I try to move the car. It lurches to the side.

Okay. Two of my tires are now in the gutter on the side of the road.

"Yoko! Do not do this to me!"

Wait. I've named the car. Why Yoko? I have no idea. Yoko was always there for John, unlike the way the Subaru is here for me.

"Come on, Yoko. Let's imagine there's no gutter. It's easy if you try. No empty air below your tire. Above it only car."

I put it in reverse. I put it in forward. I try to rock the stupid car back and forth. I shut off the Green Day. Maybe Yoko doesn't like Green Day?

"I hate Maine!"

I smash my fist against the steering wheel.

The horn blares, probably scaring all the little squirrels in the woods. I don't care. I hit it again.

"Stupid, stupid Maine," I mutter and bang the steering wheel another, time and then another until red marks start showing up on the sides of my hands.

Things are *so* not good. The sun is going down. It's freezing out. My car is all stuck and tilted like everything in the world is somehow horribly skewed and wrong, which I guess it is.

I mean, I am in Maine in a car stuck on ice.

I am beating up Yoko, which is just so wrong.

And I can't use my cell phone.

Why? I forgot to charge it.

Could life be worse?

I try to move again. The car lurches but slides right back.

The air screams of burned-rubber smell.

How ridiculous.

"I hate ice!"

I smash my head against the steering wheel and that's when I start to cry, bawl really. I cry and cry and cry. Because I'm stuck on the ice and my dad is dead and my mom sent me here, without her, where there are people who seem normal but are capable of suddenly believing in pixies, and I miss Charleston and warm air and flowers and roads that *have no ice on them.*

I used to be the type of person who was always in motion, always doing things, writing letters, running through the streets, laughing with my friends, moving. Always forward. Moving.

Then I got stuck. My dad died and the only words I hear are *death, deadly, stillness.* To never move. No forward. No backward. Just stuck. Gone forever, like my dad, a blank screen on the computer, an old photograph in the hall with no spirit in it, an ice patch on a road to nowhere, nothing. Just gone.

The sun is setting and it's only five o'clock.

How do people live here? It should be against the law to live anywhere that the sun sets so early. If I were a dictator I would totally make that law. Since I am not a dictator, I stumble into the cold with one of the flares from Betty's emergency kit and light it. I check out under the tire. I get back in the car.

Someone knocks on Yoko's window.

I jump in the seat and scream. I probably would have hit the ceiling but I'm wearing my seat belt. I cover my face with my hands, horrified. Someone raps on the window again. Finally, finally I get enough nerve to look.

Nick Colt stands next to my car, all casual, like standing in the ditch is part of his everyday routine. I put down the window. Cold air rushes in. I shiver.

"What are you doing here?" I ask, stunned. He saw me scream. He looks like he thinks it's all funny, his cheek twitching like I'm some big joke.

"Is that any way to greet your rescuer?"

He smiles. His smile is perfect.

"I'm sorry. I'm just— Oh, I don't know what's wrong with me." I shake my head. "I'm freaked out. I'm sorry."

"Obviously." His voice is steady and low.

I wipe at my face. "I've never driven on ice before. Back home I'm a perfectly good driver."

"I'm sure you are."

"I am. I am a very competent person."

"I'm sure." He has a dimple on his left cheek when he smiles.

I force myself to look away from the cute boy, look away from the dimple. "Really. And I don't usually scream when people knock on my window, either."

I start to open the door but he puts out both his arms to hold it shut.

He glances at the woods up the road a bit. "Stay in your car, Zara."

"We're not going to be able to get it unstuck. You'll have to give me a ride to my grandmother's house."

"It's better if you stay in the car."

I glare at him. Things shift inside me. What a bossy jerk. "I can decide if I should stay in my own car or not."

"Let me try to push you out. It's better for both of us if you can drive your car home," he says, looking up the road again.

This time I follow his gaze. My gasp rips through the quiet. A shadow leaps off the road and disappears into the trees. Oh my God. "Was that a man up there jumping into the woods?"

Something flashes in Nick's brown eyes. Anger? Will? I don't know. God, I don't know anything. "It was nothing. Put up your window. Put your car in neutral. I'm going to try to push you out."

"But the man up there. He could help us?"

"There was no man up there."

His jaw tightens.

I swallow. "And if he wanted to help he wouldn't be jumping into the woods, right?"

"Right."

"Okay," I say. "Fine. But there was a man." My voice comes out angry and raw and then I add, "You aren't strong enough. This is a heavy car. It's a Subaru."

"I know it's a Subaru, Zara. Just let me try."

He glances up at the woods again. The tension in his shoulders eases a bit and then he reaches into the car and touches my cheek. His voice comes out much softer. "You were crying?"

I jerk my head away, late, just a little too late. His fingers feel like electricity against my cheek, like a magnet I can't be near.

"I don't cry," I lie, and start to put up my window.

His voice stops me. "It's okay to cry. It's frustrating getting stuck, and you're probably not used to ice."

"I wasn't crying."

He shakes his head, obviously not believing me, and then walks around to the back of the car and yells, "Now. Put it in forward."

"Okay, just don't hurt Yoko."

"Yoko?"

"My car."

"You named your car Yoko? As in Ono?"

"You have a better name?"

"How about Subaru?"

"I'm shifting!" I shift the gear and the entire car lurches up and onto the road. I press the brake, amazed. The car is not tilted anymore. I'm not stuck. Yay!

Nick trots up to the car, wiping his hands on his jeans. He bends down and smiles all cocky. "Told you I could do it."

His eyes aren't so hard.

"Thank you," I say. I bite my lip and look away and then look back. The center of my palms tingle. Why does he have to be so handsome? "You didn't get hurt or anything, right?"

"Do I look hurt?"

He looks good but I'm not about to say that.

I keep my foot pressed down on the brake and put the car in park.

I manage to pull myself together. I pivot as best I can, putting my hands on the windowsill, and face him. He's so cute. He helped me. I have to try to be nice.

"Thank you," I say. "I wouldn't have wanted to abandon Yoko and walk home."

His eyes shift again.

"Zara," he says. "You ever need a ride you can call me, or Issie. Okay?"

His hands move so they are on top of mine, completely covering them. They're really huge and warm but they make me shiver somehow. I don't move away, though. I don't want to.

"I don't have your number." My words come out slow, stunned.

"I'll give it to you. It's my cell."

He writes it out on an old gas receipt and hands it to me with a flourish. I take it.

"What are you? Mr. Protector of New Students?" I laugh when I say it so it doesn't come out sounding mean.

"Not all new students."

I try not to melt inside. "Just me?"

He cocks his head.

"Maybe?" His voice trails off. He's searching up the road. "You really saw someone go into the woods up there?"

I nod. "Didn't you?"

He doesn't answer. Instead, he wipes his hand through his hair.

I suddenly remember how to be polite, like the semi-Southern lady I am. He *did* move my car, after all.

"Thank you," I say, "for moving my car and everything."

He smiles at me again and out of the corner of my eye I think I see something up the road. I can't stand it. I can't stand not knowing. I smash open the door and dash up the side of the road, toward where I saw the man.

"What are you doing?" Nick yells after me. "Zara!"

"I saw him again." I keep running, looking along the ground. Nick flies after me.

"What are you doing?" he says again.

"Looking for evidence," I say and stop. I point at the ground. There, on top of dried-up mud and ice and twigs, are tiny specks of gold powder, like glitter, but even smaller. I stagger backward into Nick. "Oh my God."

He squeezes my shoulders and then lets go to bend down and touch the powder. "It's like dust, but gold."

"Pixie dust," I say. "How can it be pixie dust?"

"Pixie dust? What do you mean?"

"Devyn and Issie, they have a theory about some stuff that's been happening to me. There's this guy who keeps showing up. They think he's a pixie. I know it sounds stupid. Pixie kings are supposed to leave dust like this."

He brings his glittering finger closer to our faces. My face warms from his breath. It's minty. His finger trembles, just the tiniest tremble. "Like this."

"Yeah." I step back and search his face to see if he thinks I'm ridiculous. "The whole pixie aspect of it is kind of whacked, but it could be a serial killer or someone who is completely mental. It could be his calling card or something. I don't know. I don't like it."

"Me either." He tugs on my sleeve. "Let's go back to the car."

"You don't want to go see if he's in there?" I gesture toward the woods.

"You don't have boots on."

"Oh. Right." We walk back to the car and that's when I see it on the back of his jacket, little gold flakes . . . like dust.

He follows me home to make sure I'm safe. In the driveway, I park Yoko and tell it, "John would be proud."

I turn off the ignition and check out the scene. I did not make it in to register the car, but I think under the circumstances this is totally acceptable. It's not every day you start believing in pixies or psych yourself out about opening the door and walking twenty feet to your grandmother's house.

"Paranoid, Zara. You are being paranoid." Telling myself this does not make it feel any better.

The sun has almost completely set. I open the door and start across the ice toward the front door. Grandma Betty has left on the porch light and has spread some grains of blue chemical stuff across the ground so the ice dissolves in little clumps, which was very nice of her. I should do that tomorrow, help out, you know?

Something cracks a twig in the woods just beyond the driveway.

I squeal and fast-walk to the porch, lunging up the steps in a totally ungraceful and wimpy way.

I slam the door open and lock it behind me.

I check the lock.

Okay, let's face it, Maine is creepy. That's all there is to it. Creepy, creepy, creepy and too damn cold.

For a second I wish that Nick Colt *had* followed me all the way up the driveway. He's cute and he has that whole I'm-going-to-keep-you-safe thing going on. Not like there's anything to be scared of. What do pixies do? They frolic in flower gardens, right?

Only this guy points.

I walk over to the window that looks out at the driveway, the woods, the lawn. "I'm being ridiculous."

I stare out into the dusky lawn. The woods at the edge of it seem full of secrets, full of unexplained things.

I never should have read all those scary books when I was little. What was my dad thinking keeping them in the house? Pain wells up in my heart and then the ache comes.

My dad. It is so hard to just think of him.

I turn away from the door and sit on the couch where he used to sit. I put my face in my hands and rock back and forth a little, but I do not cry.

No more.

Betty crashes out of the kitchen, bringing the smell of burned meat with her.

"I murdered the pork chops, just fried them to death," she says.

"That's okay."

"I have Campbell's soup . . . chicken noodle."

"Cool."

She eyes me. "Okay. What's going on?"

"Tell me about the boy who went missing last week. What happened?"

Betty turns to glance out the windows. "It's almost dark. You should be back before dark. You don't know these roads. They're dangerous."

"I was at Issie's."

"Oh, that's good. She's a sweet girl. Jumpy. Her parents work at the bank."

"Uh-huh. Yeah . . . I kind of sort of went off the road a little bit. I didn't hurt the car! I swear. Nick pushed me out."

"Nick?" She wipes at her face with the moose dish towel and motions for me to follow her into the kitchen. "Nick Colt?"

I nod.

"You didn't get hurt? Were you speeding?"

"It was ice."

She takes it all in. "He's a good boy. Cute. Don't sigh at me. He is."

"Tell me about the boy. Please?"

"He was out alone at night. He was an eighth grader. He didn't show up in the morning."

"So what? Everything is all business as usual?"

"No. We had search parties. The state police came in." Her shoes slap against the wood floor. "You're getting all motivated again. Maybe Maine has already been good for you."

I decide to ignore her psychoanalysis. "Do the police have any leads?"

She opens the cabinet and pulls out two microwavable soup containers. "No."

"And what do you think?"

She pops the plastic top off the containers and starts prying off the metal lids. I wait while she puts it all into two bowls and plops them in the microwave for sixty seconds.

Finally she says, "I think he ran away."

I wait. She turns around and leans against the counter, like it's too hard to keep standing up. "Okay . . . a long time ago this happened. Almost a couple decades ago. Boys turned up missing. No girls. Just boys. One a week. Always at night. It was in the national news."

The timer on the microwave counts down the seconds, getting closer and closer to zero.

"Mom and Dad never told me that."

"They wouldn't. It's not something anyone around here wants to remember."

"And now you think it's happening again."

"I hope to God not."

"But it might be."

The microwave beeps. She chucks the pork chops into the trash can. "It might be, but he may have just run away."

"Seriously, why did Mom send me here? A boy went missing."

"People don't go missing in Charleston? I bet the murder rate's a lot higher there." She swallows. She pulls in air through her nose like she expects she'll never breathe again. "She thought she was doing the right thing. It wasn't easy for her, Zara. You weren't acting alive anymore. She thought a change of scenery would help."

"Was I that bad? Really?"

She stares out the window above the sink, past the old glass insulators she collects. "Yes."

Right after dinner my cell phone goes off while it's charging and I rush over to the counter to get it, even though it's probably just my mother, but the display says it's a Maine number.

I flick it open. "Hello?"

"Hey, Zara. It's me, Ian." His voice sounds all happy.

"Hi, Ian." I lean against the counter. Betty makes bug eyes at me like she's all excited that a boy is calling me. I refuse to look at her.

"Hey. Sorry to bother you. I hope you aren't eating."

"Nope. We're done."

"Good. I was just thinking about how hard it must be for you to be in a new town and everything . . ."

I bump my butt against the counter because it's hard to be still. "It's not that bad," I lie.

"Well, anyway, I was thinking maybe I could show you around after cross-country tomorrow? You know, give you a grand tour of the excitement that is Bedford, Maine."

"Oh. Tomorrow?"

Betty perks up and starts hustling around, taking dishes off the table.

"Say yes," she whispers.

"I have to go register my car tomorrow," I say, which I do.

"Oh," Ian says.

"I'm sorry."

Betty yanks the faucet to turn on the hot water and groans.

"I could come with you," Ian says.

"To the DMV?" I am stunned.

"Yeah. It's boring as hell in there, but it's better with someone else."

"Sure. Okay." I don't know what to say. "If you don't mind."

We hang up and Betty asks me who it was.

"This guy named Ian that I met at school. He wants to go to the DMV with me."

She hands me a plate to dry. "Well, there's true love."

I snort.

She says, "He's the Ian who is a runner, right? The point guard of the basketball team?"

"I don't know. I know he runs and he's in a ton of clubs."

"Classic overachiever. He comes from an old Bedford family. His father lobsters. His grandfather logged. They have hardly anything; live in a glorified shack, basically. It's amazing to see what that boy has done."

While I rub the plate with a dish towel, I think about Ian and all his clubs and all his energy. "Yeah."

"And he's obviously got good taste if he already has his eye set on you." She points at me with a fork.

I put the plate away and grab the fork from her. "He's just being helpful."

"Ha. Right."

. . .

I wake up in the middle of the night. There's a noise downstairs, soft tapping across the floor. I grab the big metal flashlight that's next to the bed and slip out from under the covers. I don't turn the flashlight on, though. I grab it like cops do, ready to bash someone over the head. I tiptoe down the stairs and that's when I see her, Betty, standing by the front windows.

Her body is fierce, tight, strong. She looks like an Olympic athlete, a warrior, not a grammy.

"Betty?" I whisper her name, afraid to startle her.

She motions for me to come all the way down. I stand next to her, peering into the darkness.

"What are you looking for?" I whisper.

"Things in the night."

"Do you see anything?"

She laughs. "No."

She pulls me against her and kisses the top of my head. "You go on up to bed. I've got everything under control."

I walk away a step and stop. "Gram? Are you really looking for things in the night?"

"People are always looking into the dark, Zara. We're afraid of what we might see. It might be the dark outside, it might be the dark of our own souls, but I figure it's better to get caught looking than to never know. You get me?"

"Not really."

She steps away from the window, pushes me toward the stairs. "Go to bed. School tomorrow. Okay?"

"Okay."

Couplogagophobia

fear of being the third wheel

That night I dream about my dad, all night long. He's standing at the end of Betty's driveway. It's snowing. There are giant paw prints on the snow. His mouth is open and moving, but no sound comes out.

I make myself wake up. The room is cold. The wind blows tree branches against the house, making scraping noises. I turn on the lamp next to the bed, trying not to freak out.

"It's just a dream," I whisper, but the truth is that when my dad died, his mouth moved and no sound ever came out.

When my dad died, we had just come in from our daily morning run. We always ran before breakfast, before the Charleston heat overwhelmed us and made running too much effort. We were talking about gay marriage. He was the one who got me started on writing letters for Amnesty International. I was maybe in first grade, complaining about writing being boring and stupid and a waste of my six-year-old time, and he sat me down at the dining room table and told me stories about people who were suffering. He told me writing was never a waste of time, and that's when I wrote my first letter.

But when he died, we weren't talking about Amnesty, we were talking about his friends Dave and Don. Don, the artist, needed health care and Dave's company wouldn't cover him. My dad opened the door and let us into the house.

"It's ridiculous. Get me some water, honey," he had said, smiling, bending over to catch his breath and leaning on his knees for balance. He'd already taken off his Red Sox hat and his silver hair beneath it was wet from sweat.

I grabbed two Poland Spring waters out of the fridge and pivoted around, and it was like my dad wasn't there anymore. That's the only way I can describe it. He cringed. White and gray erased the normal ruddy color of his skin.

"Daddy?"

He didn't answer, just sort of lifted up a hand to wave me off. Then he pointed toward the sink. "The window. He's . . . I saw him. Run."

"What?" I said.

"Don't let him take . . ."

"Daddy?"

I started to turn and look at the window but then he fell over on his side, his mouth wide open, trying to grab air. His blood didn't know what to do because his heart had failed him.

I dropped the water bottles on the floor. One rolled into his shoe, the other went back toward the fridge, hiding, I guess. I wanted to hide too. My own heart started beating crazy rhythms, out of control, against my ribs. I reached out for his hand and grabbed it. He squeezed back but not hard, not tight and strong like normal. He was weak.

"Mom!" I screamed. "Mom!"

She thundered down the stairs and stopped at the entrance to the kitchen. She sucked in her breath and grabbed the big palm plant next to the sink. Her words came out like a whisper, "He's having a heart attack."

My own heart stopped then, and my dad's eyes widened and he looked at me, pleading. He had never looked at me that way before. His mouth moved. No sound came out.

At school Issie and I sit together at lunch and in all the classes we share. Devyn sits with us in the cafeteria too, and he and Issie laugh so much about the stupidest things it's hard not to laugh with them, even as I check to make sure I haven't gone transparent.

It's actually hard to get annoyed by them because they are so cute together.

"So," I say. "I think I might believe you about the pixie guy."

"Why?" Issie asks.

I chew on my bagel. "I got stuck in the ice yesterday. I went off the road."

"Nick told us," Devyn says.

"Did he tell you about the dust, too?" I ask, watching Devyn rip into a roast beef grinder.

"Yep," he says with his mouth full.

"It's weird," I say. "Especially with the boy that went missing last week. I think they might be connected."

"You know about the Beardsley boy?" Issie asks.

"Betty told me that it happened before," I say. "I'm thinking about going to the computer lab and looking for info."

"I'll come with you," Devyn says, mushing the rest of his grinder in.

"Me too," Issie says, collecting his garbage and her own.

"You should be a couple," I tell Issie as we throw away our trash. "You aren't already a couple, are you?"

"Me and Devyn?" she squeaks.

"Yeah, you and Devyn," I say, elbowing her in the side. "I think he likes you."

She drops her soda can into the recycle bin and turns to stare back at Devyn.

He waves.

Her smile is huge.

"Really?" she asks.

I toss my apple core into the garbage bin. "Really."

She links her arm through mine. "I'm so glad you're here, Zara. I'm glad you aren't hanging out with Megan and her people."

She glances over at Megan, who is holding court over a throng of admirers.

Megan lifts up her eyes and meets mine. I swear if she could shoot fire at me she would, or at the very least, laser beams.

"She hates me," I say. "No big loss. I'd rather be your friend any day."

This is so corny, but Issie eats it up.

"Really? You have to come over again, you know. There's so much stuff I want to tell you." She pulls me back to the lunch table, almost hopping the entire way. "Devyn, guess what Zara just said."

"That she adores snow?" Devyn asks. "And is no longer a victim of cheimaphobia?"

Issie licks some honey that's run off her sandwich and onto her fingers.

"No."

"That she has called her mother and no longer resents her for sending her to Maine, thus ending future decades of therapy and massive loss of revenue for my revenue-hungry parents?"

"No."

I stick out my tongue at him.

"That she has indeed freed all the political prisoners throughout the globe?"

"Devyn!"

He laughs. "Okay. Okay. I'll play nice."

He turns to Issie and says all sweetly, "What did Zara say?"

"She said that she'd rather be my friend than Megan's, any day."

"Zara's no idiot," he says. He raises his eyebrows at me. "I knew you had it in you."

I'm totally confused. I take a sip of my soda. "What do you mean?"

"To make good choices," he says. "You'd choose Issie even if Megan didn't hate you, right?"

I glance at Megan and her frosty eye shadow, her perfect hair, her happy laugh, and her group of admirers. "Megan is cold."

Devyn nods. "Exactly."

We google like crazy. Most of the pixie hits are crap about role-playing games. Then we hit paydirt.

> People believe pixies are tiny, happy fey with just a streak of mischief. They are not. Closer to the vampire's callous disdain for the sanctity of human life, pixies should be avoided at all costs. The only protection against their wrath is their mortal enemy, the were.

"The were?" I say.

Devyn and Issie exchange a look and then Devyn turns to me. "Not *were* as in the verb 'we were' but *where* as in 'where the heck have my sunglasses gone.' It's werewolves, werebears, that sort of thing."

He smiles like it's no big deal.

"You *are* kidding me." I rock back in my chair, shaking my head.

"Weres are protectors of humans and each other," Issie explains. "It's like their sacred duty or something."

"And we know this how?"

"Eighth-grade cryptozoology project." She turns back to the screen. "Does it say anything else, Devyn?"

We all read the page silently. Devyn must read faster than we do, because he points at a far-ahead paragraph.

> Pixies tend to congregate in wooded places. Some pass as humans and interact with humans under the bene t of a spell often known as a glamour. They should still be avoided. When not mated with a queen for an unspeci ed amount of time, the pixie king will demand tributes given to him in the form of young human men.

Devyn reads the next part. " 'Whom they kill after using them for their blood-hungry pleasures.' "

"Not cool," Issie says.

"Not cool at all," I agree.

I read a tiny bit more, " 'The tortured boys gradually fall prey to hysteria'—Duh? Wouldn't you?—'and then they lose pieces of their souls, gradually becoming an inhuman husk prior to death.' "

"That's so freaky awful," Issie whispers, grabbing onto Devyn's arm.

His eyes get sad and scared but his voice is brave. "It'll be okay, Is."

"What if that actually happens?" I whisper. "What if it's already happening?"

I look into their pale, motionless faces. I try to brave myself up. "But it's just a Web site, right? Anyone can write something on the Web."

The bell rings.

"Right." Devyn erases the history on the Web browser.

Everyone looks so disturbed I decide to make a joke. "I guess the weres around here aren't doing a good job."

They don't even crack a smile.

"Come on," I say. "You don't actually believe this, do you?"

Issie rubs at the bridge of her nose with the side of her hand. "Kind of."

I stare down Devyn. "You believe in werewolves and pixies? Like there's not enough real-life badness to be freaked about, you what? You want more?"

"Zara. Can you explain the dust?"

I pull in a breath, remember it by my car, near the woods, on Nick's back. "No."

"Do you think people are so brilliant we understand everything?"

"No," I say, and I stare at him. "What does Nick think about this? Does he believe that guy was a pixie?"

His voice comes from behind me. "Oh, I'd say I believe it."

Devyn clicks off the screen while I stare at him.

"Your mouth's wide open, Zara," Issie whispers.

Nick reaches down and hauls me up. "Have you guys eaten yet?"

I nod.

"You want to come with me anyway?" he asks.

I nod again, staring at my hand touching his hand. Issie starts giggling and Nick lets go.

The snow has mostly melted, so the cross-country practice is held outside. The trail is what you'd expect in Maine. You run across a big field and then on a narrow winding path that loops through the woods, where the pine trees seem to hover over you, ready to grab at you. It would be a perfect place for some kind of freak guy to jump out and grab you.

But that is not going to happen. Still, I kind of wish I had some pepper spray or something. We all huddle around the coach, who puffs up his body like he's terribly important, like some sort of dictator making laws, which I guess he is. It all smells like Christmas and deodorant and baby powder. I think Megan's the baby powder.

"We're going to buddy up," he says. "Megan, you go with the new girl."

She looks horrified. "No way."

"I'll go with her," Ian and Nick both say at the same time.

"Oh, so popular," Megan snarks while the coach shakes his head.

"Fine," he says. "Colt, you go with her."

Nick nods. I bite my lip. Coach says, "What? That not okay with you?"

"No," I mutter. "It's good."

Everyone else partners up and Coach Walsh sets us out two-by-two. "Easy runs today. No PRs."

"That means personal record," Megan says.

I touch my toes. "I know what it means."

We're the last group to go. Nick stays a step or so behind me the whole time and it drives me crazy, like I'm not good enough to run alongside or something.

"Do you have to run behind me?" I finally say when we're long-legging it up a hill that twists through the forest.

"It bother you?"

"Yeah."

"I'm not checking out your butt or anything."

I stop. He rams into me and we both topple down. My arms go to break my fall, but I don't have to. His right arm loops around my rib cage and he rolls us so that his back takes most of the fall. I'm on top of him. For a second his arm doesn't move. When it does I push myself up. He stands up too, turning around, trying to figure things out, I guess.

His voice is a bark. "What are you doing?"

"Checking out your butt," I tease, and then I leave him behind me, sprinting across the field so the coach can register my time and I can go home.

We all hang around, stretching, sort of, while the coach does coach things that involve muttering beneath his breath and checking his clipboard.

Ian walks over next to me and smiles. He pulls his leg up toward his butt, stretching out his quads. I reach for my toes but don't actually touch the ground because it's cold and snowy.

"Nick giving you a hard time?" he asks.

I grunt and reach up toward the sky.

"I think he likes you."

"Really?"

"Yeah. He's a loner though. He's never had a girlfriend."

"Seriously?"

Ian raises his hand. "I swear."

"Good."

"Good?"

Ian's foot thuds back to the ground. I glance over at Nick. He's walking in circles, not even pretending to stretch. Nick stomps over, doesn't even glance at Ian.

"I think I should follow you home, make sure your car doesn't slide off the road," he says.

"I'm not going home."

Nick cocks his head to one side. "What?"

"I'm taking her to the DMV, so she can get her car registered," Ian says. He's standing right next to me, smelling like cologne.

Nick's nostrils flare. He looks at me. "Oh. Okay. I'll see you later then, Zara. Be careful on the road, okay? It's icy."

"But the snow was melting earlier."

"It melts for, like, a second and turns to water and then it freezes. It's called black ice. It's dangerous, so just be careful, okay?"

"Okay." I watch him walk away. Every single cell in my body wants me to run after him, no matter how tired I am.

Philophobia
fear of love

That night I pad down the stairs into the living room and there's Grandma Betty standing at the front window again. Her hand holding the drape shakes. She stares outside into the dark.

"Oh, Jesus . . . ," she mumbles.

I touch her shoulder. She jumps, whirls around, almost growls, eyes flashing.

"Gram? What is it?"

"You scared the bejesus out of me."

"Sorry."

She puts her hands up to her heart.

"What are you looking at?"

"Nothing," she says. She forces a smile. "I have to go call your mother. We owe her a call. How about you get started on dinner? I bought one of those precooked rotisserie chickens from Shaw's and a box of stuffing."

"Gram?"

"Everything is under control, Zara. Don't you worry about a dotty old woman staring into the night."

Yeah, right. I peek out the window. Darkness greets me.

"Why isn't Nick hanging out with us?" I ask Issie and Devyn in PE.

Issie and I are lounging around waiting for the PE teacher, Coach Walsh, to show up. According to Devyn, he's in the locker room, hollering at Ian about something. We just sit on the lower bleachers and wait.

Devyn's fingers tap against the side of the chair. "I think he's just trying not to draw attention to you. You know if he likes you then everyone notices you. Plus, it's just part of his image. He's all bad boy."

"Sexy stud with a heart of stern," Issie banters. She starts tying her sneaker.

Her fingers fumble around. I kneel down in front of her and start tying them for her. "You guys are cute," I say.

Devyn laughs. His dimples show. Whenever his dimples show Issie starts blushing like crazy.

"Sexy stud with a heart of stern," he repeats what Issie said while I start on her next shoe. "That's brilliant."

"He's never even kissed a girl, so I don't think that one works," Issie says.

My insides stop working for a second. "Seriously? C'mon, how would you even know that?"

"He told Devyn. Devyn told me," Issie says. "So that one doesn't work. Okay. Moving on. How about hometown hero with high standards?"

"Hometown hero?" I say, yanking at the knot. "Nick?"

Devyn shrugs. "I think so. He saved me."

I raise my eyebrows and start to ask how, but Megan slinks over, all sexified in her tiny shorts and tank top with spaghetti straps. Spaghetti straps are a violation of the school dress code, not like Megan cares. Coach Walsh obviously doesn't care either.

Something in my throat tightens as Megan stands above me, blocking my view of Nick.

She smiles.

I do not trust that smile.

Issie coughs and twists her hands together. I slip a fingernail into the knot in Issie's laces, and loosen the knot, as if I have all the time in the world. Then I look up and meet Megan's eyes. They don't match her smile. She obviously is not a good enough actress to make them friendly.

"Zara?" She twists a long lock of strawberry-blond hair around her perfect finger. "You're from Charleston, right?"

I nod and wait for it to come.

"It must be hard adjusting to Bedford," she says.

I glance at Devyn. He gives me sympathetic eyes.

"It's okay."

"Some people never adjust, you know," she says.

"That's not true," Issie says. "Thanks for getting the knot out, Zara."

Megan glares at her. "Yes it is. Some people can't fit in."

I start working on tying the lace. One rabbit ear. Another rabbit ear. Done.

"Why would I *want* to fit in?" I cross my arms in front of my chest.

Megan steps closer to me and bends a little so her face is close to my face. She's put white mascara on her eyelashes, which makes her blue eyes a little creepy. It's not a good look for her. "You obviously don't want to since you keep hanging out with these freaks. Wheelchair boy and hyper girl."

She starts walking away but I reach out and grab her by the arm. It's icy and cold. "What did you say?"

She doesn't answer. My fingernails make half moons on her skin, but I don't loosen my hold. I say, "Don't threaten my friends. And don't insult them."

Ripping her arm out of my grasp, she stares me down. Then she flounces her hair back over her shoulder and says, all condescending, "Oh, little princess. It's not me you need to be scared of."

She bounds up the bleachers to go sit with her people. They all start doing the popular girl laugh. I ignore them. She yells down, "You know all that peace and love crap went out decades ago. And John Lennon is dead."

"You're shaking." Devyn says. "Zara, it's okay. Sit down."

I look down at my T-shirt. Something inside me breaks a little and I must gasp or something because Issie grabs my hand and tugs on it. I can't figure out how to sit down. Why would I want to sit down with her staring at me? I want to run, to just get away from here. Where can I run? I start looking for ways to escape. My breath pants out and my heart beats eight hundred beats a second, I swear.

"Zara . . . ," Devyn repeats. "It's okay."

"I grabbed her," I manage to say. "I never grab people. Never."

Issie opens her mouth, a little panicked looking, but then Coach Walsh saunters into the gym with Ian. Ian runs ahead and stands by me.

"I'll be your partner for the sit-ups," he says. "Hold your feet."

I nod. "Sure. Fine. Uh . . . Megan won't be cool with that."

"So?" He stares hard at me. He has little crinkle lines by his eyes.

"So, you're friends and everything and I don't want her to get mad at you."

"Megan isn't my keeper, Zara."

I eye him, struggle to find words to fit together. "Yeah, uh, right. Um. That okay with you, Issie?"

"Yep." She scrambles up. Her shoes, I must mention, are beautifully tied, with no laces flopping on the floor. "Devyn, can I tuck my feet under the sides of your wheels? Will you count for me?"

"Anytime," Devyn says. His dimples show. Issie starts blushing. Again. I wish I could be that cute with someone.

Ian puts his arm around my shoulders and steers me to a spot on the mat. "So, Megan's giving you a hard time."

"I'm fine," I say as I settle into sit-up position on the mat. It smells like wrestler sweat and chalk. Ian scowls. I don't know if it's at me or at her.

I glance to my side where Nick and Megan work on their crunches. Nick whispers something to her and her face scrunches up, annoyed. If he likes me why is he helping Megan? Whispering to her? If he's friends with Issie and Devyn how can he even talk to her? Issie is so clueless sometimes. My heart stabs at me a little bit for some stupid reason. I do not like Nick Colt. I will not like Nick Colt. Or, maybe I'm afraid of liking him.

"Hey, Ian," I say, pulling up to look at him. He has nice teeth, really white and even. "Issie and I are starting this Amnesty International school chapter. We write letters to try to free political prisoners and stuff. You want to join?"

"What do I get in return?"

I slam back to the floor and up again, faster and faster. "My undying respect?"

"Good enough," he says. "And maybe you'll go out with me Friday?"

I smile at him and we switch off. I hold his feet and wonder what he'd think about our pixie theory, what he thinks about the Beardsley boy. He could be in danger too. Every single guy in here could be in danger.

"Well?"

I finally answer him. "Maybe."

It's not like I have a chance with Nick anyway.

"So, I hear you think I'm ignoring you," Nick says, folding himself into a chair at the cafeteria table.

My mouth must drop open, because Devyn reaches over and pushes my chin back into place while he says, "Uh-oh."

Issie cringes and leaps out of her seat. "Oops. Sorry. I'm going to go get a cookie. Anyone want a cookie?"

No one answers. Issie pulls on Devyn's arm. "Devyn, I *know* you want to help me get a cookie."

"What?" He finally gets it and he throws his napkin on the table. It flops there, dead. "Oh, right."

"They've abandoned me," I say.

"Us," Nick corrects. "They just don't want us to fight."

"I don't want to fight either. I hate fighting."

"Really?"

"Yeah, really. Why do you look all surprised?"

"Because I'd say you like fighting."

"You obviously don't know me well."

"I'd say you like fighting but you hate that you like it."

"Oh, thank you, wise one."

"You handled Megan today."

I run my hand over my eyes. "That was horrible."

"You didn't slug her."

"I grabbed her arm, and I never grab people's arms."

"She was attacking your friends."

"Yeah. She was. And then you helped her with her sit-ups. That was rude of you."

"Why was it rude?"

"Because they're your friends too. It's like you went all traitor or something."

He shakes his head. His hair flops over his ears a little. A muscle twitches near his jaw. "Zara, I would never go traitor."

"It's okay. She's pretty."

"I was talking to her. I was telling her to leave them alone. Leave you alone."

I stab at a piece of lettuce. My fork pierces all the way through but when I bring the fork up to my mouth the lettuce rips, flutters down. Everything seems to be fluttering down: Devyn's napkin, the lettuce, my heart, my ego, my everything. When I talk again my voice is soft. "I just don't like that I grabbed her arm. I don't like that I had to yell at her. I hate yelling. I'm not into conflict. I promised myself a long time ago that I would never hurt anyone for any reason . . ."

He leans away. "What? Like you wouldn't attack the creep who keeps pointing at you?"

I shrug. "I don't know. I don't know if I could hurt someone else."

"C'mon, Zara. You don't value yourself that little, do you?" He leans back. His thigh touches my thigh. Neither of us move away.

"That's not it. I don't really know how to explain it. It's more like, who am I to decide that my life is worth more than someone else's?" It tingles where our legs meet.

A cafeteria light flickers and makes a buzzing noise high above us. Trays clatter in the background. People murmur about tests and dates and here we are talking about this.

He smells like the woods. I try not to smell him; it makes me dizzy. I try to focus.

He's talking. "You wouldn't attack a person who was trying to kidnap someone? Or hurting a baby? Or—"

"Enough," I interrupt. "I don't know if I would, okay? I mean, I know all about self-defense and everything, but I don't know if I could do it, if it's morally right to do it."

"You'd do it." He grins, so certain he's right. "If someone was attacking Issie you'd do it. If someone was attacking your grandmother you'd do it. Or Devyn. Or probably even Ian."

My eyes close. This is probably true. "I don't want that to be true."

"Why?"

"Because I don't want to be violent."

"It's not violent to protect your friend."

"It doesn't matter. It's not like someone's going to go attack Issie."

"We don't know that."

"What? You think Is is in danger?"

"No." He raises his hands up in the air. "I think we're all in danger."

"From that guy? The pointing guy? You think he's seriously bad?"

"Yeah," he says. "Yeah, I do."

I lean forward, closer to him. "But how? How do you know?"

"I feel it here." His fist taps his stomach.

We stare at each other for a second. There's something about his eyes that makes me frightened, yet not frightened. That makes no sense. It's like every part of me needs those eyes to look into my eyes a certain way, but I'm afraid of that. I want to ask about the dust I saw on his coat, but I'm afraid of that, too.

"I'm such a wimp," I say.

He must think I'm still talking about the pointing man because he shakes his head. "No you aren't. You just don't want to be brave."

"What?"

Nick doesn't answer because Devyn rolls back to the table. Issie bee-bops right behind him. He's got a pile of cookies spread across a napkin in his lap. "Is went a little crazy."

"I didn't know what kind everyone would like," she explains, plucking cookies up off the napkin and putting them on the table. She glances at us. "Oh no. You two are still fighting."

"No, we aren't," Nick says.

Devyn eyes us.

"Really," I say. "We aren't fighting."

"Then what's all the doomy-gloomy vibe going on?" Issie asks, sitting down. She offers me a cookie, M&M's mixed with chocolate chips.

"I scared her," Nick explains. He grabs an oatmeal raisin.

"Good," Devyn says. "She needs to be scared."

"What?" Issie turns on him.

"Fear makes us stronger, puts us on our toes. We've got to embrace it."

Issie snaps her cookie in half. "Guys can be so stupid."

True. Devyn's face turns red but Nick just laughs.

"So," I say really quickly, "are we going to go to the library after school today?"

"There's no cross-country?" Devyn asks.

"It's our day off," Nick explains. "Should we carpool or what?"

I turn on him. "You're going?"

"Yeah. Of course I'm going. That's okay with you, right?"

I nod. "Yeah, that's okay and yes, we should carpool to lower our carbon footprint and all that."

But for some reason knowing that I'm going to be in the library with Nick makes a knot form in my stomach, and it's not because the cookie is bad. The knot is becoming a familiar feeling. It's fear.

That dust on his jacket? It doesn't necessarily mean anything, right? And the way my insides feel all crazy weird whenever I look in his eyes? That doesn't mean anything either.

There is something about libraries, old libraries, that makes them seem almost sacred. There's a smell of paper and must and binding stuff. It's like all the books are fighting against decay, against turning into dust, and at the same time fighting for attention.

I touch the cover of one book, *ESP Your Way*. "It's like they're all crying out, 'Read me. Read me.'"

Nick turns around to look at me. "The books?"

"It's like they're lonely," I say. I shrug on purpose so he doesn't think I'm too weird.

"Books get lonely," he repeats, not looking at me anymore, scanning the titles above his head.

"What?"

"It's sweet."

I am sweet. My heart flip-flops and I bite my lip a little bit. Sweet as in a lollipop, or sweet as in a girl you would like to kiss passionately in the stacks? That's the question.

I squat down, checking out the numbers. "Found some."

Nick squats next to me and whistles low. "Wow."

We start pulling them out, *Fae Lore, Fairy Charms, An Encyclopedia of Fairies.*

Nick carries most of them to the back table by a big bay window. Dust particles swirl around in the sunbeams. Devyn and Issie almost look enchanted, like storybook heroes.

"You guys find stuff?" Issie asks too loudly.

A guy by the magazines shushes her.

"Sorry. Sorry!" She holds up her hand in an apology and then whispers at us. "What a grump. We found stuff too. Right, Devyn?"

Devyn nods but doesn't actually verbalize anything, just keeps reading the book he's got. It's ancient and smelly. I sneeze and settle into a chair. Nick grabs the one next to me. He splits our book pile in half and thrusts three books at me. "Dig in."

I dig.

We read and read and read and then Nick says, "Got something."

I sniff. "What?"

Issie hands me a crumpled tissue she's fished out of her bag. "It's clean."

"Thanks," I blow my nose. "I'm sorry. I'm allergic."

"To books?" Devyn raises his eyebrows like he can't believe it.

"Old books," I explain and lean closer so I can check out the book that's splayed in front of Nick. "What did you find?"

"It's about the tributes," Nick says. He is almost snarling. "It's vile."

"Just read it," Devyn demands.

"Quietly." Issie looks over at Magazine Man, who is leafing through a copy of the *Economist* and glaring at us.

Nick lowers his voice and reads, " 'So you are being chased by a pixie?' "

"It does *not* say that," Issie squeals, snatching the book away from him. "Oh my God, it does."

"Issie . . . ," I warn, looking to see if Nick's pissed. He isn't. "It doesn't really say that."

"It does!" She shows me the book, pointing.

" 'Of all of the Shining Ones—pixies, elves, fairies—it is true that the preservation of the princely bloodline is integral to their survival. They all share the sidhe heritage. In fact, their name is derived from the pict-sidhe. They are the Caille Daouine, or forest people. If you have been singled out by a male of their race, be proud. You are singled out to help continue the bloodline. It is unusual for this to happen. It is especially unusual for this to happen to humans. You might have some sidhe blood already flowing through your veins.' " I shut the book. "Oh, I am so honored."

"That's amazingly bizarre," Devyn said, staring at me like he's never seen me before. "Do you think you have sidhe blood?"

"What? No." I stare at all of them. "You guys aren't believing this."

Nick and Issie both put their hands on my arms. Issie reaches all the way across the table.

"I know this is a little freaky," she says, all calm.

"A little freaky?" I pull my arm away. "It's super freaky!"

"Will you please be quiet!" says the man reading the *Economist.*

"Sorry. Sorry." I sit down. I try to breathe slowly.

"Maybe he wants you to be his queen," Devyn says. "Continue the line."

"That's crap," Nick says.

"Yeah." I glare at him. "Why would anyone want *me* to be their queen?"

"That's not what I meant." The front legs of Nick's chair slam back down.

I can't even look at him. "Right."

"I just don't get what this has to do with boys going missing," he adds in a whisper that is low and serious. "What do you think, Devyn?"

Devyn rubs at his nose and stretches his arms out like he's been lifting weights and the muscles are tired. "The Web site said if the king doesn't have a queen he needs blood tributes from boys."

Issie shivers. "Creepy."

"What does that mean, though, blood tributes?" I grab one of Nick's books out of his pile and look at the index. "Oh. It's in this one. Page 123."

I flip to the page, scan the lines, and suck in my breath.

"What does it say?" Devyn asks.

When I look up from the words I can see him staring at Nick, like he's trying to get strength from him somehow. His face pales.

Nick nods at me. "Read it, Zara."

" 'When unable to mate with a queen, the pixie king has no choice but to take blood tributes from young males.' " My voice starts shaking and Nick puts his big hand on my shoulder, steadying me. " 'The entire court will help him hunt down the boys, absconding with them to the king's home, where the boys' blood is slowly drained.' "

I stop reading. Devyn's face is pale, almost all the dark, good color of it just gone, washed away.

Issie's eyes widen more than usual. "That's sick."

She sits back. She leans into Devyn, who still looks like he might pass out or puke or something.

Nick squeezes my shoulder. "Anything else?"

I flip the page. I don't want to keep reading, not if it's upsetting Devyn.

"It's okay," Devyn says.

I clear my throat and whisper. " 'Eventually, the boys die, their bodies overcome by the horrors brought upon them by the pixies. The pixies, this narrator might add, have no will to fight this overwhelming need. The pixie king can be without a queen for only so long before he succumbs to the dark, torturous side of his nature, and with his weakness the other pixies also become more debased and deprived, roaming the woods, hunting for potential queens and blood tributes.' "

"Look," Nick points. "In the margin."

"What's it say?" Issie asks.

I squint at the faded pencil marks. " 'Stay out of the woods.' "

"Good call," Nick says. His hand drops from my shoulder. I feel abandoned, colder somehow. I go to the back of the book where the due dates are stamped. No one has taken it out since they've pasted in a new sheet on the back page. But there's writing underneath it.

I start peeling off the edges while Issie says, "I am really not into this pixie thing. You guys think this is right, don't you? About the blood tributes?"

"Yeah, I know it's right," Devyn says. "But what does it mean that he's pointing at Zara all the time?"

"That's obvious," Nick adds. "He wants her to be his queen."

I swallow, but I don't look at Issie when I talk. Instead I stare into Nick's eyes. "Why not? It doesn't say that the pixie queens are bad."

"It doesn't say they're good!" Devyn almost yells.

The magazine guy throws his *Economist* on the table and stomps away.

Issie lowers her voice. "We probably just haven't read the part about the pixie queens being murdered and raped and turned into blood tributes."

"Right," I say.

"Zara . . . ," Nick warns. "You're thinking something."

"No, I'm not," I lie, standing up. I grab the book we've been reading and a couple others. "I'm going to go check these out. It's almost dark. Betty'll kill me if I don't get home before dark."

"Do you think she knows?" Devyn asks.

"Knows?"

"About the pixies?"

I imagine Betty with her gruff flannel shirts and her fact-gathering nature. "No way."

Nick gives me a ride home to where Yoko waits alone since we carpooled. We are silent a good part of the way.

"I don't know if I really believe this," I finally say.

"But?"

"But if it's true . . ."

"It sucks."

"Basically. Yeah."

He puts the MINI in park. "Maybe once we figure it all out we can set a trap."

"A trap?" I pick at the back of the book, where the due date is. The little wheels in my head are working overtime.

"What are you doing?"

"Nerves, I guess," I say and then it peels away, revealing the way that people used to take out books from libraries. There's a list of people who had the book, all their names handwritten in neat lines. I gasp.

Nick leans over, dark and forest smelling. "What?"

The words blur on the paper. "On the take-out list. The last name."

"Matthew White?" He looks at me.

A tear escapes out of my eye before I can trap it in there. Nick reaches out with his thumb and wipes it away.

"That's my dad," I stare at the name, written in his scratchy tall letters. "That means . . ."

"He knew."

"He knew about the pixies?"

Nick nods, "But look at this."

Written in pencil scratch around all the names like a border or something, it says, *Don't fear. Here there be tygers, 157.*

"What does that mean?" I ask.

"Is might know. It sounds familiar, doesn't it?" Nick says, but his eyes shade as he pulls out his cell phone.

"You're not telling me something."

"What?"

"You're hiding something."

"And how would you know that? You're psychic now?"

"Your cheek is twitching. I have this, um, this theory that your cheek twitches when you lie or you're hiding something. It's like you're trying to run out of your own skin."

He shakes his head, keeps punching buttons. "I don't know what to do with you."

I smile. "You could just tell me what you're thinking."

"Hold on," he says and then tells Issie what we found. She says something back and he hangs up.

"Well?"

He shifts his weight and slips his cell into a little nook between us. "She thinks it's a reference to the old medieval line, 'Here there be dragons.' It was used on maps and stuff to warn sailors away from dangerous places."

"I knew it sounded familiar."

"Mm-hmm."

"But that doesn't make sense."

"Why?"

I point at the first two words. "It says not to fear."

"And it's not dragons."

"It's tigers."

"Weird."

Betty comes to the front door and yells, "Are you two going to sit out there forever?"

I blush. "I should go."

"Yeah."

I step out of the car. The cold air bashes against me as I stuff the library book into my bag with all the others. I hoist the bag onto my shoulder, buckling under the weight.

Nicks jumps out of the car so quickly that I don't even notice it, and he's suddenly beside me, taking the bag off my shoulder. "Let me get it."

I am all for equal rights and everything, but it's pretty heavy. "Thanks."

"No problem," he says, walking with me to the porch where Betty's still standing, arms crossed over her nonexistent chest, smiling at us. Nick lowers his voice to a whisper. "Don't do anything stupid."

"You either," I whisper back.

Betty snorts as we clomp up the steps. "Well, Mr. Colt. Would you like to join us for dinner?"

"She's cooking," I warn.

Betty swats me with a dish towel. "Spaghetti. What can I do to spaghetti?"

Nick puts my bag just inside the door and actually looks scared. "That's okay. I've got a steak planned at home."

"Fine," Betty winks at him and then winks at me. Nick blushes. "I'll let you two say your good-byes."

"How embarrassing," I mutter.

Nick laughs. Dimples crinkle up the skin near his lips. I will not look at his lips. How can he never have used those? That's a crime against humanity right there.

"Bye," he says. "See you in school."

"Bye," I say, and he walks away. The sun is pretty much gone. The woods are dark, tall masses that lock the sky to the ground. Anything could be hiding there. I watch him get in the car. I watch him drive away. The whole time I expect something to jump out, grab him, and take him away, a blood tribute. I shake my head. The taillights disappear around a curve.

Betty's hand comes around my waist and I jump.

"You're letting the cold in," she says, and she shuts the door.

"So, John McKee's son has a ruptured appendix," Betty says as the water for the spaghetti boils.

I put forks on the table. The tongs of my fork touch an old water stain that looks like a cloud on wood. "That's too bad."

"It's more than too bad," Betty grumbles. "It means that I might get called in. We're the only paramedics in town. We're the only ones who can handle anything big. The first responders are just the drivers. They need John or me to deal with the big stuff."

"So?"

"So? So?" She tosses the pasta into the pot in one big clump. Half of it pokes out above the rim. "So that means I have to figure out what to do with you."

My words come out slowly the anger right beneath the surface, bubbling. "What to do with me?"

"If I have to go."

I push her out of the way, grab the pasta spoon thing, and push at the spaghetti so it goes down beneath the boiling surface. "You can leave me here. I'm a big girl."

"I don't want to leave you here alone."

"Why?"

"People get more depressed at night. Almost all my suicide calls are at night. We just want . . . we want you to be okay, Zara."

I turn the heat off high so the water doesn't boil out of the pot, down to medium. "Is that why Mom sent me here? Because she thought I was going to kill myself some night?"

Betty's eyelid twitches. "She was worried about you."

"I'm a big girl," I mock. "I'm fine."

"You miss your dad."

"Of course I miss my dad!" I point the pasta spoon at her, which feels way too melodramatic. I put it on the counter by the coffee maker. "That doesn't make me suicidal. That doesn't mean I have to have some freaking EMT babysitter standing over me all the time."

Betty's face crashes down but her thin, wiry body hardens up like she's made of steel. "Is that what you think of me?"

"No. I'm sorry. That was mean." I swallow hard, look away from her hurt face, and turn back to the stove. I grab the stupid pasta spoon again and swirl it around in the water, pretending like it's really important that none of the spaghetti noodles stick together. "I could come with you if you have a call."

She sighs. "That would work, maybe. But not if it's something complicated. You couldn't come into the building. You'd be sitting outside in the ambulance all by yourself. Plus, it's illegal."

"Illegal?"

"To have civilians in the ambulance."

I turn up the heat a little more and face her.

She smiles. "I could call that Nick boy and have him come over."

"No!"

"What? You don't like him? I've heard tell you and him and Devyn and Issie are running around all over town together. You went to the library today, right?"

"You're spying on me?"

"No. It's a small town. People talk."

I shake my head, grab some glasses, and open the fridge. "You are not going to phone Nick."

She takes some paper napkins from under the sink and flops them on the table. "There probably won't even be a call."

Halfway through dinner Betty's beeper goes off.

"Crap!"

We listen to the scanner. There's a possible cardiac arrest at the Y.

"Sorry," she says. "You stay put till I get back. Okay? I'm calling Nick on my way in."

"No, you aren't!"

"Yes, I am. And don't let anyone else in. I'm serious, Zara. Crap." She kisses me on the top of the head and pushes a bracelet on my wrist, all hectic. "Your mom's thinking about coming up for a visit."

I lift up my arm. An iron bracelet dangles there. "What's this?"

"A little gift."

She hauls on her jacket. "I'll be back as soon as I can. Don't worry about cleaning up."

"Do not call Nick!" I touch the cold metal of the bracelet.

She ignores me. "Lock the door!"

. . .

I could do the Urgent Action appeals for Amnesty. But I don't.

I could call Nick and tell him not to come. I don't do that either.

"This is One. I'm 10-23 at the Y," Betty's voice sounds from the radio she has on the counter.

The dispatcher, Josie, comes on. "10-4, Unit One. 10-23 at the Y, 1845 hours."

In ambulancespeak 10-23 means "on location." Anyone else would just say they were there. Unit One is Betty; 1845 hours is the time, military-style. It's all kind of corny.

So Betty is at the Y. It is 6:45 p.m., also known as 1845 hours. How can I know this stuff? There's a list of ten codes Betty posted on the fridge. I swear I've memorized half already. Maine is turning me into such a geek.

I push away from the table, dump our dinner plates into the sink, and start scraping off the spaghetti. Betty hasn't finished hers because she dashed out, so I change my mind and wrap it up, storing it away in the fridge. She might be hungry later. I keep scraping mine away. It is no fun eating alone.

I stare out the window above the sink at the dark woods. The moon is full and it makes everything glow and look almost pretty. Even the snow looks nice, not so cold. I bet the guy is out there, the pixie guy. And I bet if I go out there he'll find me, and then maybe I'll get some answers. And I'm not a boy, so I don't think I'm in any real danger.

Betty's voice is back on the radio, "I'll be 10-6, taking one forty-five-year-old male to Bangor. He's CH3. 10-4?"

Cardiac issues. Chest pain. Just like my dad.

"10-4," says Josie at dispatch.

"10-4," I say to the radio, as if they can hear me. "I'll be 10-6, going running, looking for a pixie guy. 10-3?"

I rush up the stairs into my room and start pulling out running clothes. I have tights for the cold weather and a layer of Under Armour to wick the sweat away from my skin. It's the sweat that makes you feel cold. I find a wool hat in Betty's closet and put it over my hair, which is the worst look imaginable when you have lots of fine hair like I do, but it isn't like I'm going to a beauty pageant, trying to be Miss Maine or something. I'm going running in the dark, nobody will see me. Until Nick gets here.

That's right.

I am going running and maybe I'll find that boy-stealing pixie guy. I pull the hat on and pause for a second without really thinking about it, and look in the mirror at the paler, thinner version of me that I've become. Even my eyes are dull. Blue, but not as blue as they used to be. If my dad were here he'd be taking my temperature and trying to feed me French onion soup. But it isn't my body that's sick. It's my insides. My insides are hollow. My insides are hollow because I've been too scared of living and going on, which is totally self-indulgent and awful, because think of all those people in prisons for nothing—for blogging, for speaking, for thinking differently. They'd probably give anything to move forward, to go on.

Is there a name for this fear? I'm not sure; I should look it up. There's tachophobia, which is a fear of speed, of moving too fast.

I shake myself out of my haze and lace up my sneakers. This is the first step in moving forward, the first step in pixie hunting, the first step in taking control of my life, because I can.

I text a message to Issie, telling her I'm going for a quick run and that we should do some more Internet investigating tomorrow at lunch. Then I text Nick.

`Gone running. See you ON ROAD.`

There, my bases are covered and I'm going pixie hunting.

Scotophobia
the fear of darkness

My mother is afraid of the dark.

When I was little we had nightlights all over the house, not just in my bedroom and the bathroom. There were two in the upstairs hallway, one in every guest room, one in the kitchen, the dining room, the downstairs bathrooms, the living room, everywhere.

I asked her about it once. We were in the kitchen. I was sitting on the counter, feet dangling, wearing my Elmo pajamas and watching her cook. "Why are you scared of the dark, Mommy?"

She'd been making pancakes, stirring up the batter. She spilled blueberries into the bowl and stirred and stirred.

"I'm not."

"Then why do we have a million nightlights?"

She banged the spoon against the big ceramic bowl, the one with the two maroon stripes around the rim. "That's so you don't get scared."

"I'm not scared," I said. "I like the dark."

"No, you don't."

She stared at me, her face hardening into something unrecognizable. She'd stirred the batter too much and broke all the blueberries apart.

"The pancakes are blue," I told her.

She looked at the bowl, frowning, and let go of the spoon. "Oops!"

"It's okay. Blue is pretty."

She kissed me on the nose and said, "Let me tell you something, Zara. Sometimes there are things that people should be afraid of."

"Like the dark?"

She shook her head. "No, more the absence of light. Understand?"

I nodded, but I didn't understand, not at all.

I slam out the door and down the steps. I don't warm up. I don't stretch. I just start jogging under the light of the moon. Frost crystals form on the windows of the house. The trees seem heavy from the weight of the air.

There is a definite absence of light, but I've rigged up one of those headband flashlight things, so I won't trip as long as I'm careful.

Something about the cold air just rips through my lungs when I run. Every breath is like an ax into my chest. Every breath is a decision I have to make, a decision to live, to go on.

It hurts but I push through it and then the pain numbs. It isn't like it's gone, but more like it just isn't so wrenching anymore. I don't think there's any other word for it than wrenching.

Breathing should always be easy, but nothing is easy in Maine. Nothing is easy in the cold. I keep running though; turning out of the driveway and onto the main road. It's easier to run on the asphalt than it is on the dirt because of foot placement. But it is harder on my joints and scarier too, like something is watching.

My legs stretch out and I pick up the pace, but that feeling comes back. A noise thuds in the dark forest beside me and I keep running. Maine makes me skittish. I've never been such a wimp. I ran through all sorts of neighborhoods in Charleston and I never got scared there.

I hate being scared.

"If you can name something, it's not so scary," my dad always said. "People are afraid of what they don't know."

I turn my head and scan the woods, but all I can make out are trees and shadows. I can't see anyone in there or anything.

My mind fills with visions of bears and wolves, but the only bears Maine has are black bears, and they're pretty much terrified of people. The Maine Department of Inland Fisheries and Wildlife swears that there are no wolves in Maine, just coyotes. I know this because I checked their Web site after I saw the huge paw prints in the snow my first morning. I told Grandma Betty about them. What had she said?

"They're afraid to admit there are wolves here, but everyone knows it's true. Anyway, it's nothing to worry about. Wolves don't bother people."

That's what I tell myself, *Wolves don't bother people. Wolves don't bother people.*

It doesn't help.

Wolves don't bother people. Pixies bother people.

That spider-crawly feeling comes back along the palms of my hands.

Then I hear it.

My name.

"Zara."

I stumble a little, trip over a rock or something that's in the breakdown lane of the road. Why are there no cars out here? Oh, that's right. Maine isn't the most populated state in the country, especially Betty's part of Maine.

I keep running, picking up the pace, listening. Then I hear it again. It seems to echo off every tree in the forest. It seems to come from both sides of the road, behind me, all around. Still, it is soft. A soft whisper, commanding.

"Zara. Come to me, Zara."

It sounds so cheesy, so much like a bad musical line, that it's not really that scary. Oh, that's a huge lie. I'm totally scared. Crap. Crapcrapcrap.

I wanted this. I wanted to draw him out. But now? Fear pushes my feet faster, makes my heart speed up too fast. It pounds against my chest, trying to escape. But from what? A voice? A shadow? I came out here to find him. He's found me.

The truth slams into me:

I didn't imagine that man at the airport.

I didn't imagine the way my skin felt each time I saw him.

I didn't imagine that dust or make up the words in that book.

The sound of large wings slashing through the air makes me look up. An eagle flies over my head and then ducks into the trees. Its white head gleams.

"Stupid," I say. "I'm so stupid. I probably just heard the eagle."

If my dad were here he'd laugh at what a wimp I'm being. *I* laugh at what a wimp I'm being and I keep running. My breath comes out in ragged puffs. I push it in and out, focus on my feet.

"Zara!"

I stop. Anger fills me. To hell with wimp. To hell with Booker T. quotes.

"What?"

I plant my feet and wait.

The cold air chills me. I shiver. My hands turn into fists.

"What do you want?" I yell. "Why are you following me?"

I force my eyes wide open and look for something, flashing my light around. What am I looking for? Maybe a man? Maybe a man in a dark European suit? Maybe the kind of man who points at planes and makes your skin feel like it has become a spider parade route?

The forest seems to look with me. Each tree branch reaches out as if trying to sense what is there in the road with me. Then something in the woods moves. I grab a stick from the side of the road, hold it in front of me, and turn to face the noise. The light swings with me and I keep searching. It isn't a real noise, more like a sense, a feeling of movement.

"I'm not scared," I say, staring into the side of the road. "Just come out and talk to me. I've been reading about you. I found a book."

My voice shakes when I speak. The hand holding the stick is not too steady either.

"Zara," the voice says. "Come to me."

"Right."

"Please."

"No," I say. "You want to talk, you come out here."

The eagle screams out a warning.

Something snaps in the woods behind me, the opposite direction of the voice and the first noise. I twist around, ready for anything—crazy men, wolves, bears, dinosaurs.

"I know you're a freaking pixie, and if you think that scares me, you're stupid!" I yell. "And I know that you're following me."

The woods are silent. The spider feeling goes away.

"What? You just leave? You're toying with me? That is so lame."

Nothing.

"If you want me to be your stupid queen you should stop hiding. But I've got to tell you something, Mr. Pixie Guy, there will be no more torturing boys while I'm here! Got it?" Anger hits me in the gut and I roar, really, I just roar like some sort of crazy actor in a wrestling match. I scream out my rage in some steroidal guttural way. I came out here because *I* want to find *him,* because *I* want to know what's real, because I want to stop it.

Blinding light flashes into my eyes and a MINI Cooper engine roars as it rounds the curve in the road. A horn blares and I jump sideways out of the way and into the ditch. A rock scrapes my cheek. It takes me a second to figure out what happened. I stand up. I've dropped the stick. The world waves in front of me, hazy and unfocused. The light falls off my head and I can't find it.

"Zara!" Nick slams the door of his now parked car. He rushes to me and stands in front of me. I can't see his features because of the headlights shining behind him. He is just a massive silhouette, but I'd know that silhouette anywhere.

"What are you doing out here?" His voice comes out angry.

My voice is whisper weak. "I wanted to find him."

"What?" His hands ball into fists and his whole body quakes. "What the hell is the matter with you?"

I shrink back. Nobody has ever yelled at me like that. Never.

He's so mad, I almost expect him to hit me. I must have swayed because he grabs me, puts an arm around my waist, and leads me toward the MINI.

"I just wanted to stop it. I wanted to save someone like I couldn't save my . . ."

"I'll take you home," he says, a lot more quietly.

The inside of his car smells like him, like pine wood and the sea. I touch my face. Blood covers my fingers.

Nick grabs a wad of tissues and presses them against my cheek.

"It's okay," I say.

His eyes tell a different story.

"Don't be mad at me." I move my fingers up to the tissue against my cheek. My fingers graze his fingers. Something electric—good and shocky—surges through me. Maybe he feels it too, because he pulls away. He stares at the blood on his fingers and his jaw hardens.

"Lock your door," he orders.

I do.

He puts the car in drive and takes me to Betty's. It doesn't take long, but he doesn't say anything the entire way and the silence presses against me.

Everything inside of me tingles and waits and dreads.

Next to me, Nick drums his fingers on the top of the steering wheel.

"You want to tell me what happened out there?" Nick asks.

I stare out at the road. The moon hangs above us, waiting maybe. The trees are dark. I touch my head where the headlamp should be.

Finally I say, "I don't know. I think the pixie guy was out there calling my name, like in some horror movie, and then I yelled back at him, and there was an eagle, and then I yelled some more, and he was gone."

"You scared the pixie away? Is that what you're saying?"

"I don't know."

"Why did you go out there?"

"I wanted him to take me. I don't want you to get hurt or Devyn or anybody. So I figured . . . It sounds so stupid."

"You were going to sacrifice yourself to save everyone else?"

I cringe. "Then I wimped out."

Nick pulls up to Betty's and hops out of the MINI. I unlock my door and he lifts me out, placing both of his big hands on either side of my waist like I'm a little kid or something.

"I'm fine," I say, trying to pull away. "I can walk."

He arches an eyebrow but lets me go and watches me sway on the driveway. "I think you've had a shock."

"Well, you almost ran me over."

"You were standing in the middle of the road," he argues, hustling me inside.

"You were speeding," I tease.

I open the door to Betty's house and turn.

"I was not speeding," he says, fixing his hat. It has a big *B* on it for Bedford.

"I'm sorry," I say. And I am. I lean against the door that is quiet and doesn't complain about things or your behavior or anything like that. Doors are very good that way. Blood has seeped through the tissue. I hold it against my cheek.

He watches me and doesn't move. So I add, "I went out in Charleston all the time."

"This is not Charleston."

I laugh. "That's for sure."

"Zara, this is serious." He pushes me lightly into the house.

"Why, because it's about pixies? 'Zara, this is serious,'" I turn and walk toward the sofa, feeling ridiculous because I've totally lost my cool and acted like some diabolical dictator or something, and I've got to hold on to some dignity. I plunk myself onto the corner of the couch. I grab onto the armrest. He stays standing. Of course. Not like he'd want to hang out and stay awhile, maybe have some hot cocoa, talk about why everyone in this annoying town is so deranged and paranoid and can run so darn fast.

"What?" I manage to say. "Aren't you leaving?"

"I promised Betty." His jaw firms up and then he says in a calm but forceful tone, kind of like an actor trying to play a cop, "You can't go out after dark."

"I'm not a boy."

"No? Really?" His mouth loosens up. "But you are what the pixie guy wants."

"You think so? Then why doesn't he just grab me? Why does he just call my name?" I pull the tissue away from my face. Blood drips.

"Maybe that's the rule. I don't know. I feel like I don't know anything." Nick yanks me up by the arms and brings me into the kitchen. It still smells like spaghetti.

He grabs a dish towel and shoves it under the faucet, then presses it against my head. The water drips down my face.

"Sorry. Forgot to wring it out," he says and blushes, actually blushes, as he wrings it out over the sink. His fingers twist and squeeze the cloth. Then he brings it back up to my skin. His touch is actually almost tender and his eyes seem to soften a little. I stare up at him, leaning against the counter. He is so very close. With his free hand, he cups my uninjured cheek and tilts his head, staring at me, staring into me.

"I can't figure you out," he says.

I swallow. His eyes watch my neck move and then they harden as they look at the dish towel over my cut.

"Are you trying to drive me crazy?" he says.

"No."

If I keep my eyes open and take a little time maybe I could figure him out, but do I really want to try?

Probably.

"Betty is going to kill you." His thumb moves slightly against my cheek but it's enough to make me tremble, and not in a bad way. Something is so going on but I don't know what.

I reach out a hand. "I was scared. I was scared before you came. I thought I heard . . . I think I'm going crazy. Does Maine make people crazy? Does the cold or something get into people's brains and not allow them to think rationally or I don't know, maybe freeze their neurons or something?"

I stop talking because even I can hear this sort of hysterical edge taking over my voice. My hands grab onto air, nothing but air, looking for words or something to hold on to.

He shakes his head and his hair moves in the air the way a dog's does. "You're not crazy."

"I feel crazy."

"Why?"

"It's just . . . I don't know what's going on. Ask me about the situation in Darfur, I can tell you all about it. You want to know how many people are waiting on death row in the United States? I know that too. But no, I can't understand why there are pixies in some hick Maine town."

"I don't really understand it either."

I sigh and touch my hand to my cheek, then rub it across my eyes. I'm so tired. The floor sways a little and I manage to shuffle into the living room and flop down on the couch. He moves beside me instantly, putting his hand on my shoulder, peering at me. He moved so fast I hardly noticed it.

"I'm a little woozy," I say. "Which is probably why I'm acting like . . . like . . ."

"Woozy?"

"I know, it's a dumb word. My mom says it all the time. My mom sent me here, you know. She said that word, woozy."

He pulls a wool blanket from the back of the couch. "You miss her?"

"Yeah. She was spunky before my dad died. I'd like to be spunky. Do you like spunky girls or unspunky girls? I always wondered that. Not about you, but about guys in general. Am I spunky?"

"You're spunky."

"Yeah, right. I feel the opposite of spunky."

"Which would be, what? Spunkless?" He wraps the blanket around me and sits down next to me, right next to me. I move closer to him without thinking about it.

"I hate this," he says, "not being able to figure out what's going on."

"Because it makes you feel helpless?" I ask.

He touches the thread on my finger. "Yeah."

"We'll figure it out." I inhale the pine smell of him, like Christmas trees.

"We better."

"I was scared," I say, remembering the voice.

"You said that." He puts his arm around me. Right over the top of my shoulders the way Blake Willey did on our first date in seventh grade when we went to see one of the *Shrek* movies.

I let him keep his arm there and bite my tongue so I don't start babbling again. And I don't think about what Ian would think. Ian, who wants to go out with me. Ian, who, despite his weird friendship with Megan, is always nice, totally unlike Nick.

Nick.

Nick has thick dark hair.

Nick has big chestnut eyes.

Nick has nice white teeth.

Nick has a big chest with runner's lungs so he could huff and puff and blow my house in. And I do not care. I lean in. He's so cozy warm but I shiver anyway, remembering the woods. My eyelids just don't want to be open and I really want them open, because Nick is so cute when he isn't bossing me around.

"Thank you for getting me," I try to say. My lips are so tired they don't want to move.

"Anytime, Zara. Really. I mean it." He seems to be smelling my hair.

"I know you hate me and everything but we should be friends," I tell him, closing my eyes.

"I don't hate you," he says. "That's not it at all."

"What is it then? Are you a victim of parthenophobia?"

"Parthenophobia?"

"Fear of girls."

"You are so strange." He moves back even closer to me, this wicked glint in his eye like he's trying hard not to snort-laugh at me. His hand presses against the side of my head. Nobody has ever touched me like this before, all gentle and romantic, but strong at the same time. "I'm not afraid of girls."

"Then why haven't you kissed any?"

For a second his eyes flash. "Maybe the right one hasn't come around yet."

"That is such a line," I say. I watch his lips. For some bizarre reason I say it again. "We should be friends."

"Yeah, we should," he agrees and something warm seeps over me, making me nestle even closer.

"I mean, I'm not going to be like one of those annoying women in movies who falls in love with the guy who rescues her, because I don't think you even rescued me, okay?"

"Rescued you?"

My stomach cramps. "Whatever."

He starts laughing. I tap him on the thigh. "Stop it."

"I can't."

His whole body just bounces up and down and he looks little and younger and cute. Once when my dad and I were watching this silly NASCAR movie my dad transformed like that. It was like he was a little boy all of a sudden and everything he was worried about—like bills, and me, and human rights relief—was all gone, lost in a fart joke.

Nick takes in a deep breath, so deep I move with it too, since I'm leaning on him. When he exhales he says, softly, almost so low that I can't hear it, "I don't want to hurt you, Zara. I don't want anything to hurt you."

I smile.

"Good. But I'm not a damsel and there is no distress."

Then I fall asleep, which was ridiculously bad timing of course, because the conversation is just getting interesting.

Philophobia

fear of falling in love or being in love

I wake up the next morning in my own bed. Not the couch, but my bed. Which means?

I've dreamt everything!

Right?

Wrong.

My hand reaches up to touch the wound on my cheek. It's bandaged with gauze and tape. There are marks on my hand from when I broke my fall. They aren't too deep but they're funny looking. Sitting up is not easy. All my bones creak and pop like I've run a marathon. My abs hurt. I pull myself out of bed and pad over to the mirror. The white bandage almost blends in with my pale face, but not quite. Betty must have bandaged it last night, but I can't really remember that. I can't remember Nick leaving. Color spreads across my face as I think about him. Oh God, I asked him to be my friend. You don't ask people to be your friend.

Catagelophobia is the fear of being ridiculed. I think this is a very normal phobia. It is a phobia I should actively cultivate.

"Needy. Needy and pathetic," I say to my ugly mirror reflection.

My ugly mirror reflection mouths the same words.

I yank my fingers through my hair and give up.

Catagelophobia.

Why do I care? There is absolutely no reason to care about Nick. He is just a cute boy who almost ran me over in his beautiful MINI. Sure, he smells good—like comfort and warmth and safety, but he isn't safe. I know that. I know that absolutely. Plus, why would he like me anyway? The girl in my mirror is too pale, too plain, and has a big bandage on her head. I am not exactly supermodel material, or even Megan material.

I start yanking at my hair, trying not to look at myself, trying not to care.

Grandma Betty's hand on my shoulder makes me jump. "Zara?"

Turning around, I lean against the dresser. I'm afraid to meet her eyes.

She lets her fingers drift to my hair. "You need to put some conditioner on it to get these tangles out."

"I know."

Outside a dog barks.

"Damn dogs," she mutters, looking away and then back at me. "That Nick is a nice boy."

I eye her. "He doesn't like me."

"Really? Are you trying to convince yourself or me? Because I found him with his hand pressing a bandage to your head while you were passed out drooling on the couch."

"I was drooling?"

She laughs. "Not too much."

I hide my head in my hands. The air in the room is stale and smells like crusted-up blood and doubt. Betty pulls my hands away. Her face is smiling. "He likes you, Zara. He took care of you. That's what men do when they take a shine to you."

"He obviously has some rescue-the-damsel-in-distress gene, which is totally inappropriate because I am hardly a damsel in distress," I say, a little too bitterly. Even I can hear it.

"Hardly. You're too busy trying to rescue people you don't know." She points at my pile of Amnesty International papers.

"Like that's a bad thing?"

"It's a good thing, Zara. It's just. Well . . . we all need a little bit of rescuing from time to time. It doesn't make us weak."

"He doesn't *like me* like me."

"You know, there's nothing wrong with admitting he likes you. There's nothing wrong with feeling good things, Zara. Your dad doesn't want any of us to stop living."

My bedcovers are all tangled up on the mattress. None of them are in the right place. I try to straighten them. My pile of books and Amnesty International human rights reports topple against my foot. The book with my dad's name in it awaits.

"This place is such a mess," I mumble, trying to stack the reports up again. "I'm sorry I'm so messy. I bet my mom wasn't messy when you guys took her in."

"She wasn't messy, but she never put the cap back on the toothpaste."

"She still doesn't!" I shake the human rights report at Betty for emphasis. There are so many numbers in those reports, and each number represents someone's pain, someone's story. My stomach crumples and I put the book gently on the pile. Then I pick up the book from the library. "Dad took this book out. His name is in the back."

She takes the book and stares at it. After what seems like forever, she says in a quiet voice, "Do not fear. Here there be tygers."

"Do you think he wrote that?" I touch her arm. She suddenly seems frail.

"Looks like his handwriting."

"What do you think it means?"

"It was a Ray Bradbury story." I must give her a look because she adds, "He was a science fiction writer. One of the best."

"Oh, I'm not really up on my science fiction."

"Hmm." Betty becomes serious, shuts the book, and hands it back to me. I hold it against my chest for a second, even though it sounds super corny. The book feels kind of special. Like it's a message left from my dad to me.

Betty eyes me. "You went outside, alone, last night."

I place the book on top of the pile of human rights' reports. "I know, I—"

"Zara?" Betty's voice turns into a warning. I haven't responded as quickly as I should have.

"I'm sorry," I rush out. "I told Nick and Issie what I was doing. Well, I left them text messages so they couldn't talk me out of it. And I . . . I just wanted some answers."

"And you thought you'd go looking for answers in the dark?" She picks up a pillow.

I haul in a massive breath. "Look. I was trying to find someone."

"Someone?"

"That man on the side of the road. We saw him when you brought me home from the airport." I keep smoothing the already pretty smooth sheets. They feel cool against my hands, soft and stable.

Betty sucks in her breath. "Zara, that is not a good idea."

I straighten up. "Why?"

She stops fluffing a pillow. It dangles. "He's dangerous."

"How? How do you know he's dangerous? How is he dangerous?"

She takes a step away from me, backing into the bed. She starts making it all over again, tucking the sheet corners tightly into the mattress. "I think he's the one who kidnapped the Beardsley boy."

"I think so too. So why don't we arrest him?"

"You have to be able to catch someone to arrest them." She fidgets more with my pillow, jerking it around with quick, aggressive movements. The sun shines onto her gray hair and makes it glisten like snow. "And he seems to leave no trace, no tracks, just appears and disappears. I'm surprised we even saw him that evening. I'd like to see him again."

"Why?"

"To catch him," she snarls, and for a moment it's like my grandmother is gone. It's like she's someone different, primal, and then she snaps back. "Anyone who can kidnap boys."

"But you aren't positive it's him."

"No. I'm not positive."

I want to tell Nick and Issie and Devyn. "I'm super late for school."

"I'll drive you."

"You don't have to," I say, whirling back around to look at her. Her shoulders are broad, like a swimmer's, but skinny. I don't know how she can be an EMT heaving all those people around, saving them when she's so old herself.

"I want to," she says, smiling. "Let me be your grammy for a day and take care of you. Okay?"

I smile back. "Okay. If you make me hot cocoa."

"Plus, you might have a slight concussion."

"I do *not* have a slight concussion."

"Of course you do."

Betty drops me off at school. We sit in the truck for a second even though I'm already tardy and I'll have to go get a note from Mrs. Nix.

"Your mother misses you, Zara," Betty says out of nowhere.

Something tightens inside me. "Uh-huh. Did you know that some people are afraid of ugliness? Really. There's a name for it and everything. It's called cacophobia."

"And some people are afraid of talking about their mothers."

"Oh, nice one."

"Don't roll your eyes," Betty says, but not in an angry way. She taps her fingers on the steering wheel. "I'm just a little worried about your relationship. It seems like you're avoiding her."

I close my eyes so I don't roll them again. "She sent me away."

"Because she was worried about you. You lost your spunk." Betty reaches over and squeezes my knee. The skin on her hand is fragile and paper thin. "I think you're getting your spunk back."

I raise my eyebrow, just one, on purpose, to show her what I think of that. She slaps my knee and laughs. "There's talent right there. Now, get going."

She honks her horn good-bye and leaves me, off to go rescue the world for another day. I drag myself through the freezing wind into school and down the corridors, past the big wooden Eagle statue and the art students' self-portraits. I really don't want to be here, but it's better than being home alone all day thinking about the voice in the woods.

The school secretary's office door is closed but I open it and stand by the counter waiting for Mrs. Nix to turn around and notice me. She's filing and trilling out a country song about wasting time and driving in cars. I clear my throat so she'll know I'm here.

It works. She turns around and smiles. "Zara!"

She puts down her papers on her desk and walks to the counter. Her eyes narrow in concern as she glances at my bandage.

"Zara, are you okay?"

I nod. "I fell when I was running last night."

Mrs. Nix shakes her head and signs a late pass for me. "Well, I hope your grandmother told you to wear your coat inside out."

The pass dangles from my fingers. "What?"

She slowly meets my eyes and her mouth opens. Her words come out winter slow. "Oh. I thought Betty would have told you that."

I shake my head.

"Your mother didn't either?"

"No. Why would she?" I ask, feeling more and more confused. I know Mrs. Nix is really sweet, but she's acting a little crazy weird, like she's the one who can't believe what's going on.

"Why would she? Everybody's in denial, but it's happening again," she mumbles. Her arm knocks against the top of the counter and a box of colored paper clips tumbles to the floor and scatters all over the picture of the school's mascot drawn into the tiles.

"Such a ninny!" she says and crouches down to pick up the clips. I squat down to help her and our knees almost touch as our fingers scoop up the clips. I can't believe she said "ninny."

"It's okay."

"You are such a sweet girl, Zara, just like your mother." She stands back up. "Thank you for helping."

"Not a big deal." I tuck my hair behind my ears. It was flopping into my eyes so I couldn't see her and I really want to see her, to figure her out. "So, why do you wear your coat inside out?"

She blushes and dismisses her own words with her hand. "You wear your coat inside out when you're alone outside at night. It's an old wives' tale. A superstition. I thought everyone knew that."

"Why?"

Her face grows even redder and the phone rings. She looks thrilled to hear it. She gives me a little wave and answers the phone in an overly happy way. "Hello, this is Mrs. Nix, school secretary, and how can I help you this fine day?"

I take my note and leave.

Maine just keeps getting stranger and stranger.

Devyn finds me after Spanish. Ian's hanging on my elbow and Devyn says, "Hey. I need to talk to Zara for a second."

"Sure," Ian says, not changing his pace.

"Alone?"

"Oh," Ian fumbles. "Right. See you later, Zara."

"Sure," I say, watching him stride away. "Poor guy."

"He's fine," Devyn says. "I've been thinking about the book. Do you have it?"

"Yeah." I juggle my books around and show him.

"Can I borrow it?"

My heart drops. "Sure, yeah . . ."

"I'll take care of it, Zara, I promise. I know your dad wrote in it and that makes it special."

I put the book on his lap while we move down the hall. "I'm that obvious?"

"It would be special to me if I were you," he says. "I just want to read it whenever I get a chance."

"Yeah," I say. "I've been thinking about the quote about tigers."

"And?"

"It seems important."

"I know."

Issie stomps toward us. "I am so mad at you!"

I point at myself. "Me?"

She grabs my elbow. "Yes, you. *You* went running alone at night. *You* are an idiot."

"Thanks, Is." I pull my arm away.

"He could have taken you," she whispers. She looks to Devyn for help.

"It was dumb," he agrees. "Nick told us what happened. About how the guy said your name."

I don't say anything. Issie softens, puts her arm around my waist. "We know you were just trying to be a martyr."

"I wasn't—"

She interrupts, "We don't want you to be a martyr. We'll figure this out together. No one gets to be a martyr. Right, Devyn?"

He nods. "Right. At least not alone."

. . .

"Zara, this is great," Issie says, bouncing up and down between some desks. "Check out all the people here."

I look around the classroom that we get to use for our Amnesty International lunch. Nick is not here.

"There are ten people, Issie," I say, sighing. "Ten is not much. There are thousands of people who need our help."

Ian waves at me. He has a monster smile on his face, and he swaggers over like he's responsible for all ten people here, which, to be fair, he probably is.

"Ten's really good," Issie says and then points at Ian with her elbow. "Uh-oh, look who's coming."

"At least he's here," I say, putting down some pens and pre-stamped envelopes. "Unlike other people."

Something in my stomach drops when I think about Nick not being here.

"At least *he* cares," I add as Ian comes closer.

Ian smiles down at me. "Hey, Zara. Good turnout."

I glance at Issie, who gives me an *I told you so* look. "It's only ten people."

"Ten is good up here. We're psyched if five people show up for Key Club," he says, nodding at my Urgent Action reports. "Can I help you pass those out?"

"Yeah." He is being so nice. "You could."

It isn't until I've explained all about Amnesty International's important mission and people start writing letters that Nick decides to show up.

Ian is already sitting next to me. So Nick stands in front of my desk.

"Nice of you to show up, Colt." Ian sneers. He suddenly looks like a snake. It is not a good look, all scaly and coiled.

Issie puts her hands over her eyes like she's afraid to see bloodshed.

I stare up at Nick. "You're late."

He smiles at me. There's a piece of spruce branch stuck to his sweater.

"I had things to take care of," he says, all growly, looking away from me and staring Ian down. They do the whole *I'm alpha—No, I'm alpha* thing, with the staring and pulling the shoulders back and posturing.

Devyn whispers to Issie, loud enough for us to hear, "They're so sad sometimes."

She whispers back, "I know."

Nick picks the spruce branch off his sweater and says in a normal voice, "We are, aren't we?"

Then he smiles at me and my heart starts beating harder, which I'm ashamed to admit, but it's true. Hearts betray you like that. This is why it's perfectly acceptable to be cardiophobic, afraid of hearts.

"I'm sorry I'm late. Tell me what to do, Zara," he says, casually rocking back on his heels. I swear Ian almost breaks his pen in half, but I just stand up and get Nick settled in with an Urgent Action appeal and some paper.

During school the sky is bright and blue, the kind of Maine sky that painters always recreate, the kind of sky that makes even a Charleston girl like me relax and smile. The colors crisp on the trees that I stare at during art class. I'm supposed to be working on a paper collage of an eagle, but my thoughts keep drifting off to pixies and political prisoners.

I rip a piece of red brocade paper to create a splash of excitement on the eagle's left wing. When I'm applying the glue, Nick glides into the room. He sits down at the table next to me.

"Is it okay if I sit here?" he asks.

I nod. My heart pitter-patters a million crazy, happy rhythms. My brain wonders why he's sitting next to me. There are a million trillion places he could have sat, not to mention where he usually sits. *Do not get too excited. Do not make this into something. It's probably just to talk about pixies.*

Nick goes back to the supply closet and grabs his project. He sets it up on the table. It's a wolf stalking through the forest. He's done it all with coiled-up paper.

"That's good," I say, pointing.

He smiles. "Yours too."

We sit there without talking for a minute. I wish he'd say something. Anything. Well, not anything, maybe something nice.

"You're too quiet," I blurt out.

He laughs. "Like you aren't?"

"I didn't sit down with you."

"True, but last night *you* asked *me* to be your friend." His eyes twinkle.

"Shh. There are some things that should just never be repeated."

He clutches at his heart, pretending to be hurt. "What? You didn't ask me?"

"It just makes me sound so needy."

"No, it doesn't."

"Yes, it does."

He smiles and the smile comes through his voice. "Zara, you are not needy."

I rip another piece of paper and edge it finely with an X-Acto knife while I groan. "Yeah, right."

"Plus," I say after I work a little bit on the wing and my logic. "A real friend would not bring up something that would so obviously embarrass his friend because of its innate patheticness."

He starts laughing, but it sounds like a snort. "Innate patheticness?"

I pretend like I'm going to stab his chiseled forearms with an X-Acto knife. Of course, our art teacher notices.

She points at me with a glue gun. "Zara."

"Just kidding!" I say.

"Do I need to ask Mr. Colt to move?" She wiggles her lips. "Are we having a little love in the afternoon?"

Everybody titters—not laughs, but titters. I can feel my face turning red. "No. No, it's fine. He's fine."

"He sure is," mutters some girl with mall bangs at the next table. Her table mate slaps her five.

"Back to work, people." The art teacher pulls on her smock so the top of her cleavage shows. "Let's leave Nick and the new girl alone."

I scowl and stab the knife into the newspaper. "I hate being the new girl."

"Why?"

I glance up at him, trying not to get all crazy fluttery about his eyes or his jawline or his hands. I don't answer.

We sit there another minute working. I am so ridiculously, intensely aware of him there, right next to me. It's like I can feel the heat he generates. It's nice.

"Okay, so when I came into school Mrs. Nix was acting really weird. She told me if I'm going to go out at night I should wear my coat inside out."

"What?"

"I know. Weird, right? So I googled 'wearing clothes inside out,'" I say.

"Yeah?"

"It says that pixies can confuse humans alone in the woods at night, but wearing clothes inside out protects us."

He presses paper to glue, paper to paper. "That's weird." He pauses. "I talked to Betty about stuff."

"Yeah, you said that."

"She's going to let you in on some things tonight."

"Why don't you just tell me now?"

"Because."

"Because why?"

He gestures around. "People might hear."

"You have to give me a hint what it's about."

"You're pouting. Pouting is not allowed. It's too cute."

My heart opens wide and then his face shifts. His eyes narrow. He suddenly turns serious.

"Tell me now," I insist.

"No way."

"Please."

"I promised Betty."

"So?"

"You know you can't cross Betty."

"True." I give up.

Then after another little bit I get enough courage to say, "If we're friends I should know things about you."

He opens up his arms. "Go ahead."

"Um." I think for a second. "What do your parents do?"

"They're nature photographers. They travel a lot."

"Really? Where?"

"All over. Right now they're making a film in Africa."

"No way."

"Really."

I start with the glue. It squirts on my finger a little. "So you're all alone?"

"Yep."

I shudder. How awful. "Don't you hate it when they leave you? Don't you feel left behind?"

He shakes his head. "I'm meant to be here."

"Very philosophical," I say and touch my head where the bump is. It still hurts. I wonder if Betty's told my mom about it.

His eyes seem concerned. "No, just the truth."

It's pretty obvious that he's all through with that subject. But I continue on, because I hate it that we're so different.

"It must be nice to know where you're meant to be," I say.

"You'll know someday, Zara."

I shrug.

"I doubt it." I've always had friends, but I've never felt like I fit with the rest of the world. My mom said that it was a normal adolescent thing to feel. I hated her for saying that. I just pounded right out of the room and went running down at the Battery.

"I don't think I'll ever find a place," I say slowly, turning back to stare at my collage instead of Nick. I have to stop staring at him all the time. "I'm just not a person who fits in. That's okay."

"I'm positive you will."

"Really?"

"Absolutely sure."

He motions to the glue brush. "Can I have some?"

I start to grab it so I can it pass it to him. He reaches for it at the same time. Our fingers touch, and the moment they do the fluorescent lights overhead flicker and then fizzle out.

Everyone moans, even though we can all still see. There's enough light from outside filtering in, just not enough for us to really focus on the finer details.

Nick's fingers stroke mine lightly, so lightly that I'm almost not sure the touch is real. My insides flicker like the art room lights. They do not, however, fizzle. I turn my head to look him in the eye.

He leans over and whispers, "It will be hard to be just your friend."

The lights come back on.

"Just a little brownout." The art teacher smiles and holds out her arms. "Welcome to Maine, Zara. Land of a million power failures."

Nick's breath touches my ear. "I heard you didn't drive to school. I'll bring you home after cross-country, okay?"

"Okay," I say, trying to be all calm, but what I really want to do is leap up and do a happy dance all over the art room. Nick is driving me home.

Devyn is waiting for us outside art class.

"What?" Nick says. His face changes into worry. "Issie okay?"

"Yeah," Devyn says, motioning us to follow him. "I found something."

He brings us to a little cubby in the hallway, a place just off the main hall. There's a red door to a supply closet and another to an electrical room. We all barely fit in the nook. Nick squats down to Devyn's level. So do I.

"Okay," Devyn says. "It's not good."

"Just tell us."

"They kiss people," Devyn says.

I laugh. "Who kisses people?"

"The pixies," Devyn explains. He lifts the book from the library. "This is serious, Zara."

"Sorry. Okay. They kiss people," I repeat. I look up at Nick, who has never kissed a girl.

Devyn must notice me looking at Nick's lips because his voice frustrates out, "This is not a good kind of kiss. This is bad. It can kill you."

"Powerful kiss," I say.

"Zara . . . ," Nick warns.

I raise my hands again, leaning my back against the wall for support. "Sorry."

Devyn points at me. "No more interrupting and no more attempting to hide your fear behind pathetic attempts at sarcasm, although I do appreciate it. Anyway, the kiss gives the pixie king some of the power over the woman's soul. And it changes her into a pixie."

"Which means?" Nick asks.

"I'm not sure," Devyn continues. "But if she's all human and has no pixie blood it can kill her."

"Wait," I say. "So, the pixie guy kisses some woman. She either dies or becomes the queen. Either way part of her soul becomes his?"

"Yeah."

"That sucks," I say. "And you said *if* she's all human? What else could she be?"

Devyn shrugs. "She could already have pixie blood. According to this book there are a lot of people who are descended from the Pixies. Or . . . ," he looks up at Nick and then says it, "she could be were."

"Weres again? Werewolves?" I shake my head and stand up. My bracelet slides down my arm. "This is crazy."

"Zara?" Nick stands up too. He grabs my hand. "You already believe half of it."

"I know! But kisses that take away your soul? Pixie blood? Weres? It's crazy." I grab the book off Devyn's lap and walk away. "It's way too crazy for me."

Malaxophobia

fear of love play

Nick and I leave practice early because my head is still spinning from clonking it and maybe, just a little, from the pow-wow with Devyn by the electrical closet.

"I can bring her home," Ian says when he sees Nick leading me off the trail.

Nick raises his arm. "Nope. I got this one."

Coach Walsh meets us in the parking lot where the trail ends. He leans on his old maroon pickup truck, holding his clipboard. He takes one look at me and his whole PE coach posture changes. It goes from straight to slumped.

Shaking his head at me, he says, "Don't push yourself so hard, Zara."

"I'm not."

He stares hard at me. I stare back. He has crud in the corner of his eye, just a little bit. I don't know whether or not I should tell him or pretend I don't notice.

"Yes, you are. No practice tomorrow either," he orders. "My fault for believing that you could run today. Betty's going to kill me."

"But— "

"No buts." Pointing at Nick he says, "Take her home."

Nick fake salutes. "Sir, yes sir."

"Sarcasm doesn't become you, Colt," Coach Walsh says, but he smiles when he says it, so obviously he is only mad at me, not superboy Nick Colt, beloved of coaches everywhere. If I were a guy he would let me run tomorrow.

"I want to go to practice, Coach," I say. "I'll be fine tomorrow."

"We aren't practicing tomorrow," he says.

That makes no sense. "It's on the schedule."

Mr. Walsh exhales and rubs the top of his head. "I might as well tell you two now. We've just gotten word. Jay Dahlberg's missing."

"Missing?" The world spins. Nick grabs my hand.

"He never came home last night after practice. His parents haven't heard from him." The coach starts rubbing his neck. "He's not the kind of kid to run off."

"Maybe he'll show up." I reach out my free hand and touch the coach's shoulder.

"The other ones didn't," he says, slouching even more. He starts rubbing his eyes now. "God, I never thought this would happen again."

I swallow and look at him, look at Nick. Beneath my feet is an old Cheetos wrapper, and the little orange cat mascot's smile is smashed from feet and dirt and ice. He is discarded, forgotten. I drop my hands, bend, scoop up the wrapper, and stand back up, a bit woozy. I stash the wrapper in my pocket.

Nick opens the door of his MINI to let me in and Coach

Walsh eyes his clipboard. Then the coach yells after me, "Don't do anything stupid, Zara."

I slam into Nick's car. What does that mean? Don't do anything stupid? I bet he wouldn't tell Nick not to do anything stupid. But because I am a pacifist I say nothing.

I pull on my seat belt as Nick says something to the coach. God, someone else is missing.

Jay Dahlberg. He's tall with blond hair and a goofy laugh. He seems like a good guy. He hangs out with Ian sometimes.

Swallowing, I check out the MINI. I hadn't paid attention to it the night before. The dark maroon seats are sort of the color of blood. It smells like Nick, woodsy, manly. I shift my feet around a bunch of school books scattered on the floor. My foot tip touches a small clump of brown fur.

Nick must have a dog. It smells faintly of dog, but mostly of the Christmas tree air freshener. I pick up a book, Edward Abbey's *Good News.* A little postapocalyptic ditty. Interesting.

What if Nick is a pixie? He had dust on his coat. He's never kissed a girl, supposedly. Although he's not the guy who points, but he could be one of his minions. Is that the right word? Minions?

I put the book back down on the floor.

Nick and Coach Walsh seem to be arguing a little. I turn the key dangling from Nick's ignition and put down the window to hear, but I can't get any of the words.

Cold air rushes in. The air chills against me so I zip up the window and turn on the heat. The warmth blasts out of the heaters, rolling the tuft of fur underneath my seat.

Nick jumps in. He looks human. He is so human.

"Took you long enough," I tease, brushing all my doubts out of my head.

He glowers and puts the car in reverse to get it out of the parking spot. "Coach and I were having a little talk."

"It looked like you were arguing."

"It was just a talk," he says slowly, shifting again so he can speed out of the parking lot like a tornado is chasing us or something.

"Whatever."

"I didn't think we should practice anymore. He, of course, disagrees because he wants to win state." His mouth steadies into a line and then he speaks again. "I'm freaking sick over the Jay Dahlberg thing, Zara. I haven't slept since Devyn was attacked last month. I've been trying to figure out what's going on and I haven't been able to piece it together. Pixies! I mean, who would have thought there were actually pixies?"

"It's okay, Nick." I grab his hand and squeeze it. "It's not your job to save the world."

"But I have to." He lets out this man growl that sounds like a professional wrestler gone bad. All the veins in his neck bulge and pop. "I'm trying, okay. I am really trying."

"Why? Why are you trying so hard?"

He keeps holding my hand. His eyes meet my eyes. "Why are you?"

Anger rushes out of me from somewhere inside. And I'm surprised, because I had no idea it was there. "Because I couldn't save my dad. There. I said it. Okay? You happy?"

I try to pull my hand away but he won't let me. He pulls over and stops the car.

"No. Not happy. I'm honored that you told me, though." His jaw is so straight and his eyes are so deep, like a tree where the bark is all textured.

"I'm sorry. I don't know why I was so mad."

"It's okay." His thumb drags across the skin of my hand, the one that's not scraped up.

He unbuckles his seat belt and turns his body so he faces me, blocking out the entire window of the driver's side door. God, he's huge. He rests one arm on the steering wheel. The other lays across the back of the seats. His solid fingers thrum against the upholstery. I turn to face him.

"How's your hand?" he asks, like everything is all normal.

"Fine."

"And your head?"

"Fine," I say. I want answers. "You're changing the subject."

He smiles. "I know. Most girls around here would take the opportunity to tell me all about their injury, then they'd tell me about their clothes and shopping, and the way their parents mistreat them."

"I'm not most girls."

"That's true."

"I'm not into pity parties."

He raises his eyebrows and I turn my hand up so I can see my scrape from last night. It isn't too bad at all, just a bunch of lines.

Nick grabs my wrist. I shiver. Nick gentles his hold.

"Do you know what these lines look like?" he asks.

I shake my head.

"The rune for protection," he says, not touching the lines, but tracing the air above them.

"You know about runes?" I'm ridiculously shocked. He looks like all he knows about is working out and sports. But he does have Edward Abbey in his car. Who exactly is this guy?

"Do you?"

Sorrow hits me hard. I remember my mom trying to read my fortune, tossing the bone-colored rune stones on our coffee table, teasing me about all the boyfriends I would have someday. Then my dad trying to read the future of the world.

I swallow.

"My mom liked them. And my dad, my dad was really into them. My stepdad."

"Betty's son?"

"Yeah."

I take my hand away and settle it into my lap. Then I realize he's doing it again. "You're still trying to distract me."

He shrugs and doesn't look contrite or anything.

"That's not fair," I say.

"You expect me to play fair?"

"Heroes are supposed to play fair."

"Heroes?"

"Isn't that what you're trying to be? Mr. Rescue Man?"

I reach out to fidget with the dial that shifts the air into the cab of the MINI. I open and close the heating vents. I run a finger along the dust on the dashboard.

"Okay. Ask away," Mr. Rescue Man finally says.

"Really?"

There are a million questions I could ask him. What happened to Devyn? Why is Maine so damn cold? How can we find Jay Dahlberg or the Beardsley boy? Why does he have such a hero complex?

But I don't ask any of those. I ask the silliest question of all, the shallow question. It just comes off my tongue.

I am not proud of it.

My finger draws a line in the dashboard. It starts to curve like a heart. I stop it and then I just ask him my question.

"Do you like me? You know, *like me* like me?"

I cringe the moment I ask and cover my face with my hands. The smell of blood and trail dirt wafts into my nose. Something sinks inside me. What is it? Oh, I know, any dignity I could possibly have left.

"Can I take that back?" I ask softly from behind my hands.

Nick's voice is low and warm. "No."

I peek between my fingers. "No, I can't take it back or no, you don't like me?"

His fingers wrap around my fingers and he pulls my hands from my face so he can look at me, I guess, or else so I can look at him.

"No, you can't take it back. That's your question," he says in a voice so deep and warm and full of things that I can't get mad anymore. This has to be what people mean when they say they "melted." I feel all wiggly.

"Oh," I say. "Okay."

I swallow. His eyes are deep and brown and . . . How can a man's eyes be so ridiculously beautiful and gorgeous, so full of things that I want to know?

"So, what's your answer?" I whisper, afraid I might still screw it all up.

Those eyes of his widen a little bit.

I hold my breath.

"I like you, Zara," he says.

I breathe out. Something like joy surges up inside me. I remember leaning against him on the couch. I remember the feel of his chest beneath my head. It had felt so good and safe.

Had I really not been just hallucinating? Maybe my concussion hadn't thrown me all out of whack? Maybe what I was hoping for was something that was actually possible?

The wind blows some old leaves across the driveway.

"You like me?" I repeat, because, well, I want to be really, really sure that I heard him right. This is not the sort of thing you want to get wrong.

He nods and says, "Very much."

"You like me *very* much?"

He lets go of my hands and touches my check. "Too much."

"Too much?" Trying to keep my voice calm, I say, "No such thing."

"If you only knew . . ."

"Tell me then."

He leans closer. One inch, another, oh God, oh okay. Yep. I think he's going to kiss me. Okay. Okay. Another inch. Obviously not a pixie, right?

And then he jolts up straight, rigid, like he's been shocked. His eyes glaze over. I swear his nostrils flare, like he's repulsed by the smell of my hair or something, and then his words rush out, "Get in the house now. I have to go."

"Go? Go where?"

What? What had just happened? Wasn't he going to kiss me? Had I imagined that? My heart thuds and falls silent. I am not sure if it is beating at all. It's a great big hole there. He doesn't like me at all . . . does he?

I want to clutch at his arm, to make him stay, but I don't. I won't. I am not that pathetic. "Where are you going?"

"The woods. I'll be right back."

He leaps out of the MINI and rushes off toward the forest, not even shutting the door. I bound out after him, shutting my door and running to his side of the car.

"Nick? What is it?"

He tosses the words over his shoulder but doesn't slow his pace. God, he's fast, faster than at cross-country or in gym, almost superhuman fast. I think he's even faster than Ian. "Go in the house. Don't let anyone in except me and Betty. I'll be right back."

Everything inside of me just crashes, all my internal organs fall, but it's not the hollowed-out pain that I'm used to these last few months. No. It's the same kind of pain that I felt right when my dad died: sharp, piercing, all over.

"I'll be back," he yells and then he is gone, rushing into the trees, swallowed up by the density of the forest, by the darkness.

I shut his door and shiver. The sun has started to set.

"Go in the house, Zara!" he yells one more time. I can't see him, but his voice comes to me, faint and far away. "Go in the house."

So I do.

Autophobia
fear of being alone

I know I should try to spend the next hour inside Betty's house doing chores and not worring about things, but it doesn't work out. Dread makes its home in my sternum. Just kind of nestles there. What if Nick goes missing, like Jay Dahlberg or the Beardsley boy?

Why hadn't I asked about this?

It is all too horrible to think about.

I put some mashed potatoes in the oven to warm and start on a letter about Vadivel and Valarmathi Jasikaran in Sri Lanka. They have been in jail a long time and not been charged. Valarmathi had surgery before she was arrested. She could be dying. They are trapped there, uncharged, in jail, probably tortured and alone.

I simmer and start to write. My fingers clutch the pen so tightly that the wound on my hand throbs, but I don't care. It's nothing compared to what the Jasikarans are going through, what

Jay Dahlberg might be going through. What Nick might be . . . No. He's fine.

I still don't know how people could do this to each other. How can we survive knowing that we do these things? How can we not help?

Nick is out there in the woods alone.

And I am in here doing what? Writing a letter.

I need a plan.

Okay. If these things are really pixies there's got to be a way to fight them, right?

I log on. It takes forever because Betty has dial-up. I swear to God. But finally I get on and I type in "fight pixies" in the search engine. All the gaming sites come up. It's not until page eight that I find something that looks legit.

I scroll past the explanation that pixies are not Tinker Bell, but dangerous, very dangerous, and do not attempt to contact them on your own. I snort. Then I find what I'm looking for:

> The only thing that can defeat pixies is iron. Iron can be found in steel. It is essential for the composition of railroad ties, skyscrapers, and cars. Pixies will avoid iron at all costs.

So that's probably why they're here. Most of the houses are made of wood, framed with two-by-fours, not steel. There are no skyscrapers anywhere, just trees. There aren't even that many cars because there are hardly any people.

I can't wait to tell Nick, but first I have to find him.

Okay. Iron is the basic component of steel.

My eyes scan the room and latch on to the woodstove, made of cast iron. It's not like I can haul that around. But I can take the fireplace poker thing that we use to turn the logs.

Trying to be quick, I call the ambulance house and ask for Betty, but she is out on a run in Trenton, where a logging truck has smashed into a minivan.

"She'll be tied up some good for a long time," Josie tells me.

"Okay. Just ask her to call me. It's Zara."

" 'Course it is, dear. I'll give her the message."

So that leaves me home, alone, with all my million questions and absolutely zero answers.

I walk outside again and stand on the porch, listening. No birds sing or even twitter. The wind howls and rustles through the tree branches. A pine cone drops onto our roof and rolls down by my feet, making me jump. My hand clutches the poker.

"Wimp," I mutter.

I march over to Nick's MINI and put my injured hand on his door handle, pulling it open. It smells so much like him. I touch the steering wheel with my fingers. Something inside me shudders again, and not in a good way. I don't want him to be in danger. I pull my hand away from the steering wheel. It stings. The lines do make the rune for protection. How weird. I turn around in a circle so I can see all around me. A prickly feeling creeps through my hand and up my arm, marching toward my heart.

"Nick?" I whisper.

I push the hair out of my face. The wind whips it back. I grab an elastic band off my wrist and yank my hair back into a ponytail. The sun has almost set behind the trees. It casts an orange glow, a last stand against the night.

"Nick?" I say louder.

No answer.

I try it even louder.

"Nick? You out there?"

That's when I hear it, the angry howl of some kind of dog. I freeze.

And then I hear something even worse. From the edge of the forest comes a hoarse whisper that is not Nick's voice, but I recognize it. I heard it last night when I went running.

"Zara," it says. "Come to me."

Phonophobia

fear of noises or voices

I take a step toward the voice, just one step. "Nick?"

"Zara . . ."

I stop and look around. The clouds darken with the setting sun, turning into something somber and full of potential dangers. The trees lean with the wind, the younger ones almost bending. I wrap my arms around my own trunk, trying to make the spidery feeling go away.

"Zara . . ."

"Nick, is that you?"

No answer.

"Who are you?" I yell.

"Come to me."

"Tell me who you are!"

"Zara . . ."

I stomp my foot down. "Look. This is crazy. Tell me who you are and I'll come, okay? But I've got to tell you that if you've hurt

Nick—or if you are Nick gone psycho—I am not going to be happy."

My words dangle like a warning in the cold air. My insides warm up like I am on fire. Anger will do that to you.

"Zara . . ."

"Enough with calling my name!" I scream, raging now. "It's ridiculous."

I storm into the woods then, not thinking about it, just powered by rage, ready to beat someone up, even though I've never beat anyone up before. Friedrich Nietzsche says, "He who fights with monsters should be careful lest he thereby become a monster."

I race maybe fifty feet into the trees and then I stop, feet skidding on the hard surface. I am doing exactly what everyone has been telling me not to do, what I'm not supposed to do, exactly what I had promised Nick that I wouldn't do. I almost scream.

I am so angry at myself, angry at the voice, angry at Nick. My hand clutches the poker.

The voice whispers out from behind me. "Almost there, Zara. Don't stop now."

I whirl around. I can't see anyone standing among the trunks.

"Where are you?" I demand.

No answer.

"Who are you?"

"You know." The voice comes from my right this time. I pivot. It doesn't sound like Nick. The voice is older, slicker.

"How do you know my name?" I ask, listening hard.

"I've always known your name, princess."

Zara means princess. Right. I don't care what my name means. I rush toward where I think the voice is coming from, flying over stones and pinecones and tree roots.

"Where are you?"

Nothing breaks the endless tree trunks, no swath of cloth, no eyes, no hair. Trees are all I see. Trees. Trees. Trees. I pivot, looking for the house, which should be to my right, but it's not there. Just trees. Damn, it's dark in the woods.

Fear grips my stomach, only this time it isn't just fear for Nick. It's fear for me, too. I can't be lost. I can't be lost that quickly.

"Where are you?"

"This way." The voice comes from my left this time. I bomb after it, darting through the trees, going farther and farther into the increasing darkness. It is almost night.

"Did you take Nick? Because I swear to God, I'll kick your ass if you took Nick."

I blast into a small clearing. A circle of small spruce trees stands as sentinels. Snow begins to fall from the sky. I stop, standing there alone in the middle of the circle as the snow comes down, faster and faster.

"You're trying to get me lost," I say. My fists clench. I release them. I won't show him I'm afraid. I won't be afraid. "You're really annoying me!"

There is no answer.

"I am not imagining you!"

Still no answer.

My head pounds. There is a name for this, this fear of a voice. But I can't remember it. Damn.

Phobophobia, fear of phobias.

Phonophobia, fear of noises or voices.

Photoaugliaphobia, fear of glaring lights.

Photophobia, fear of light.

That's the one. And what's the next fear, alphabetically?

Phronemophobia, fear of thinking.

I am not afraid of thinking. Thinking calms me down. I search the periphery of the trees, looking, looking.

Where am I?

I am in the woods.

Where is Nick?

I have no idea. Not taken. He can't be taken.

Where is the voice?

I check my pocket for my cell phone. It's still in my cross-country bag. I shake my head because, really, how could I be doing this? I am probably following the voice of some psycho pixie serial killer into dark woods worthy of a Stephen King novel, and I *did not bring* my cell phone.

A noise escapes my lips—guttural, panicked, pathetic. I swallow, straighten. That is not how I am going to be. I am not going to die a wimp while waiting for the killer to get me.

The snow plasters itself to the spruce trees. It touches my hair, coats my jacket and my pants, presses itself into my sneakers. It comes down so quickly it's already covering the ground, which means there will be footprints to follow or for someone else to follow.

"Zara," the voice comes again. "Come to me."

I shake my head. I've already been totally irrational. I'm not going to make it worse. "No."

I brush the snow off my face.

"This way."

I cover my ears and refuse to move.

"I'm lost. You made me lost," I say, my voice weak, "and that is a super jerky thing to do."

Then I hear it: amused laughter, and beneath that laughter something else, the howl.

Of a wolf?

It is a dog. It has to be a dog because I cannot handle a wolf right now.

I listen again. Maybe those old books I read back in fourth grade are right. Where German shepherds and Saint Bernards always rescued people in dire circumstances. Maybe a nice doggie has come to rescue me from whoever or whatever is in the woods. Maybe he'll even have a barrel of beer under his neck. I don't care. I'll even take a werewolf right now. I'll take anything.

Hope is a crazy thing. It will make you believe.

I rush toward the dog's howling noise, searching for some friendly fur, maybe some drooling jowls. The howl seems closer, coming from behind me. I plow toward it, ignoring the snow and how it covers the ground, hiding the tree roots and rocks, making every footfall a danger.

Stopping, I suck in my breath. I have no idea where I am. My head is spinning from my minor concussion.

Breathe in, Zara.

Breathe out, Zara.

List the phobias.

I can't. I can't think of any.

Breathe in.

Mrs. Nix!

She said to put your coat on inside out to avoid getting lost. Sure, she's a flake and it's a stupid superstition, but I am willing to do it. Right now, I am willing to do anything.

I yank off my jacket and turn it inside out. Then I pull off my sweatshirt and flip it around too. The arms feel all weird and bunched up.

"Can't make it worse," I mutter to the trees and start running again.

I'm not sure how long I run through the woods. I run blind, bumping past trees, hair snagging on low branches, feet somehow managing to keep me upright, my headache throbbing against my skin.

I can hear the dog.

I follow it, getting closer and closer, until bang—just like that—I've escaped the woods. I'm out on my own front lawn.

I pump my fist in the air. I'd kiss the ground if it wasn't so damn snowy. I did it. I did it. I did it!

Yay for me!

Yay for dogs!

I do a little victory dance worthy of any NFL running back. Uh-huh.

Then I look around. The front porch light is still on. Grandma Betty's truck is still missing and the MINI is still parked in the driveway covered in snow. No footprints disturb anything.

Heart sinking, I swallow and glance behind me for signs of the man who belongs to the voice that knew my name.

Just woods.

"Nick?"

His name echoes out into the snow-filled air like a worried question. I trudge through the snow, one step, another. My running shoes have soaked through. I didn't notice until now. I shove my worries about frozen toes out of my mind. Why isn't Nick back yet?

"Nick?"

I sense something to my right and turn, fists up, ready to kick, to punch, to pummel, to run. But it's not the psycho guy. There, coming from behind Nick's MINI, is the largest freaking dog I have ever seen. It's leaner than a Saint Bernard, but taller and more muscled. Its brown fur looks like a wolf's, but wolves aren't that big. Are they? No. They are not.

Maybe this is the dog who led me home, my rescue dog.

I reach out my hand and it turns to look at me head on. Its eyes are beautiful, shining deep and dark from its snow-plastered fur.

"Doggy?" I say. "Here, sweetie. Do you know where Nick is?"

That's when I see it, there in its shoulder: an arrow, lodged and stuck. Blood has seeped out and dripped down the dog's fur, clotting a bit where the arrow entered. Who the hell would shoot a dog with an arrow? Rage sweeps through me and I grit my teeth, trying to shove it down and away. Then the dog whimpers and all that rage turns into something else.

"Oh, honey," I say and rush toward him, not thinking about how big he is or that he is probably a wolf. I flop to my knees in the snow in front of him.

"Does it hurt?"

The dog/wolf sniffs my hand. I scratch his muzzle and peer into his eyes. I am totally in love with this doggy. He does the dog equivalent of a shrug with his front shoulders, but the pain of the arrow must be too great because then he lets out a long, hard groan. The poor thing.

My cold fingers stroke beneath his chin. He's warm under there.

"We have to get you out of the cold," I say, standing up and hitting my leg, hoping he'll understand. "Come."

I start walking slowly toward the house, checking over my shoulder to see if the dog/wolf has taken some obedience classes somewhere and is following me. It could happen. Right?

I hit my chest and say it again, "Come."

With a strong, graceful swoop of his head he stares up at me. His eyes meet my eyes. I am not sure what I see there. Something feral? Something strong? Something very intelligent? Oh God . . .

"I just want to take care of you," I say softly. I shelter my fingers inside my sleeves. The cold and the snow has numbed them. "Please, come with me in the house. I'll take out your arrow. Get you warm. Please. Let me save you."

My eyes take in the dog, then stray to look at the rapidly falling snow, and Nick's car. My voice catches in my throat. Again.

"And then I can call my gram, and go out again and look for Nick, the guy who owns the MINI," I explain.

The dog cocks his head when I say Nick's name.

Hope foolishly crashes into my heart. "Did you see him? Did you see Nick?"

The dog doesn't go all Lassie, but his tail moves weakly, almost like he is trying to wag it but can't quite commit. Of course, the dog doesn't answer. I am really losing it. It's like I do believe in weres and pixies. It's like something deep inside of me, something in that deep-down part has always believed in weres and pixies and that belief has finally struggled out even though I've tried to smash it down.

Pointing at the door, I say, "Inside. Now."

The dog flattens his ears against his head. His muscles twitch and then he jumps, straight past me and onto the porch in one bound. He whimpers when his front paws touch the porch floor.

I cannot figure it out. The dog must have jumped at least thirty feet. How can that be possible? I struggle up the stairs and tentatively place my hand on the top of the dog's head.

"Okay, sweetie," I tell him, shouldering the front door open. "Let's get you fixed up."

The house is warm and inviting and the dog seems horribly out of place, standing by the front door, dripping in the cold. I yank off my wet shoes and grab a blanket off the couch, throwing it over him.

"Okay," I say, walking backward, hands out, trying to make a plan. "You warm up. Okay? I'm going to call a vet."

I grab the phone and the phone book in the other room and bring it back to where the dog has slumped down on the floor by the front door. I sit down next to him. He puts his head on my lap. I lean down and kiss his nose. It is black and dry. He shivers.

"Oh, doggy, it's going to be okay," I murmur as I flip through the phone book. There is only one veterinarian listed, but it has an emergency number. I dial it.

An annoying tone comes through my phone. "Your call cannot be completed as dialed."

I hang up. Actually, I smash the phone down because I take my anger out on inanimate objects. Which is better than taking it out on people, right?

I pull in a breath and try to calm down and think. Okay, so I must have dialed the wrong number. I do that sometimes, flip the numbers around. I try again and get the same damn recording.

"Your call cannot be completed as dialed," the computerized voice tells me in a condescending way. How can something that's not alive be condescending? I have no clue. But it is.

The dog whimpers as I hang up again. I forget about the phone and examine the arrow that's sticking out of his sweet doggy self. It's made of some sort of black wood and has green leaves etched on its thin shaft. It would be beautiful if it wasn't stuck into flesh and muscle.

"Who did this to you?" I whisper.

The dog snuffs out a breath of hot air almost like he's answering. He seems hurt. Really hurt. Anxiety starts to take over, hyping me up like I've had eight cups of espresso. I rub my head. Think, Zara. Think. I sink my hands into his fur.

The answer comes.

"I'll call my grandmother," I tell him. "Betty will know what to do. She's really practical. You'd like her."

I punch in the numbers to her cell, which I'm not supposed to do. I'm supposed to call Josie. But this is really important, and the amazing thing is, she actually picks up.

"Gram, there's a dog here. He's hurt. Someone shot him with an arrow. I called the vet but it's not going through. And I can't find Nick but his MINI is here. You've got to come home," I rush out.

"Zara, slow down, honey," her voice comes through the phone all steady. "Tell me that again."

I tell her again. As I speak the dog snuggles his sweet doggy head on my lap. He shudders. Oh God.

"He's shuddering," I tell her.

His breath speeds up to something fast and shallow. His eyes turn up to gaze into mine, trusting. He trusts *me* to save him. For a second I blink back to when my dad's heart attacked him, to when he clutched his chest, crumpled on the floor. I hadn't been able to help him. Who am I fooling? I can't help anybody.

"Gram," I insist. "You *have* to come home."

"I am on my way, sweetie, but the roads are bad. It's going to take me a bit."

"But the dog? He's really really hurt, Gram. And Nick . . . Nick is missing."

"What?"

"Nick drove me home and we heard something in the woods and then he raced off and told me to stay inside and he hasn't come back."

"And he hasn't come back? But there's a dog there now?"

"Yeah. I went out and looked for him and I heard a man in the woods and he was saying my name."

"Zara!" she interrupts. "Are the doors locked?"

I check. "Yeah. But he's missing and the dog is so hurt and . . ."

"First, calm down. Take a deep breath. You aren't going to be any help to Nick if you're panicking. Okay?"

Embarrassed, I take a deep breath and say, "Okay."

I stroke the dog's head. He opens his eyes. Something about his gaze makes me feel calmer and stronger. He trusts me. I can trust me.

"Good," Betty's voice takes a hard, calm official tone. "I have just had Josie dispatch a unit to the house, okay? And I am on my way."

"Tell me what to do."

"First you've got to go wash your hands with hot water and the antibacterial soap. You don't want to cause an infection."

I gently lift the dog's head off my lap and place it on the floor. Stepping around his great bulk, I rush back into the kitchen and scrub my hands.

"Done."

"Good. Get a towel and put some water on it and get the Neosporin. It's in the bathroom cabinet."

I race back into the kitchen and wet a towel and grab the Neosporin. The oven is still on. I don't turn it off. There's no time. "Okay."

"The first thing you're going to have to do is pull the arrow out."

"Oh, Gram. I don't know—"

"You have to. You can do this, Zara. Be strong and steady. I'll be right here."

I stare at the arrow and touch it with my finger. The dog moans softly but doesn't open his eyes.

"I have to put the phone down," I say.

"Go ahead and put it down, honey."

I put it on the oriental carpet on the stairs that are next to the front door. Then I wrap my hands around the arrow. It's thin and hard, cold against my hands. I give a tiny tug. It doesn't move. It doesn't move at all, but the dog shudders and makes a little moan. I swear, my heart is breaking.

Something acidic moves up into my throat.

"You can do this," I tell myself.

I tighten my grip and pull slowly, trying to apply even, smooth force. The arrow fights against me and the dog shivers again, moaning in such a horribly sad way that tears start to tumble down my face. It must hurt so much. I must be hurting him so much.

"Almost there," I say. "Almost done, doggy. You're a brave, brave doggy."

There's this horrible sucking nose and the arrow squinches out, bringing with it a burst of blood. The dog gives a massive shudder and stops moving.

"Doggy!"

He doesn't move. Blood pulses out of his wound.

I throw the arrow out of the way and grab the phone, shoving one hand against the hole.

"I did it but now he's bleeding. He's bleeding a lot. I'm so sorry, puppy."

"That's okay," Gram answers. "Is it squirting?"

"No," I stare at the horrible red blood. "It's slowing down."

"Good, you don't have to apply a tourniquet then. Just apply gentle pressure with a bandage. Do you have a bandage?"

"I think so," I rummage through the first-aid kit, smearing blood all over the tape and the aspirin and the scissors with the funky ends. "Yep. I found it."

"Okay, Zara. Don't worry. The worst is over. I'm going to tell you what to do. When the bleeding slows down, you have to clean the wound with water. If there's any dirt or anything left in there, you've got to dip those tweezers in alcohol. They are in the first-aid kit. Okay?"

She's talking super fast, but I think I'm following her.

"Okay."

"Then you cut away any fur that's near that wound so it doesn't mess with it. Shaving it is better, but that might be too much. Then you put on some Neosporin and bandage it. Okay?"

"Okay."

"You've done a good job, Zara. I'm on my way. The police might get there first, okay?"

"Okay," I swallow hard. I wish she could come home and help me. I wish I wasn't alone. "Thanks. Do you think Nick will be okay?"

"Don't you worry about him, Zara. He's a special breed, that one. And the police will be there soon."

"Thanks, Gram," I say, pushing on the dog's wound.

"You're welcome, honey. Good job. I like it when you call me Gram."

She hangs up and the world is suddenly way too quiet. Special breed? Is that what she said?

I lean down and kiss the dog's cheek, by his jowls. "Are you thinking she means what I'm thinking?"

He moans.

"Looks like it's you and me, guy," I tell him. "But you sleep it off, okay? Do you think you like mashed potatoes?"

The dog doesn't respond. Of course he doesn't. I snuggle against him.

The dog and I are alone. But the thing is, I saved him—with Grandma Betty's help, of course. But I saved him. Me.

Teratophobia

fear of monsters or deformed people

I do everything I can for the dog. I clean his wound and heft sections of his heavy body up so I can wrap him in a blanket. I bandage him and stroke his head while he softly groans in his sleep.

"Poor puppy," I say, even though he obviously isn't a puppy. He may not even be a dog. "Do you think Nick's okay?"

The dog huffs out a sleepy breath. I shiver because there's a draft by the door and I ease the dog's head off my leg, placing it on a soft pillow I'd yanked off the couch. He's so huge.

"Are you a werewolf?" I whisper, ashamed to be even asking it.

He blinks open one eye and stares at me.

"I'm sorry I woke you." I lean down and kiss him on the top of his muzzle. "You feeling okay?"

Checking his bandage, I pull back the blanket a little.

"I think you've stopped bleeding. That's good. I'm going to go check outside. I'll be right back. I'm really worried about this

Nick guy. Don't get jealous, though. I'm also really worried about you."

The dog tries to lift his head but he's too tired, I guess, too worn out from his injury. I settle him with my hand. "You rest, sweetie."

He is so cute, with all that shaggy hair and those big canine shoulders and his jowly jowls. Maybe we can keep him. Betty's house would be a lot less lonely with a dog around all the time. And aren't all Maine people supposed to have dogs? I think that's in the stereotype book along with junked-out trucks in the front yard and a front porch held up with cinder blocks and lobster traps.

I lift up a jowl to check out his teeth. They're clean and white and huge. The dog opens his eye and stares at me reproachfully.

I let go of his jowl. "Sorry. Way too invasive, I know."

He wags his tail, just once.

"Thanks for leading me home," I say. I wish he could understand me.

He wags his tail again.

"I'll be right back."

Standing up for real, I check that the front door is locked in case any serial killers want to stop by and then I peek out the window. The snow covers everything, absolutely everything. Nick's car still sits there. The wheels are buried under. I swallow and pick up the phone book, bring it back into the kitchen, tiptoeing by the now-snoring dog. His jowls shake when he blows out the air.

"You'll be okay."

I find Nick's number in the phone book under "Anna and Mark Colt" and call. There's no answer.

I call Gram back but I can't get through. I just go right to her voice mail. I call the dispatcher, who says she's on her way home.

"Good," I say and then remember to be polite. "Busy night?"

"You're telling me," she says hurriedly as another line rings in the background.

"Any sign of Jay?" I ask.

"The Dahlberg boy?" Josie sighs. "Nope. You sit tight, Zara honey. The deputy was all the way out on Deer Isle but he's coming your way and Betty is too."

"Can they hurry?"

"They are, sweetheart. The roads are bad."

"Okay."

"You keep your chin up, girl. And don't worry too much. Nick Colt is a resourceful young man. A real keeper, that boy. You hear me?"

I bite my lip.

"You hear me?" she asks again.

"Yep."

"Damn. I have another call. You sit tight, Zara."

What else am I suppose to do? "Yep."

Useless and sighing, I hang up the phone, stare at the dirty white thread I'd knotted around my finger. My dad would tell me to calm down, that it was my overactive imagination making mountains out of molehills, or some other silly dad cliché.

I miss silly dad clichés.

"Everything will be fine," I tell the kitchen. A huge gust of wind slams against the house, howling. The lights flicker, turn off for about three seconds, and then come back on again.

The digital display on the microwave flashes the green neon

time as 00:00, which seems appropriate. A tree branch scrapes across the window. I jump and grit my teeth.

That is it.

I am going to have to go back out there and look for Nick, but this time I am going to be prepared.

Watch out, potential psycho freaks, competent Zara is ready.

I haul open the door to the basement so I can grab some of Grandma Betty's old boots and a good winter parka, and maybe some wood in case the power goes out for good and I have to start a fire. In my crazed rush, I stub my toe on one of the trillion railroad ties that Betty's got stored down there, and then I slam on one boot, then another, and shove a hat on my head. I pound back up the stairs again, boots making me sound heavy and big against the pale wooden stairs. I bite my lip and put the parka on inside out. I have to reach inside and down to zip it up. The thread on my finger catches on the zipper and pulls a little, loosening it. It's starting to fray.

"I should not be worrying about a string," I announce to the house.

The house creaks with the wind, which probably means it agrees.

I haul up three logs and balance them in one arm against my side. Wood scrapes stick to the parka. With my other hand I grab the flashlight just as the lights flicker again and go off.

With my luck it wouldn't be all that surprising if the batteries don't work, but the light clicks on with a powerful beam.

"Thanks, Betty," I whisper.

Grandma Betty is the type of prepared lady who would always have fresh batteries in her flashlight.

I stomp up the rest of the stairs and dump the wood on the kitchen counter. The air smells of mashed potatoes and something else, something raw and woodsy.

Fear shivers against my skin, like spiders crawling. Heart racing, I swing the flashlight around the kitchen, terrified of what I might find. The microwave's digital display doesn't flash anything now. It's dark and silent and dead.

I back up and open the silverware drawer, pulling out the biggest knife I can find, the one you cut big vegetables with. It has a large sharp silver blade and a black heavy handle.

A sound comes from the living room. My fingers tightens around the handle. Maybe it's just the dog.

Or maybe it isn't.

I slide my feet across the wood floor trying to make as little noise as possible, but it's hard in Gram's clodhopper boots. One hand clutches the knife, ready to stab. The other hand holds the flashlight, which is long and heavy and could probably be a good weapon. Right?

One step forward, another, and then I swing the light around the room and right into the eyes of a large naked guy wrapped in a blanket.

Hormephobia
fear of shock

I scream. The flashlight bangs to the floor and rolls away, shutting itself off on impact.

"Zara?" His voice breaks through the darkness.

"Nick, Jesus. You scared the hell out of me," I say, kneeling down on the floor and trying to find the flashlight. I grab it and turn it back on, my heart beating a million times a minute. How can a heart stand it? "You're naked."

"Really, I couldn't tell," he jokes weakly.

"Why are you naked?"

I shine the light on his face, not the lower parts, I swear. He raises his arm to shield his eyes, so I lower the beam a little, hitting the smooth lines of his chest and abs. He has the blanket that I'd put on the dog draped around him toga style, so I can only see half of his very fine physique.

That is not the point.

He nods slowly as I stalk toward him. I stand below him and soften. The way his eyes shadow is pitiful. "Are you cold?"

I reach out and touch him with the hand that still holds the knife.

"You're warm." My voice comes out frightened and I back up a step. I flash the light onto the doorknob. I locked it. I know I locked it. "How did you get in here?"

"The door," he says.

I back up some more. "I locked the door."

He doesn't say anything. His tired brown eyes meet mine.

I flash the light along the floorboards. It skitters and jumps.

"Where's the dog?" I demand.

He doesn't answer me.

"The dog," I repeat like he doesn't understand the first time. "There was a dog here. He's hurt. That blanket you're wearing, where did you get it? Did you steal it from the dog? Because that was really uncool. He's hurt."

He doesn't answer.

I whirl on him, flashlight zigzagging along with me. "Why are you naked?"

He lifts his eyebrows and walks to the white leather chair that sits beneath the front windows. He sinks into it, wincing. I soften a little, but only a little.

"Are you hurt?" I ask, clomping over.

"I'm okay."

His voice tells me this is a lie. I don't know what's going on, but I decide to pretend to trust him, try to draw whatever it is he's hiding out into the open.

"Nick, I'll stop being mad. I'm sorry," I say, placing the knife down on the floor, and the flashlight on the end table. I reach out toward him. "I was worried about you. Strange stuff happened. I went looking for you in the woods and some guy followed me."

He catches my hand in his. His grip crushes my fingers. "I told you to stay inside."

"I was worried about you," I say, trying to be patient. "And I was right to worry."

His hand loosens and suddenly feels nice around mine, and I bring it to my lips and kiss it, just once, like a peck my mom would give me when I didn't feel well. I don't care if he's naked, I'm glad he's safe and that I'm not alone.

"And there was this dog," I say, trying to see what his reaction will be. "He was huge and someone shot him in the shoulder. Did you see him? Maybe he went up the stairs."

Nick shakes his head.

"I don't think so," he says slowly.

"Uh-huh. Okay. I'm not worried about the dog right now," I explain, taking my fingers out of his. "I'm worried about you. Where are you hurt?"

"I'm fine. I'm healing already."

"Oh. Right. Healing from what?" I asked.

He looks away.

"You stay there," I say, pulling myself away. "I'm going to build a fire in the stove."

I start walking away and then think better of it. "Promise not to move."

He coughs. "I promise."

"Swear?"

"I swear." He laughs lightly like I'm amusing.

Grabbing the flashlight, I hustle back to the kitchen and bring in the logs. I crumple some newspaper in the big black Franklin stove, toss some kindling on, and find one of the long matches Betty keeps in an iron basket thing near the stove. Once the fire starts I put a log on. The flames light the center of the room with a soft, warm glow, but the edges are still dark and mysterious.

The burning wood smell seems comfortable and comforting, like everything is normal, like I didn't get chased by some crazy guy in the woods or pull an arrow out of a dog's shoulder or have a naked guy sitting on the chair.

"I can't believe you can build a fire," he says.

I wipe my hands on my pants. "I'm not completely hopeless, you know."

He smiles. "I know."

"I'm also very good at letter writing."

"And running."

"True. And I'm stubborn."

"We're both stubborn."

Yanking off my boots, I take a deep breath of the woodsy air and then I stand up.

"Show me where you're hurt," I order.

"It's nothing."

"Let me see it."

I walk toward him and he cringes. Really. Big man Nick Colt cringes.

"I'm not going to hurt you, and Betty should be here soon, and the police." I reach out and move a lock of his dark hair off his forehead. "You're hot. You might have an infection."

"I'm always hot." He shifts uncomfortably in the chair.

"That's modest."

He laughs and the movement makes him wince. "That's not what I meant."

"I know."

We stare at each other for a moment and then I let my hand

rest against his warm cheek. He was out in that storm. He could be really sick. And where the hell are his clothes? And the dog? And how did he get in the house? I don't want to think about what I've been trying not to think ever since I saw the dog fur in the Cooper, but I do. I think about it.

"Nick, you need to trust me. I'm actually quite trustable."

He swallows. He takes his hand and places it on top of mine, leading it to his covered shoulder.

"I know."

I shiver. Something inside me surges up and makes me want to run away, but I stay there, steady. "Where are you hurt?"

With a small movement of his arm, he makes the blanket shift off his covered shoulder. I freeze. Competent Zara pretty much vanishes. There's a bandage there, crusted with blood. The bandage is familiar, too familiar.

My hand jerks away all by itself, but that's the only part of me that moves. Nick's eyes stare at me, waiting.

Swallowing, I try to force my fear and confusion somewhere else. It's all I can do to not stand up and run away. That's what my mother would do, not me. I am not my mother.

"But . . . ," I whisper. "That's impossible. Isn't it?"

I cock my head, studying the bandage, and then I reach out and rip it off with one quick jerk of my hand. There it is, a puncture wound made by an arrow, already crusted over and healing.

My breath sticks inside my chest.

Slowly, slowly, slowly, I turn my head to meet his eyes. He looks scared and resolute, steady but ready somehow.

The bandage dangles from my fingers as the question leaves my lips. "Nick? What are you?"

. . .

I am so afraid I already know what he is. But he can't be. My heart seizes up like someone is squeezing it, but no one is. It's just me, afraid.

Nick closes one eye and turns his head to peek at his wound, then faces me full on.

"Where'd the dog go?" I ask, panicky sounding.

"That wasn't a dog, Zara," he says, words whisper strong.

I jerk my head up. "What was it then? A cat? A gerbil? A geriatric hamster?"

He takes my hand. "You're getting hysterical."

Jumping away, I point at him. "I am not getting hysterical. I'm making a joke. Why do the good-looking guys never have a sense of humor?"

"Zara . . ." He reaches out toward me.

"That was rhetorical," I say, stepping away, afraid. The fire crackles and I jump again. The fear of fire is pyrophobia. Ranidaphobia is the fear of frogs, which is just ridiculous. Rectophobia is the fear of rectum or rectal diseases, which is just disgusting.

No more phobias. Real life is scary enough.

"What happened to the dog?" I demand, planting my feet.

"It was a wolf, Zara," he says. He seems too well-behaved and patient as he shifts in the chair.

Then he stares into my eyes. "And you know what happened to it."

I grab the poker and move the log over in the fire. Then I push another one in. Sparks and burning embers flutter in the air. My hand slams shut the stove's glass door.

"Be careful," Nick says.

"It's a fire. It's warm. I like warm."

The flames lap against the glass panel, "licking it" is how my dad always described that motion. The flame licks at the glass panel. It shifts colors from dark orange to brownish black to a lighter orange and back again.

"Zara," Nick's voice licks at me like those flames. Everything in me aches for the promise of that warmth, but nothing, nothing makes sense. Turning to look at him takes all the effort I have. Deep breaths force me to calm down. I can deal with this. I will not be afraid of this.

"Nick?" My voice comes out pleading. He has to tell me that there's a perfect, logical reason for everything.

"Zara," he says. "Come here."

Reaching out his hand, his eyes mingle with sadness for a second, aching and lonely. Teetering forward, I wonder if this is the same arrogant guy I met the first day of school, the guy who seemed so tough and confident. His vulnerability frightens me even more than the implication of the wound on his shoulder.

I take his hand. He pulls me in toward him, gently turning me so I land in his lap.

"I'll hurt you."

His voice deepens. "I'm already healing. Look at it."

The wound tightens up, almost closing as I watch.

"We usually heal fast," he says.

"We?"

I swallow and search his eyes, but I can't figure out what I want to see in there.

His eyes stay steady and match his voice. "Shifters."

"Shifters?"

Almost against my will, I lean into his warm chest.

He nods.

"Okay, what are shifters?"

"Shape shifters. Weres."

I snort. He sighs.

"I'm serious, Zara."

"Uh-huh. And what kind of shape shifter are you?"

"Well, I, personally, am a werewolf."

I laugh and flick a tiny piece of white lint off his bare shoulder. "That's not very original."

"I'm not kidding, Zara." He jostles me a little. "It's not a prank. Look at my shoulder. Think about the wolf you saved."

"Dog."

"Wolf."

I shudder, remembering the noise the arrow made when I pulled it from the animal's shoulder. "It doesn't prove anything."

He arches an eyebrow. "It's the same wound."

"Yours is smaller."

"That's because it's healing."

I try to stand up but he won't let me. "I do not want to believe this."

"But you do."

I pull away. He lets go. I walk over to the door. A quick flick of the fingers unlocks it. A nice pull opens it up. Wind blows snow inside. The world glows from the snow and the only tracks that I can see are filling with snow already. The only tracks are mine and a dog's. My hand is grabbing the threshold of the door, bracing me against the wind, against the truth, but I still think I might have to fall down, pass out or something, because this cannot be happening, this cannot be real.

Nick stands behind me. He puts a hand on my waist.

I yank in a breath. The world seems to swirl around me.

"Are you going to faint?" he asks.

I back into him and blurt, "But you're so cute. Werewolves aren't supposed to be cute. Vampires are, I think. They are in the movies. But the werewolves are pretty much ugly and they wear leather jackets and are all dirty with these monster sideburns."

"That's all you have to say? That I'm cute?" He takes a stray piece of my hair and curls it around his fingers. "Most people faint or shriek or never talk to me again."

"Have you told a lot of people?"

"Not many."

"Your parents?"

"Yeah, they know." His face tightens. "It's genetic."

"Your dad?"

"Both."

I nod, thinking for a second and then lifting my hands up to the sides of his body. One hand touches the roughness of the wool blanket. The other hand touches his smooth skin. "Does your shoulder hurt?"

He shakes his head and his hand leaves my chin and moves to the back of my head, cupping it there. "Thank you for taking the arrow out."

"It's okay," I say, trying to calm down. I'm really not sure if I am more freaked about the fact that he's telling me he's a werewolf or that his lips are so close. "I save people who think they're werewolves every day, didn't you know?"

"No," he says, leaning in. "I didn't."

His eyes are so beautiful and dark and they do look like that dog's—I mean, that wolf's. They are kind and strong and a little bit something else and I like them. I like them a lot. No, I like them way too much. Something inside me gets a little warmer, edges closer to him.

The fire crackles and I jump again, jittery, nervous, but I don't jump away from Nick. I jump toward him. Nick in the firelight with just a blanket on is a little hard to resist, no matter how crazy he might be. His skin, deep with heat, seems to glisten. His muscles are defined and good but not all steroid bulky. He is so perfect. And beautiful. In a boy way. Not a monster way. Not a wolf way.

"Are you going to kiss me?" My words tremble into the air.

He smiles but doesn't answer.

"I've never kissed a werewolf before. Are were kisses like pixie kisses? Do they do something to you? Is that why you never kissed anybody?"

He gives a little smile. "No. It's just I never kissed anyone because I never thought I could be honest about who I am, you know? And I didn't want anyone to get attached to me because . . ."

"Because you're a werewolf."

"Because I'm a werewolf," he repeats softly. Watching his lips move makes me shiver; not in a scared way, in more of an oh-he-is-too-beautiful way.

I put my hand against his skin. It is warm. It's always been warm. He smells so good, like woods and safety. I swallow my fear and move forward, and my lips meet his, angel-light, a tiny promise. His lips move beneath mine. His hands move to my shoulders and my mouth feels like it will burst with happiness. My whole body shakes with it.

"Wow," I say.

"Yeah," he says. "Wow."

Our mouths meet again. It's like my lips belong there . . .

right there. One tiny part of me has finally found a place to fit. We pull away for air.

"Are there a lot of you? Because I think there could be a market for these werewolf kisses," I ask.

He laughs. "There are a few."

I pull away, just a little bit, adjust my shirt, try to make sense. "Are there any more in Bedford?"

"Yeah. Actually, there are a lot in Bedford, more than other places. Some have moved away."

"Why are there more here?"

"Genes. Inbreeding back in the eighteen hundreds or something, I don't know." He touches his wounded shoulder with the palm of his hand. "But it's not like the only place there are weres."

"Do I know anybody else who is one?"

His eyes stare into my eyes. "Betty."

"Betty?"

"She's a tiger."

Here there be tygers.

One second passes. Two. I slam my hands into his chest. "Get out!"

He raises his hands in the air. "What?"

"You can't go telling me my grandmother is a freaking tiger, okay? Just get out!"

"Zara . . ."

"It's too much," I tell him, slumping away and throwing myself on the couch. "Okay? It's just too much."

Algophobia
fear of pain

Let's just say I'm a wimp. Okay?

Here:

I'm a wimp.

I get off the couch and pace back and forth, chanting.

"Oh my God. Oh my God. Oh my God."

I rush over to the fire and put my hands out to see if I've gone mad or if I can feel its warmth. A fire is real. Crazy people often lose touch with reality.

"This is not happening."

But it is.

A hysterical laugh bursts out of me. I cover my mouth with my hands.

"This is fine," I mutter. "This is okay. You can deal with this. My grandmother is not human. Nick is not human. There are humans who are not human."

Nick doesn't say anything. He sits on the edge of the coffeetable, watching me. He's all rigid, like he's a soldier ready to be ambushed, ready for the painful shot to the gut. Finally, I stop pacing.

"Thank you for trusting me," I whisper.

He cocks his head and relaxes. Then he raises his finger for me to wait and trots into the kitchen. I stay where I am and in a moment he comes back, paler than normal, wearing the blanket around his waist and one of Grandma Betty's oversized navy blue hooded sweatshirts. He yanks the metal zipper up and then crosses his arms over his chest, leaning against the wall, just past the woodstove.

"So . . . ," he says.

"So."

"So, I'm a werewolf and your grandmother's a weretiger. You all set with that?"

I nod like a good girl, like this is all perfectly normal. "It appears that way. Are you hurting?"

"I'm okay."

My hand flutters up to my forehead. The world seems to spin again. He must notice because he grabs my hand and leads me over to the couch, the ugly, ridiculous plaid couch. We sit down together.

"I thought you weren't going to faint." He scowls at me. I hate when he scowls at me.

"I'm not."

I lean back against the armrest and grab a pillow, hugging it against me, like a barrier between us. That's what he thinks it is, too. I can tell because his eyes get all hurt looking, so I put the pillow back on top of the couch. It tumbles down on Nick's head. I laugh. He laughs too and bonks me with it. Dust swirls into the air and I sneeze.

"It's just weird, okay," I say, tearing the pillow out of his hands. "It's weird finding out someone's a werewolf. I don't even believe in werewolves. It's impossible. It's physically impossible."

"Not really."

"Well, obviously."

My hand flits in the air, gesturing at him. I pull it back down into my lap. "And Betty is a were too, and if it's genetic that means that my dad—I mean my stepdad—was probably one."

"Brilliant deduction."

"Shut up."

He is being annoying; smiling at me like it's fun to watch me squirm. A million questions rattle inside me. I ask the first one, "So how do you actually become a werewolf?"

"Born that way. Or bitten." He wiggles his eyebrows. "You interested?"

I shriek and jump back, knocking my hip into the side of the sofa and almost falling onto the floor. "No!"

He catches me around the waist with his too-big hands and hauls me back on the sofa, laughing a real laugh, all big and hearty. "I was kidding, Zara. I'd never let that happen to you."

"Really?"

His eyes melt me. "Really. I'd never let *anything* happen to you."

"Oh. Right. Hero-complex thing. You're a werewolf with a hero complex. That's so funny."

He doesn't answer. The muffled light of the room gives everything a romantic sort of glow, even though the fire kind of dries the air out and makes my throat hurt. My heart pings in my chest, hope making it beat fast, too fast. His hand reaches out and touches the back of my head. His fingers entwine with my hair. It happens again, that melting feeling, the longing feeling. I want to gesture my body against his body, to explain things like need. The blanket he wears rubs against his legs and my legs.

His voice comes out husky. "I'm going to kiss you now, okay?"

I don't think I can speak anymore so I just nod.

"Okay."

His lips warm against mine. My arms wrap around his shoulders and he presses me to him. I am warm here, safe. The backs of my knees tingle and I feel absolutely the opposite of empty. I feel like my life will burst open with good.

Finally I say, "I can't believe you're kissing me."

He leans back and tucks his big hand along the side of my face. "What? Aren't you kissing me back?"

I shrug. "I just thought . . ."

"Thought what?"

"That maybe you . . . Oh, I don't know. Didn't kiss girls. Do *not* get mad. That's what Issie and Devyn said."

"That I didn't kiss girls?"

"Yeah. I thought it was because you were a pixie maybe. I saw gold dust on your jacket."

"You what?" There's an edge to his voice.

"I didn't really think. I just sort of thought it." I snuggle in, try to calm him down.

"When was there dust on my jacket?"

"After you helped me with my car."

He nods. "That was after I went through the woods searching for him. I dropped my jacket before I turned. I probably picked it up then. I can't believe you thought I was a pixie."

"Only a little." We sit there for a minute. "I think we should call Issie and Devyn and tell them."

"That we made out?"

I elbow him. "No. The pixie/were stuff."

I haul myself up off the couch and grab the phone off the brick hearth. It's warm. I start pushing in numbers. "And then maybe we should all go out looking for Jay."

The phone makes a funny noise. The display reads "no signal."

"Great," I say.

Nick gets up and grabs the other phone, listens. "The lines are out."

I flip open the cell. "No signal."

I pocket the phone.

Nick points outside. Blue lights fill the windows, flash through the windows. "The police are here."

Pogonophobia
fear of facial hair, mostly beards

Two cops come to the door, both sheriff's deputies. Their hands are on their guns, like they're ready for action.

"You Zara?" the taller one with the beard asks. His hair is red and short.

I nod.

"Sergeant Fahey," he says, taking his hand off his gun and reaching out to shake mine. He sees Nick behind me and lets himself smile. "Hey, Nick."

Nick nods and smiles.

"So, you found your way back," Sergeant Fahey says, taking in the blanket around Nick's waist. He nods to the other officer, who is beardless and really young looking. "Safe and sound. So . . . Deputy Clark and I don't have to go searching."

"Nope," Nick says. "Sorry about that."

"Sorry? It's a good thing," Deputy Clark says. Then he shivers in the cold.

"Oh, do you guys want to come in?" I ask.

"Nope. Thanks," Sergeant Fahey says, all straight-backed and official, which makes Officer Clark grimace. "But your grandmother told us you heard a man in the woods saying your name?"

I nod. "And he tried to attack Nick."

Sergeant Fahey's eyes grow all big. "Really?"

Nick glares at me and then I realize that there's no proof. His wound's already healing. "It was nothing. I ran away."

His mouth twitches. Running away is so the opposite of who he is. That lie is costing him.

Deputy Clark whips out a pad. "Can you describe him?"

Nick does. They come inside, sit on the couch, and ask questions. Deputy Clark asks a lot of questions, mostly I think because he doesn't want to go back outside into the cold. Then they get up and head into the woods with these supercharged flashlights looking for the man.

We stand at the windows and watch the light flash through the darkness, searching.

"They'll never find him," Nick says.

"You don't know that."

"He doesn't leave a trail." Nick turns away and sits back on the couch.

I don't join him. I just keep staring out at the night and the officers. My voice hitches inside my throat. "I thought you were gone."

"I'm tougher than that."

"Because you're a were?" I close the curtain again.

"Yeah."

"You got hurt even though you're a were." I turn around and

look at him, so solid and healthy on the couch, so normal looking, in a ridiculously good-looking human kind of way.

"But you read what it said on that Web site. We're the natural enemy of pixies."

"Did you even know pixies existed until this week?"

He cringes, touches his shoulder. "No. But for the last month or so Devyn and I knew there was something out there, something bad. Issie too. We told Issie."

"Your parents are weres too, right? But they're out on some photo shoot somewhere."

"Making a documentary."

"And they just left you here alone. I thought wolves were pack animals, that they hang together."

"They do, but my parents . . . We've got some interesting family dynamics going on."

"How do you mean?"

"When the son of an alpha wolf, the leader, grows, he matures into alpha himself, and then there's some tension because there's just this genetic need to be alpha."

"To be the one in charge. The hero."

"Basically. But there can only be one alpha, so my parents have been taking an extended trip this year, and next year too, until I go to college. That way my dad and I don't rip each other apart."

"Because you're both alpha?"

He nods.

"Wow. That's weird."

A truck rumbles into the driveway. I watch the police walk out of the woods and talk to Betty by her truck. Then they leave and she comes inside, all business.

She points at Nick. "Take off your shirt."

He does.

"Why are you making him take off—," I start to ask.

"She knows," Nick interrupts. "She knows I'm a were."

Betty nods, peers at the almost invisible wound. "Did you tell her?"

"That you're a were too?" I flop down in the green leather chair by the door. "Yeah, he told me."

"How is she taking it?" Betty asks Nick.

"Not well."

She laughs. "Your wound looks fine. You did a good job, Zara."

I manage to nod.

"The police haven't found anything," Betty says, putting some wood into the stove. It crackles. "But I didn't expect them to. You can always hope, though."

"We think he's a pixie, Gram," I sputter it out.

She nods. "You think right. Where's the poker?"

I find it by the front door. "I took it, um, as a weapon."

"Good idea," she says, taking it from me and using it to shift the logs. A couple of embers fly into the room and wisp out. "I've called your mother. She wants you to come back home. She thinks it was a mistake to send you here."

My throat tightens up and I flip my feet up under me, studying her face in the shadowy light of the fire. "What do you think?"

Nick answers for her. "It might be safer for you to go away."

"I'm not going to run," I say. "He'd find me anyway, right? He found me in Charleston. And he hasn't attacked me or anything, not even when I was out there in the woods. It's not like I'm in danger."

"You don't know that, Zara," Betty says.

"But she sent me here because she thought I'd be safer, safer with you," I say to Betty. "Because you're a were. And if Nick's a were too I must be doubly safe, right?"

"Hopefully," she says.

"I'm not going." I stand up and walk next to her, look up at her. "You won't make me go back."

"No," she says. "I won't. But it's dangerous here. We don't know how to stop him."

Nick stands up, puts his arm around me. "We'll figure something out."

Nick stays the night. There's no school the next morning, and when I wake up it's already day and white snow light fills up the room. Everything seems so much safer, less scary.

Nick walks down the hall, peeks in, and realizes I'm awake. He smiles. "You sleep forever."

"I was tired," I say, stretching and worrying about my hair and my breath and if there's crud in my eyes. Then I notice something. "You have pants on."

"I keep an extra pair in the MINI." He comes in and sits on the edge of my bed. "Disappointed?"

"A little."

I sit up against the headboard and rub my eyes. "What've you been doing?"

"I called Devyn and Issie. They're trying to figure out if they can come over. Devyn's parents have a snowmobile but they don't want him on it because of the whole injury thing. Betty went in to work in that kick-ass truck of hers."

"Kick ass?"

"It is. Have you looked at her tires?"

"You have a MINI Cooper."

"That doesn't mean I can't appreciate a good truck." He smiles and scruffs my hair like he's my big brother or something, which is not cool. "Anyway, I made pancakes. There's some in the oven, and I've been reading old Stephen King books."

"Oh, that's a good idea, scaring yourself more?"

"I'm hard to scare."

"So tough."

He laughs. I laugh too and then I smile. "Did you really make pancakes?"

He grabs my hand and yanks me out of bed. "Come on."

"Wow, you can really wolf it down," I say.

His fork pauses in midair. "That's original."

I start giggling. "I thought so."

His dimples show. "You're sure putting it away."

"You make good pancakes."

"Thank you."

"I think you should move in with us and just make pancakes all the time."

"Is Betty that bad a cook?"

"Yeah, and I'm not that much better."

"Maybe I should stay here until, you know, things settle down or—"

My stomach pierces me and I cut the pancake without looking up at him. "I'm not going back to Charleston."

"It would be safer."

"Only for me. He'd be picking off guys until he got a queen. I can't let that happen."

"It's not your battle."

"Right." I bring my fork to my mouth, let it hover there, and really look at him. He is so charged up, so strong, but he's still made of skin and muscle. He can still get hurt. "Then whose battle is it? Just yours? Because that is not going to happen. You are not Mr. Save the World Solo Style, okay?"

He dumps some more syrup on his pancakes and then cringes, like talking is painful. "Okay. Fine. It's *our* battle. All of us."

"The syrup's dripping on the book." I reach out and move the syrup. That's when I see the cover. "*Skeleton Crew*?"

"Stephen King."

My heart stops beating and my brain makes a connection that a good brain should have made ages ago. "I know it's Stephen King. It's just . . . There's a story in here."

I flip to it and stop, just staring at the title.

"What?"

" 'Here There Be Tygers.' "

He pulls his chair closer to the table, closer to me, and leans forward, waiting.

"My dad wrote that in the library book: 'Don't fear. Here there be tygers, 157.' "

"I remember. I thought Devyn or Betty or someone said it was some science fiction guy's short story. He didn't say Stephen King, did he?" Nick's words fly against my neck skin with his breath. It's so hard to concentrate.

"It was Ray Bradbury, I think. And no. But two people could have used the title." I get to page 157.

"Zara?"

I twist the book around so we are both reading it at ninety degrees. "Look."

"He wrote in it," Nick says squinting. Maple syrup smell hits my cheek. "Can you read it?"

"It's faded."

"Why did he use pencil?"

"He always used pencil. He was quirky," I say. I lift the book closer to my face. "It says: *Defenses: Weres, Iron. Problem: If the need becomes too great, they feed in daytime. Christine.* Great. Nice and cryptic, Dad. And he underlined this line in the story all about tigers looking hungry and vicious."

"Who is Christine?"

"Another Stephen King book. The one about the car, I think."

Nick slams his chair back. "Read it again. I saw that book upstairs."

I read it again, yelling it so he can hear me. He's fast, werewolf fast, and he's up and down the stairs in a couple of blinks, holding another Stephen King book in his hand.

"He says they can come in the daytime when the need gets too great," he says. "We should call Betty."

"Let me see that book first." I reach out. He gives it to me. I flip it open and a piece of paper falls to the floor.

Nick scoops it up and hands it to me before I can react. My hands shake as I unfold it. "It could be nothing, a report card or a note to my mom . . ."

"Read it, Zara," Nick's voice gentles out in the kitchen. It feels like even the air waits.

I read.

"*If you have found this it means that the need is back. He says he doesn't want the need. He says he fights against it and*

I'd like to believe it, but does it even matter? When he loses control over his need he loses control over his court, and they demand blood and soul to satisfy their cravings, cravings they have when the king comes of age and needs a queen. Mom, you know why we ran. I could only let her sacrifice so much and his anger at our deal was so great. We were afraid to trust. I am so sorry it was not enough." I look up at Nick. "Do you know what this means?"

"Not really. Is that all?"

"No, there are a couple more lines," I say and keep reading. "*You've got to be warned that when the desire becomes too great, nighttime does not contain him. He will prowl in the sun like the others. Iron makes them weak. They are fast, but we are faster, and we too can kill. That's our only hope. Other Shining Ones are our only hope.*"

I fold the paper back up and place it next to my fork. Then I think better of it and tuck it into my sweatshirt. "My father wrote that."

Nick nods. "They can come in the day."

"If the need is great."

"I'm not taking chances about that," he says. "I'm calling Betty."

I grab his arm, stop him. "Nick?"

He brings his face down to my level. His eyes are all concerned and sweet. "What?"

"I feel funny."

"It's okay to be scared, Zara. But I'll call Betty and we'll keep you safe. It's okay."

"No. It feels like spiders." I try to explain. Heat rushes to my face. "It's stupid. It's just this feeling I keep getting, like spiders are running over my skin. I don't know how to explain it."

His broad hands wrap around my arms and stroke them lightly. "When does this happen?"

"I don't know. Ever since I left Charleston. Every time I see that man that I saw at the airport or when I hear that voice."

"The voice in the woods?"

I nod.

Nick lets go of my arms and rushes over to the fireplace. He grabs the poker that Betty uses to turn over the logs. He wraps my hands around it. "Take this."

"What? Why?"

He half growls. "It means he's coming. He will try to trick you into opening the door. Don't let him."

I start to argue but Nick holds up his finger. His eyes are so focused, so intent, so like a wolf's. How had I not noticed that before?

"I mean it, Zara. You cannot let anyone in. Promise me."

"Can't they just break in?" I demand. I stomp down on the floor like I'm two, but I don't care, I am so ridiculously frustrated. I want him to stop scaring me.

He doesn't answer, just starts rushing around, pulling drapes closed.

"You should grab that knife you left in the kitchen," he says, glancing up the stairs. "All the windows are locked up there, right?"

"I don't know!" I yell, waving the poker around. Fear tingles on my skin. Or is it that spider feeling? I have no idea. Nick is already racing up the stairs, taking them three at a time.

"What if they break down the door?"

"They can't!"

"How do you know they can't? That guy looked pretty strong."

He shouts down to me, "Pixies have to be invited in, like vampires. I read it on the Internet."

"Well, there you go," I mutter. "Then it must be true."

Pixiophobia

a fear of pixies

I made this up, but believe me it should be a word because it sure is a legitimate fear

I thunder up the stairs after him.

He ignores me, rushing from one room to the other, checking on the windows, pulling the shades down in each one before whisking off to the next. He moves so fast he is almost a blur. No wonder he's such a good runner. He isn't human.

I shudder, but I mean, he's still Nick.

My room is the last one he goes to. I block the door so he can't race off again, but he looks a little calmer now. His hair isn't standing on end or anything.

"The windows are all locked," he says, sitting down on my bed.

I dial Betty's cell.

Her voice snaps to attention. "Zara?"

"I think the pixie guy is coming."

"What? It's daylight."

"I know! But I found a note dad left for you. He says if the need gets too great then they can come in the daytime."

"Jesus." She waits, pausing, like she's struggling with big stuff. "He left a note?"

"Uh-huh." I let her have a second because I just know she must be trying to process that. Then I go on. "And I feel squiggley, like I do whenever he shows up."

"Okay. Nick's there, right?"

"Uh-huh."

"You put him on. I will be there as soon as I can, okay? I'm coming now."

"Okay."

I give the phone to Nick. He says, "Yep. I know. I know."

Then he holds it out from his body. "It disconnected."

"Great."

He scrunches up his face and flops down on my bed. "I like your Amnesty International poster."

I'd hung it above my bed, just like at home.

"These are your words of wisdom in our time of crisis? You like my poster? You crack me up." I schlump across the room and sit down next to him. "Move over."

I wiggle my hips so he'll edge over on the bed. It's too scary to be romantic. He puts his arm out and I rest my head against it, staring up at the poster.

I say, like the brilliant conversationalist I am, "I like Amnesty International."

"Sort of a save-the-world complex, huh?" he asks. His fingers wrap around my shoulder.

"I guess."

"I've got one too."

"Really? I hadn't noticed."

"Sarcasm does not become you." He turns on his side to look at me.

Everything inside me goes all jittery. I am on my bed with a cute boy. Sorry . . . a cute werewolf. The wind rattles the window. Once again, happy good feeling? Gone.

"Should we be scared?" I ask.

"Honestly?"

I nod.

"Yeah."

I reach out and touch his face, just smooth my hand along the side of it. His jaw tenses beneath my fingers. "Explain what it means to be weres."

He shakes his head. My hand moves with him. I am not about to let go, not this time.

"Weres have souls. We are part people. Pixies, not so much. They aren't human at all; that's what Betty told me. One theory is that they were a race that didn't have what it took to go to heaven, but weren't evil enough for hell. So they were left here, to flounder and torment for eternity."

I raise my eyebrows. He reaches out and smoothes them down. Then he lowers his head and sniffs my hair. His words blow against me. "You don't believe that theory?"

"It's stupid."

"I think so too," he says, flopping back down and nestling me into his side. "Pixies are definitely evil enough for hell."

"If hell even exists," I say.

"Right." He doesn't seem convinced. "There's another theory that there are five ancient races that came to the earth."

"What?"

"They were pixie, fairy, were, elf, and one other. I can't remember. They have a council. They are called the Shining Ones."

"Like in my dad's note."

We lie there for a second and then I swallow and snuggle a

little closer to Nick's side. I don't care what he says about pixies or werewolves or whatever. I feel safe with him.

I say, "You said that pixies can't come inside unless they're invited, like the vampires in all those Stephen King books."

"I don't know how vampires work. I'm not sure they're even real."

"Seriously?"

"Yeah."

"Well, there's a positive, I guess."

His fingers tighten around my shoulder.

I take a big breath of his wolf/man/pine smell and steel myself. "My mom sent me up here to the land of cold and pixies. Great mom."

"From what Betty said, she was really worried about you. They thought you were dead inside."

"I was. I was empty. I'm not now," I say, but I don't want to talk about me. I think for a second, inhale the warmth of him. "Why would she send me here when we never came back here?"

"You never came back?"

"Betty always visited us. The last time Mom was here was when all those other disappearances were happening."

"Yeah."

"That was right after my mom graduated college. It must've been so weird coming home to boys going missing and having me, then marrying my dad and going off to Tulane to get her master's. It must have felt like starting over. Maybe she just wanted to forget everything. I mean, she must've known some of the guys who got lost."

The tingling feeling surges. The scrape on my hand burns.

"This is insane," I say, plopping back on the bed.

He squeezes my good hand in his. “I know.”

I stare up at the flame on the Amnesty International candle. All those people in jails all across the world; tortured, imprisoned, lots of times for no reason at all, lots of times for just speaking their minds. How could this all be part of the same world? Me here with him, worrying about pixies. Them, all across the world, worrying about surviving.

What is the commonality there?

Just the flame of the candle.

Just hope.

“What happened?” I ask. “What happened the last time?”

“People kept vanishing. At night. Always when they were alone. The town had a curfew,” he says. “Eventually it stopped.”

“What stopped it?”

“No one knows,” his voice deepens. “Except maybe Betty. I’m thinking she might know something more.”

“Then she should have told us.”

“Maybe she didn’t think she’d have to.”

“Lame.” I cover my eyes with my hand and try not to think about that voice calling my name, but it echoes in my ears. “And they started taking the boys again right around the time I saw the guy in Charleston. And you, Nick Colt, somehow think it’s your job to protect people from this?”

“I can scare them away,” he says, like he’s boasting or something.

“How?”

“Weres have abilities.”

“What abilities?”

“We can hunt.”

I touch the metal zipper on his sweatshirt, flipping it up and down, and then repeat what he said, trying to understand. "You can hunt."

Werewolves hunt.

"You kill things." I move a little bit away from him.

"I don't kill *people*," he says, obviously annoyed.

I sit up on the bed. "How do I know that?"

He cocks his head. "Look at me."

Hesitantly, I look. Sort of.

"Look in my eyes, Zara. I do not kill people."

I swallow. "Okay."

"You believe me?"

Nodding, I get up and walk across the room and light a candle. I begin stacking CDs in piles. They are scattered all over the floor. My bracelet bangs against my wrist as I work.

"Zara."

"What? I'm just cleaning up, okay?" I am almost shouting at him so I settle my voice down. "This is all a little hard to deal with."

He swings his legs off the bed and walks over, squatting on the floor like I am. "I know."

His big hand pats my back and then he stiffens. I drop the CD I'm holding. A spidery feeling creeps along my hand. Nick grabs the fire poker again, clutching it in his large fist.

Then someone pounds on the door downstairs; loud, insistent.

I jump up. My voice sounds scared. "Nick?"

He gives me a steady look, but his hand tightens on the metal poker and his knuckles are white.

"Do not open the door, Zara."

"Is it—"

A new burst of pounding interrupts my question.

I stare at Nick and catch my reflection in the dresser mirror. My eyes are huge and scared, just like how I feel. That spider feeling seems all over me now, creeping along, invading.

My foot knocks over the pile of CDs, scattering them all over the floor again. My heart leaps out and scatters with them, pieces of it everywhere. I step on a bunch of envelopes I have ready to mail out to dictators across the world.

I clutch Nick's wrist.

"They can't get in, right?"

He nods. "Not unless you let them."

"And I'm not going to let them."

"Right."

Another round of pounding against the door. Another. Another.

"Nick?"

He wraps his arms around me. The cold iron of the poker chills a straight line against my back. It is nothing compared to his warmth. "You are perfectly safe here with me."

"Are you going to change into a wolf?"

"Not unless I have to."

"You don't need a full moon or anything?" I whisper, clinging to him.

"Nope."

I shiver. I wish I could crawl inside his skin and hide under there. "Do you think you're going to have to change?"

He moves me toward the bed, sitting me down. He has the fire poker in his hand. It looks scary there; ready, metallic, heavy.

"They shouldn't be able to get inside the house," he says. "Not unless they've been in here before."

"Are there a lot of them?"

"I smell five at least. The lesser ones I'm not worried about. But their leader?"

"They have a leader?"

"I'm pretty sure." He pulls away from me and walks across the room and closes my bedroom door, flicking the lock in the doorknob. He doesn't turn to talk to me, just keeps facing the closed door. His free hand spreads out against the wood frame of it.

Footsteps thud up the stairs. He turns his head to look at me. The irises of his eyes have gone slanted, like a wolf's.

He speaks over his shoulder in low, menacing rumbles that are barely human. "I think at least one of the pixies has been in this house before."

I freeze.

Nick's back shakes with some sort of effort. I don't know what kind.

"Nick? Can they all come in if one has been in before?"

"No. They're waiting outside."

"Can he come in the room if he's been in the house?" Terror hobbles me.

"I don't know."

He snarls and I don't know what to do, what to say, so I just say his name. "Nick?"

His voice is warm and aching all at the same time. "I'm trying hard not to change, Zara. But when people are in danger, I change."

"And I'm in danger?"

He nods.

I touch his back. I'm such a mess I don't even remember walking toward him. The muscles ripple and move beneath my fingers, like the fibers are struggling to stay themselves.

"Then change!" I order him.

"I don't want to scare you."

"I'm already scared!" I shriek. "I just don't want you to get hurt!"

"Me? It's not me I'm worried about. It's you."

A hand pounds on my bedroom door. The entire thing shakes in the door frame. Oh God. Oh God.

Nick swings around. His eyes fill with pain and grief. He rips off the sweatshirt and rushes to the other side of the bed where I can't see him.

"Whatever you do, Zara, *do not* let him in. Whatever he says. You can't." He snarls and there is a knock at the door, a gentle, lovely sounding knock. I step farther away from it.

The pants Nick has been wearing fly across the room. I catch them in my arms.

He keeps trying to talk. "I might be able to take him one on one in here, but I'd rather not chance it. He's stronger than the rest of them, and this isn't my habitat, you know . . ."

"Nick?" I whisper.

A pillow flies over the bed.

"We just have to make it till Betty gets here. Just hold out till then, Zara." His words rush out and the knocking on the door muffles them. But they can't muffle the fierce growl that escapes his throat, half warning, half battle cry, all wolf.

"Oh God," I whisper.

Someone knocks lightly against the door.

"Zara, let me in."

The wolf growls and stands between me and the door. His fur, thick and full, seems to bristle against the threat.

He said there were at least five. One is here in the house with us, but as long as I don't open the door we'll be safe.

Why would Nick think I'd open the door? He must think I am the most naive human ever. There is no way I'm opening that door to let the pixie thing in.

But what about the other ones?

I peek out the window, moving the shade just an inch and spot two dark figures in the snow. The snow shovels down from a grayish white sky, billowing toward them, and everything seems almost peaceful.

The knock comes at the door again, a sweet knock, like when my mom would knock when she needed to wake me and my friends at a slumber party. I stare at Nick. He crouches down, ready to spring.

They are trying to trick me. I won't let them. I'll ignore the door and I'll watch the ones outside.

Turning back to the window, I shriek. A face hovers, pale and wild eyed, attached to a body. I leap back and shriek even more. The shade flops down to obscure my view.

I sit in the middle of my bed and pull my knees to my chest, but I hold on to the poker. I will use it. Pacifism is overrated sometimes.

"This is not happening," I chant. "This is not happening."

Something scrapes against the window and I am so sure it's not a tree branch. It is something scary that wants in.

Nick circles the room, patrolling, back and forth, back and forth from window to door, window to door. His lips pull back, revealing his teeth. Another light knuckle knock sounds against the door. Nick bares his teeth even more, all the way back to the gums.

"Zara?" The voice comes, deep, a little hoarse. It's familiar and it's not the voice from the woods.

My heart leaps up, and not because of fear.

"Zara, sweetie?"

It can't be. It can't.

I sit up straighter and swing my legs off the couch.

The candle flame on the bureau flickers, then catches a draft and leaps to twice its size.

I answer with a whisper and a prayer, a hope.

"Daddy?"

Vitricophobia

fear of a stepfather

It can't be. There is no way, but it sounds just like him. My tongue seems to stick to my throat and my chest squeezes tightly, but I manage to say it again.

"Daddy?"

Nick's growling goes out of control. His body shakes with it. It rattles. My body rattles too.

A wolf growling is not something you want to be within ten feet of, and I'm much closer than that and it's scary. It's really scary, but not as scary as what is on the other side of that door.

My dad died. And yet my dad is speaking. I can hear him over the growls. I can. I can hear him somehow, right behind the door.

My feet silently move across the floor.

"Daddy, is that you?" I whisper.

He hears me somehow.

"Open the door, Zara honey, and let me in."

I want to. I really want to, but shock makes my limbs slow and heavy. Then Nick smashes up onto his hind legs and presses his front paws against the door, blocking me.

"Move, Nick," I beg and step closer, lean in, put my hands flat against the door, like I can somehow feel through to the other side and touch my dad's face, feel his skin warm again, pulsing with life. But I can't. Of course I can't. The cold wood against my hands seems so unfair.

"You can't be here." My voice sounds tiny and weak. My heart thumps in my chest.

If I opened that door would he be there? Would he smile at me and show his dimples? Would his cheeks be scruffy because he needed a shave? Would he hug me? All I've wanted all these months was for him to be alive.

But I'd seen him on the floor. I'd seen him in the coffin. And you can feel it when someone has died, you can feel that his soul is gone, just gone, the emptiness of his body. But if werewolves and pixies can be real, then maybe this can be happening. Maybe my dad can actually be here, right here, just a few inches of wood away from me.

I sway against the door. My shoulder presses into Nick's side. "You can't. You can't be here."

"I am, Zara. Let me in. I'll explain," he says.

He died. He died. I saw him die. The water on the floor. His face cold beneath my fingers.

But what if he didn't? "Daddy?"

"I'm right here, baby."

Lumps form in my throat, going all the way down into the core of me.

It's his voice. His. Right there. I reach toward the doorknob but I don't get to turn it.

Nick smashes at me with his head, pushing against my lower jaw and cheek, like a blow. His muzzle moves my head away from the door. He presses his face in between me and the wood. Fur gets in my mouth. I spit it out and push at him.

"That's my dad. My dad." I slap the door. "He's on the other side. The pixies will get him."

Nick shows me his teeth.

"I can't lose him again, Nick."

The wolf snarls like he's ready to bite. My head jerks back and away, but then I steady myself.

"Get . . . out . . . of . . . the . . . way."

Pushing against his thick neck, I slam my hands against him over and over again, pummeling him. He doesn't budge.

"Move!" I order. "Move."

"Zara, is there a wolf in there with you? Do not trust him," my dad's voice says, calmly, really calmly.

I grab a fistful of fur and freeze. All at once it hits me that something is not right. My dad would never be calm if I was in my bedroom with a wolf. He'd be stressed and screaming, breaking the door down, kicking it in like he did once when I was really little and had accidentally locked myself in the bathroom and couldn't get the lock out of the bolt because it was so old. He'd kicked that door down, splintering the wood, clutching me to him. He'd kissed my forehead over and over again.

"I'd never let anything happen to you, princess," he'd said. "You're my baby."

My dad would be kicking the door in. My dad would be saving me.

"Let me in," he says. "Zara . . ."

Letting go of Nick, I stagger backward. My hands fly up to my mouth, covering it.

Nick stops snarling at me and wags his fluffy tail.

How would my dad know that it is a wolf in here and not a dog? How would he know that it isn't pixies?

I shudder. Nick pounds next to me, pressing his side against my legs. I drop my hands and plunge my fingers into his fur, burying them there, looking for something. Maybe comfort. Maybe warmth. Maybe strength. Maybe all three.

"You're dead," I say and a sob breaks through my chest, exploding out of me. "You can't be here."

"I'm not dead, Zara."

I move away from Nick, grab a pillow instead, clutching it against me like a shield. The memory of my dad on the floor assails me. I see the water bottle rolling across the wood. I see his mouth, loose, open, aching for air.

"Yes, you are. You're dead," I say. "You left me. I saw you. You left me. And now I'm here in Maine where everything is crazy and you can't run at night and it's cold."

"Zara, let me in. I'll explain."

I throw the *Annual Report on Human Rights 2009* at the door. It wallops against the wood. Nick ducks and scrambles out of the way. I grab another annual report and smash it against the doorknob.

"You liar! You can't explain. You can't! You left me!"

Sobbing, heaving, I race at the door and hit it with my fists.

"You left."

He was the best hugger, my dad. He was an encompassing safe hugger, like a giant teddy bear, only warmer.

"Just let me in, Zara." He sounds angry now, the way he sounded when I talked back to my mom. He sounds just like my dad.

One step forward, another. Nick's wolf voice lets out a low rumbling growl. I hold my finger to my lips, trying to tell him to be quiet.

My fingers tremble but they still unlock the door.

"Open the door for me, Zara," he says.

Nick nudges me away from the door and I let him.

"No," I say. "If you were really my father you could open it yourself."

There is no answer.

I knew that. I knew there would be no answer.

Nick nuzzles my hand. My fingers plunge into the fur.

"Why don't you open the door then?" I ask. "It's unlocked."

Something shrieks inside of me, something violent and desperate and real.

"Go ahead!" I scream, wild and lost, alone but not alone. Nick pushes his side in front of me, blocking me from the door and whatever is beyond it. "Why aren't you, huh? Why aren't you opening the goddamn door?"

I stare at the doorknob. It doesn't move. He knows he can't fool me.

Nick was right. Pixies can only go into homes and places they've been invited into or places they've been in before.

My stepdad has been in this room a million times. If it were him he would have just walked right in the moment I unlocked the door.

But it isn't him. He isn't magically back from the dead.

It's someone else. Or something else, something that has

been in the house but not in the room. It's something that sounds just like my dad.

"Just come to me, Zara. I need you to come to me."

"What?"

"My need . . . I can't hold it back any longer . . . it's huge."

"What are you?" I ask, staggering backward, still staring at the doorknob. "What the hell are you?"

Whatever he is roars with rage. He storms up and down the stairs and it sounds as if he has summoned a tornado to trash Grammy Betty's house. Books crash. Glass breaks. I close my eyes and cover my ears. Nick growls.

I crumple on my bed. For a second, I believed that what I wanted more than anything in the world had come true. For a second, I believed that my dad was back. But he isn't. He's gone again. He's really, truly gone and I know it. I know I'll never see him again no matter how much I want to.

The candle in me has blown out and I'm afraid, really, really afraid, because my biggest fear is true. I have to live my life without my dad, my running partner, the guy who taught me about Amnesty and sang John Lennon songs really off-key.

I sob and clutch my stuffed bunny. Nick leaps up on my bed and squashes his body against mine, nuzzling my face with his muzzle until I lift it enough for him to lick away my tears.

While the pixie rages downstairs, I wrap my arms around Nick's furry body and cry into him. My shoulders quake from the effort of it. He whimpers once or twice and tries to lick my face some more, but mostly he watches the door, and eventually I stop with the pathetic sobbing stuff and just keep crying. And eventually the crying stops too because I am hugging myself against

Nick, hoping that everything isn't real, that it is somehow a dream, but if that were true, it means that I would lose Nick, too. It would mean he isn't real, and I really, really want him to be real. I want that even though I know that I'll probably lose him, like I lost my dad and my mom, like I lost myself.

Necrophobia

fear of death

He's human again when he wakes me up with just a small kiss on my forehead.

I open my eyes to see him smiling above me.

Groaning, I put my hands over my face. He's pulled the shades and bright light streams into the room. I moan.

"Did I fall asleep? Really? How could I fall asleep?"

"Stress and crying knocks people out. You conked out once the pixie stopped destroying everything downstairs."

"Oh." I touch my cheeks. "You licked me."

He laughs and leans over, giving a tiny tongue swipe to my hand. "You're very lickable."

I try to hit him. He laughs harder and grabs my hands.

"No fair! Mere mortal against werewolf," I complain.

"Fine."

He lets go, but first he kisses my fingers, each of them. I sigh happily.

Then I come to my senses and sit up.

"The pixies?"

"Gone," he says, standing up and stretching. He's put on clothes again. His entire body makes cracking sounds, one vertebrae at a time. "I can't smell them."

I nod like that makes perfect sense, which it doesn't, but it isn't like I'm some expert in magical creatures. My stomach sinks.

"He pretended to be my dad," I say.

Nick's eyes soften. "That must have been hard."

I swallow. My mouth tastes terrible, like old, burned wood.

"You outsmarted him, though," he says. "I'm proud of you."

I try to smile but I can't quite do it.

He grabs my hand. "Let's go see if the phones are working, okay? Maybe find something to eat?"

"Is Betty here?"

"Not yet."

"Do you think she's okay?"

"The roads are bad, Zara. Unless she changed it would be hard for her to get here quickly."

"Unless she changed," I repeat. My fingers wrap around his. They like the feeling, safe, nestled in his crevices. "Is it safe?"

"I'm with you, Zara. I promise you, you'll be safe."

I want to believe him, but I'm not sure I can. Is there really anything that's safe?

We brave ourselves up enough to go downstairs and it's awful, so awful. Maybe only one pixie made his way in, but he's done so much damage, it's hard to believe he couldn't have been a hundred or more.

"It looks like I had a party. A really big, really good party," I say, stopping on the middle of the stairs to survey the damage. "Oh God, Betty is going to kill me."

The couch is all flipped over. The white leather chair has soot smeared into it. Papers and books are scattered about the floor. Pixie dust coats the cushions of the couch.

Nick grabs my hand and pulls me down the stairs. "It's okay. We'll deal with it. It won't be bad."

He lets go of my hand and takes an end of the couch. "Let's flip this first."

Together, we turn the couch right side up and push it back up against the wall. Nick blows the dust off his hands. "Disgusting."

"It could have been worse. He didn't slash the pillows or anything," I say, but my voice sounds fake.

It fools Nick, though. "Right."

We start picking things up. I check my cell phone and the regular phone to see if they work yet. They don't. We open up the door and snow tumbles into the house. Any pixie prints are long buried.

My breath catches.

The world has a fairy-tale, Nutcracker, Christmas look. The snow covers the trees, turning them white and magical. Nick's MINI is completely blanketed. It seems beautiful and orderly, and natural and safe, the opposite of Betty's house.

"We're snowed in," I announce.

He sniffs the air. "It's a big storm. It'll probably last all afternoon, and not end until tomorrow morning."

I tromp across the living room and try to radio Betty. I get Josie, the dispatcher, who says, "She set out for home two hours ago."

"Oh, God."

"No. Don't you go worrying. I'll try to call her up on the other channel. There's been no word on the Dahlberg boy. The storm's supposed to last through tonight, and the roads are bad, so it might just be taking her a little bit of time. And the satellite's down, too, so some of the other channels aren't working."

I press the button on the radio. "Okay. Don't tire yourself out, Josie."

She laughs and it comes through the static loud and clear. "I'm not dead yet, Zara. I still got some life in me."

We all do, I think, and I go back to trying to clean up the living room.

We clean forever it seems and finally both our stomachs growl louder than the wind.

"I'm starving. You hungry?" he asks.

I pat my belly. "Yep. You think Betty's okay?"

He hugs me. "I think she's okay."

He strides into the kitchen and grabs some eggs out of the refrigerator, while I move the rest of the contents outside into the snow so they won't go bad.

He has two frying pans set up on top of the woodstove and is opening up a can of corned beef hash when I come back inside.

"Corned beef hash?" I say. "That's disgusting."

"It's good, puts hair on your chest."

"Fur, you mean."

"Exactly."

He pops off the metal lid and puts it on a paper towel. He slops the hash into the pan and stirs it around.

"This might take a while." He grabs another spoon to stir the eggs. "I was thinking we might need to get some help for this pixie situation."

"Okay, I thought wolves had packs. Do you have a pack?"

"Not in the traditional sense."

"Sorry, Nick, but when it comes to werewolves, I don't know what the traditional sense is."

"I don't run with other wolves."

I nod. I wait. I finally give up and say, "So you run with . . ."

He winces. "Coyotes. But they have some wolf DNA."

It's hard not to smile. "You are alpha at least, right?"

"Of course I'm alpha." He almost growls at me.

"Sorry. Sorry. So, are we going to ask your pack for help?" I ask. "If you're alpha, you can tell them what to do, right?"

"We'll ask them. They can do little stuff, try to divert the pixies, keep them busy. But they're just regular coyotes, Zara, and they get scared of magic." He breaks up the hash a bit. "No, I was thinking about asking somebody else."

"Who?"

He points the spoon at me. "You have to be calm about this, okay? When I tell you, you can't get hysterical or anything."

"Just tell me."

"Issie and Devyn."

I whirl around at him. "We can't do that. First, they could get hurt. Second, what? You're going to tell them you're a werewolf? Oh, yeah. That's going to go over well."

"They already know, because . . ."

The fire crackles again. The wind shakes the house. He stands alert and ready, but nothing happens, including him finishing his sentence.

"They already know because . . . ," I prompt, completely impatient.

He pulls in a big breath.

"Oh my God! Issie's a bunny, isn't she? Do they have those? Do they have werebunnies?"

"Big leap there, Zare." Nick cracks up. He shakes with laughter.

I pout. "She'd be a good bunny."

"True. But it's not her. It's Devyn."

"Devyn? Devyn is cute and normal."

He scrapes at the bottom of the hash pan. His voice comes out dead calm. "He's an eagle."

"Oh. Okay. I am not going to freak out about this, but let me say that I am surprised."

"Because he's in a wheelchair?"

"No! Because he's a bird."

agateophobia

fear of insanity

The wind rattles the house, makes the flames dance in the woodstove. I'm eating a bizarre combination of meat and diced potato with a guy who is actually hotter than the fire and what do I say?

I say, "We need to figure out how to keep the pixie from kissing me, from making me his queen."

"I know," Nick says.

"I don't suppose just saying no would work." I give a nervous laugh.

Nick starts scraping at the brown, crunchy hash that clings to the bottom of the pan. He mixes it into the softer hash parts, clumping it into a big brown, red, and white mess.

Still, it smells good, almost good enough to make me not think about pixies. Almost. Or that the only cool people in school are weres.

"Seriously, Zara," he says, moving on to his egg scrambling.

"First off, I can't believe pixies have kings and queens. That's so old school. I don't care if they are Shining Ones. It's just lame. Are they some sort of totalitarian dictatorship based on a monarchial ideal of superiority, because those are some of the worst governments possible. I mean, the human rights violations in governments like that—"

He puts his free hand over my mouth just like Devyn did to Issie once. But I don't do an Issie and giggle or lick his fingers. I just glare. Nick keeps scrambling the eggs with his free hand as if nothing is going on, nothing at all, as if this is a normal conversation for people to be having.

"Zara, these are *pixies* and when it comes to human rights violations, pixies don't really care," he explains. "One, they aren't human. Two, torture is part of their M.O."

I try to stomp on his foot, but he just pivots it away in some super quick werewolf maneuver and never stops scrambling the eggs, which are holding together now, almost finished. He doesn't move his hand off my mouth and his eyes twinkle like he thinks I am so amusing.

I am not amusing.

"I'm going to move my hand now. Okay?"

"I am not queen material," I sputter.

He wipes his hand on his shirt.

"What? Did I drool on you?"

"A little."

"You're a wolf. You should be used to drool."

"That's low."

He takes the egg pan off the top of the woodstove and places it on the brick hearth that surrounds it.

I cross my arms over my chest. "I don't care."

We stay silent for a minute while he scrapes at the hash in the pan again. The windows seem like empty white blanks because of all the snow that keeps tumbling down. Some of the flakes splatter against the house like they are trying to escape the wintry reality.

"This isn't their normal behavior, obviously. I mean, the pixies haven't been killing everyone all this time. There's a gap," I say. Nick starts to interrupt but I hold up my hand to stop him. "I know we know that. I'm just thinking out loud, trying to process it. It's got to all be connected to my dad's letter."

"And they've been without a queen for a quarter of a century. There's got to be a rule about that." He points the scraping spoon at me. "Zara, I know you're a little freaked out by all this and that's normal, but I think that—"

"Normal? What's normal about any of this? You, possibly the best-looking guy in the universe, actually like me, but you're a werewolf." I can hear the hysteria in my voice but can't stop it. "Two of my favorite people at this crazy school are a werewolf and a were-eagle. Did I get that right? Werewolf and were-eagle? And of course, my grandmother is a weretiger."

He nods and lets me spew. I pace back and forth in the living room.

"And don't let me forget, pixie man has trashed my living room, and pixies want me to be their queen. And to accomplish this, instead of being nice and asking or bringing me flowers or something, some guy whispers my name when I'm in the woods trying to make me lost and then barges into my house the moment my gram isn't here." I stop for a second. "Wait. Why did they wait until Betty wasn't here?"

Nick spoons some hash onto a plate, then starts on the eggs.

"I have no idea. They're probably afraid of her. Weretigers are tough."

He shrugs and starts scooping food onto his plate.

"Maybe they got tired of waiting," he offers, sitting down on the floor in front of the fire. I sit with him. The heat laps against us and it feels so good.

"Maybe they realized that I wouldn't let you get taken by them in the woods, so they decided a direct attack was best," he says. "Wolves fight better outside. We aren't house pets. Do you like your hash?"

I stir my eggs around my plate a little bit and then fork up some hash. It warms my mouth. "This is good."

He smiles. "Thanks."

"So you can cook, too?" I ask. "You're perfect, aren't you?"

"I *am* a werewolf," he says between bites. He bends his head.

"That just gives you a totally good excuse for your pathetic temper."

He wiggles his eyebrows. "True."

"If I become the pixie queen, you'll have to call me your majesty," I tease.

"Never."

"You'll never call me your majesty? That's mean. You are just a common ol' werewolf, you know, and I'd be royalty."

The fire crackles and a log moves. I jump but Nick doesn't move at all. I guess it's hard to faze a werewolf.

"You'll never become the pixie queen. I won't let you." He locks eyes with me.

He does have the alpha-dog thing going for him. I can't look away. Even if I did, I'd still feel them. Eyes. His eyes.

"Ugh. I hate this. I feel stuck."

I thought I was moving forward finally. I mean, I thought I was stuck in Maine, but really slowly I was edging closer to the future, a future without my dad . . . but my future still, mine. Issie and Devyn are my friends. Nick is here. All that could just vanish. I wince. I don't want to die.

Nick puts his plate down on the bricks. It wobbles a little on the unevenness. Free of things, he leans forward, hands flat on the floor, like the downward-dog yoga position.

"Zara?" His voice mellows out against me, but I decide to study my eggs. "I won't let anything happen to you."

"You can't promise that. People can't keep other people from getting hurt or killed." Swallowing, I face him. His mouth is so close to mine. His eyes seem hungry and calm and strong, so I tell him, "A couple of weeks ago, I wouldn't have cared. If I died. You know?"

He nods.

He waits.

My lips wiggle because I can't find the right words. "I just missed my dad so much."

I swallow again. Why is it so hard to swallow? "But now," I move forward. "I don't want to die. I don't want to be scared. I just want to live."

He lets my words settle and then he asks, "What changed?"

"I don't know. You, maybe? Or maybe it was watching Issie being so happy and brave all the time? Or . . . ," I move closer so my forehead touches his. "Maybe it was just being so scared. I knew. I just knew that I didn't want to die."

He kisses my nose. His lips trail to my cheek and then down to my lips, where he whispers, "I'll keep you safe, Zara."

I grab his shoulders in my hands. "But what about you? Who will keep you safe?"

"I'll be fine."

His lips brush against mine, pushing themselves into me. I push back. My hands leave his shoulders and move into his hair. Gently I tug his face away.

"Do you promise?" I breathe against him. "Do you swear?"

"I swear."

"We have to leave," he says.

We stand in the cold kitchen, putting dishes in a waterless sink. Snow keeps piling up outside. My fingertips touch the cold window. "You're kidding."

I place the corned beef hash pan in the sink. The metal matches. Corned beef hash crud cakes the bottom of the pan in a brown crunchy mess.

I rip a paper towel off the roll. "Disgusting."

"Zara? We can't hide in your room again all night." Nick reaches around me to grab the pan's handle. He swirls the detergent around in there, spreading it out, so it touches all of the crud. "We have to get rid of this problem now."

"Now?"

"While it's still daylight."

"Look at Mr. Proactive."

"I'm serious, Zara."

He puts the pan back in the sink. We can't do anything with it, not now, not without water.

"I know. I know you're serious, but I am not a snow person." I rearrange my ponytail. My hair is not at its best due to the lack of a shower. I pull up my wool socks. I wear two pairs and they scrunch beneath my toes. "And where are we going to go? And what about Betty?"

"She should have been here by now," he says and my heart tries to hide behind my lungs, not listening, but I do. I keep listening even though I'm so worried about Betty. "We'll go to my house. We'll get Issie and Devyn and make a plan."

I point out the window. "And how are we going to get there?"

"My car."

"The roads are bad. Betty said not to drive."

"I know, but sometimes you have to break the rules."

I give up. I don't want to stay here without Betty. Especially not if the pixies are going to come back for a happy little return visit. I dash upstairs and get my Urgent Action letters.

"You have mail?" Nick scoffs.

"They're Urgent Actions. They have to be sent out right away or else people could be tortured or killed or—"

He touches my lips with his fingers. "You are worse than I am."

"Not true."

We bundle up and head outside. We wipe the snow from Nick's MINI. The trees worry me. Not the trees, really, but what might be beyond them.

The snow covers everything outside. It covers the branches and the cars, the land and the water. It covers the houses. Beneath it the world is lost. Beneath it the people are lost, the animals, the grass. Everything is just white. Blinding. White. Everything is gone. The hard lines of rooftops and tree limbs, the straight lines of roads, everything is blurred, covered, lost.

"My dad would have loved this. Just pulled out some skis and said, 'Let's have an adventure,'" I say.

"He sounds cool."

"He was cool."

"Must've been a were."

"Yeah, right," I say, letting that additional piece of knowledge bounce around the room, finally spoken out loud. "He said 'Shining One' in his note."

Nick grabs a brush out of the MINI and whisks off the fine remains of the snow, but there's a crust of ice that covers the windows. He gets back in the cab and turns the defroster on full blast.

I brace myself against the hood, watching the windows clear; zoning out, trying to process it all.

"Zara?"

Nick waits by the driver's side door, which is open. Snow stains his hair white, sticks in his eyebrows. His face rivers into something warm.

"You coming?"

"Okay."

Betty's house is only a few feet away. I could rush back inside, slam the door, lock it, and hide.

I could hunker down.

I could stop moving.

Instead, I get inside the car.

"Okay," I say, slamming the door. "Let's go."

The inside of the MINI is warm already because the engine has been running and pumping out heat. I sigh into the warm air and smile. I could sit in here forever, all cozy, safe, and warm, like Nick. I reach down and touch the fur I'd seen on the floorboards the other day. It belongs to Nick. I glance at him to make sure he's not looking and sneak the fur into my pocket. No matter what happens I'll have it to remind me of him.

Not that anything bad is going to happen. Right?

Nick grabs my hand and it's like he's reading my mind. Can werewolves do that?

"It'll be okay, Zara."

"I know," I snuff in. My nose is getting stuffy. "I'm fine."

He squeezes my hand and lets go, which is totally unfair. I like his hand on mine.

"I need two hands to drive in this," he says.

His fingers are thick and long, and unfurry.

"I can't believe those become paws."

"It's weird, isn't it?"

I eye him. His shoulders expand beneath his jacket and his legs, solid and long, seem enormous. I pull my seat belt on and click it into place.

"We should get going. The driveway isn't plowed." Nick shifts the MINI into reverse.

"Uh-huh."

"We might get stuck."

He presses the accelerator and we scoot about three feet before smashing to a stop, trapped in the snow.

He tries to rock it back and forth, a little forward, a little backward. His face tightens into a cranky mess.

"This isn't good, is it?" I ask.

"Not good at all." He shuts off the engine.

"I could try to push it."

"That wouldn't work. Not for the whole driveway." He opens the door and hops out. "We're going to have to shovel."

"Shovel?"

I've never shoveled in my life. I've seen people on TV do it, and my dad had stories about shoveling for hours, trying to get out of the house during nor'easters, which are these monster blizzards that hit New England.

I jump out after Nick, sinking in the snow. My pants are soaked already, and clumps of snow fall inside my boots, nestling in there.

Snow sucks.

"We're going to shovel the whole driveway?" I ask, hands on my hips. "Just you and me? This is a long driveway. It's half a mile long."

A bird calls in the distance. It's the first bird I've heard since yesterday. Nick hears it too. He cocks his head and squints, listening just like a dog does. Something seems to register with him because his eyes shift into something more serious, more urgent.

"Nick?"

He wipes at his face like he's trying to get rid of a fly. "I know. It's a long driveway. Where are the shovels?"

He strides back toward the house. I chase after him.

"Nick? What if the road isn't passable? What if the plows haven't gotten out here yet? We can't shovel the road."

He stops, turns around. His strong shoulders slump. "I didn't think of that."

"One of us can go scout it out and the other one could start shoveling."

"No. No way. We have to stay together."

His face hardens again. I hate it like that. Panic rises in my throat, tightening it. I wince, remembering the arrow in his shoulder.

He rubs his face again, really roughly this time, and it reminds me of how a dog scratches its muzzle when it has an itch, just this gruff swipe with the whole of the hand. God, he really is half canine or lupine or whatever the word is for wolves.

"We have to do something," Nick says. His nostrils flare. "I hate pixies."

"Hate is a useless emotion."

"What?" He whirls around and glares at me.

I back up a step. The little hairs on my arms are standing on end. He scares me when he's like this, all angry power. "My mom says that all the time. It's one of her life quotes, she got it from my dad. *Hate is a useless emotion.*"

"That's such a mom thing to say."

"I know. I'm going to kick her butt when all this is over," I say. "And Betty's too."

He laughs. "I thought you were a pacifist."

"Whatever."

We give up on shoveling. We give up on driving. We decide on snowshoes.

Yes, snowshoes that I find downstairs by the railroad ties and some old barbed wire.

We stomp through the white falling snow, moving steadily, not moving fast, but definitely moving forward.

Together.

We raise our feet carefully, just a little bit and a sweeping motion forward. One foot. Another foot. Clean snow smells hit our noses, mixed with pine trees and the wood burning in Betty's stove.

The snow nestles down, flowing softer, falling from the sky.

"It's pretty," I admit, as we start trudging up a hill.

"Really?"

"But cold."

Nick bumps my shoulder with his, playfully. He kicks up some extra snow on purpose, whishing it onto my knees.

"You're lucky you're cute," I tell him.

"Really?"

"Especially with that doggy breath."

He scoops up some snow, makes it into a ball, bounces his hand up and down. "Take that back."

I giggle. "Nope."

I bend down to grab some snow and topple headfirst. The cold of it bites into my cheeks. I try to push myself up, but I can't. I'm all awkward and clumsy with the snowshoes on.

Nick laughs.

I struggle some more.

He grabs me under my arms and hauls me up. Smiling, he sticks out his tongue, and with tiny little movements starts licking the snow off my cheeks. It should be disgusting. It's not. It's all warm, and good feeling, and amazing. I close my eyes and let him.

"You smell good," he whispers.

"I haven't showered."

"Doesn't matter, you smell good."

His voice, sensual and warm, mellows me.

Our lips touch and part, touch again. I breathe him in. He moves his face away a little and studies me. I smile. I can't help it.

"I like you," I say. "A lot. Even with the whole werewolf thing."

He smiles back. "I like you too."

"A lot?"

"Mm-hmm," he says, leaning in for another kiss. "A wicked lot."

It doesn't matter about the snow. It doesn't matter about the pixies. I could stay here forever, steadied in Nick's arms, kissing his lips, feeling his warm, scruffy cheek next to mine. All the sorrow and the fear don't matter at all anymore. That's it. No melodrama or anything. That's just it.

Merinthophobia

fear of being bound or tied up

We kiss for a long time, a good long time. I don't even notice that it's cold and I forget to be afraid because that's just how good a kisser he is. His lips move above my lips. My lips ache for the touch of him, the softness of his skin. We keep kissing. My hands wrap themselves in his hair. His hand presses me close into him, as close as I can be against him, and he is solid, strong, amazing. My hands leave his hair and journey down to the sides of his face, still tingling.

"We should keep going," he says, voice gruff and husky again. I love when his voice sounds like that, deeper than normal. His lips puff out a little more, too. "You're blushing."

I pull my lips in against each other like I'm still trying to taste him. I move my snowshoes off of his snowshoes. It's tricky.

"You're a good kisser," I say.

"So are you."

We walk and walk and walk. We make it out of the driveway

and onto the main road, which hasn't been plowed for a while. It's got about four inches on it still.

"I was thinking about Ian," I say, sliding my snowshoes along.

"Great. Just what I want to hear."

"No, no. I was thinking about how he'll be sad about this."

"Oh, poor Mr. Homecoming King." He teases and bumps me with his hip.

I bump him back. "Mean."

An eagle shrieks. Still, I miss all the signs. Somehow Nick does too.

Something falls over our heads and Nick snarls, an animal, guttural sound. It terrifies me more than the thing on my head. But I can't stop the snarl. So I attack whatever is on my hair. I yank at it. My fingers snare into small metal loops. It's a net. Someone has thrown a net over us.

Nick clutches me, still snarling. His eyes have already turned. His forehead creases.

"Nick?" His name comes out slowly. I'm pushing panic away, trying to will everything to be okay. Like I can.

"Pixies," he manages to say as he pushes at the net above our heads, all around us. "The net is silver."

"Silver?"

He shakes his head. All of him shakes as he tries to maintain control.

"Nick!" I shriek at him, terrified.

Hands yank me away from him. They come from behind me and I can't see what they're attached to. They hold onto me with iron grips, far too tight, menacing.

I twist against them. "Let go."

They don't, they just grab me tighter. It's like they're trying to break my ankles. I'm yanked out of the net. They tumble me toward them across the snow. My body slips over one of the metal snowshoes I've lost in the confusion. I grab it and throw it backward, trying to hit someone.

There is a lovely, satisfying sound of snowshoe hitting flesh and muscle, but the hands don't let me go.

I am obviously no longer a pacifist.

My fingers try to grab onto the net. I'm pulled away too quickly, dragged through the snow. Everything is white and flying and painful.

"Nick!"

I claw at the snow, trying to slow down. There's nothing to hold on to. I kick and kick. The hands clutch my ankles. Flipping my torso over I get one quick glance of their backs. They're wearing parkas and hats and look normal, like people, but faster. I smash onto my face again and lift up my head just in time to see Nick snarling inside the net. He's transformed again.

"Nick!" I yell, but snow pours into my mouth. Sharp cold pain smashes through my teeth and into my skull. I cough and try again. "Nick!"

He raises himself up onto four legs and howls, a long, searing cry of anguish and rage.

My heart breaks for him, caught there. I have to help him escape. I have to get free.

I kick again. "Let me go."

Pain shoots through my head. Fireworks. Explosions. All inside my brain. The white world goes dark and I know what's about to happen. I'm the one leaving. I am the one gone.

Nyctohylophobia

fear of dark wooded areas or of forests at night

I wake up in a room that's vacant, large and cold, with just one air mattress on the floor. My head thrums and I lift my trembling fingers to touch a large lump on the side of my head. Did I hit a rock? Or did someone hit me? And Nick? Where is Nick?

I sit up, pushing my hands against the cold blue air mattress. The world spins and I close my eyes for a second, but think better of it. The walls seem made of concrete, with big rivets in them, bolts that once held something. There's one door, but it's large and wooden and shut.

Terror grabs me and doesn't let go.

I pull myself up to a standing position. My feet touch the cold cement floor.

Jesus. Someone has taken my shoes.

And my coat.

"Nick?" I whisper, kind of hoping for the unhopeable.

But he isn't here.

The memory of him, howling, stuck beneath the net, hits me in the stomach, spinning pain into me.

"You better not have hurt Nick!" I yell at . . . oh, I don't know what I'm yelling at.

Striding across the cold concrete until I come to the door, I try it again. "Hey! You better not have hurt my friend!"

I grab the wooden door handle and yank it. No go. I try pushing it. It doesn't budge. Damn, why am I not stronger? The door has to be barricaded or locked or something on the other side. I step back and run at it with my shoulder, which is not only not helpful, it hurts. It never looks like it hurts when cops do it in movies.

"Hello?"

No answer.

"You guys went to a hell of a lot of trouble to just lock me up in a room," I say and try the door again. Still nothing.

"This is stupid," I announce. "Really stupid."

Pulling in a deep breath, I try to think of something calming, something that would make me focus. Somehow, listing phobias dose not seem like a good choice. There is this quote they sometimes use in Amnesty stuff: "The secret of happiness is freedom, and the secret of freedom, courage."

Thucydides, a Greek philosopher, wrote that a hundred million years ago.

So, I have to find courage.

Walking back to my air mattress again, I survey the room. It isn't much to look at. It's about ten feet by ten feet, all concrete. No window. A bare bulb hangs from the ceiling but there isn't any light switch to turn it off. There's a heating grate in the floor, the kind that old houses have sometimes.

I crawl over to it and peer between the slats. No heat comes through, but a little bit of light does. The sounds of faraway voices hit my ears.

The opening is about three feet wide and maybe two feet deep. Can I fit in it? Maybe? Hope lifts my heart. I can escape and find Nick, maybe save him.

Four screws hold the grate in place. I stick my nail into one and twist it. It turns. It turns a little bit.

This will take forever, but it's worth it. I pull in a deep breath. I wonder if Amnesty would send an Urgent Action appeal on my behalf if they knew: *Maine Teen Unjustly Held Captive By . . .*

How would they fill in the blank?

I move the screw a little more, until I can grab the screw head with the tips of my fingers. I turn it and turn it and it pops off. One down, three to go.

Giggling, and possibly a tiny bit hysterical, I start on the second screw, using the same procedure. I have it halfway out when the locks outside the door slide out of place. I pocket the one screw I've freed and scurry over to the air mattress just as the door opens.

I take a big breath and get ready. I don't know what I expect to come through that door. But I sure don't expect Ian.

"Zara, you look shocked." Ian smiles.

He's wearing normal clothes, a navy sweater with a shirt underneath it and jeans. His reddish hair is rumpled, but in a deliberate I'm-in-a-boy-band way.

He shuts the door behind him and stands there for a second, just staring at me. "You really don't know?"

"Know what?" I ask through clenched teeth. I make myself

relax my jaw and uncross my arms. Ian doesn't need to know how angry I am, how scared.

Ian leans his shoulders back against the wall, looking relaxed and happy. "That I'm a pixie?"

My jaw must have dropped or something because Ian starts laughing. "You look shocked."

I don't say anything, just try to adjust to this newest twist. He's a pixie. Ian.

"Where's the dust? I thought you all left dust?"

"Only the kings." He sort of snarls it. Then he changes his face into something calmer, less feral. His voice matches and suddenly it's like he's back to being the nice guy who showed me to classes on the first day of school. "Are you cold, Zara?"

"I'm okay."

Was Ian the one who went into my house the night before? Was he the one who pretended to be my dad? Hate spills into me, useless emotion or not.

"You're lying. I can smell it. You're cold," Ian says. "I'll go get you a blanket."

He turns and starts toward the door. He knocks on it twice and it swings open.

"Wait!"

He looks back and smiles again at me. "Don't worry, Zara. I'm not leaving you. Okay?"

I slump down on my mattress, trying to stay in control, to not tackle him.

"You think everybody always leaves, don't you?" he says, his tone softer. "But pixies aren't like that. We always come back. I promise. We never let anyone alone. Even the ones who get away we hunt down. Your mother could tell you that."

"What about my mother?"

"Really, Zara? You haven't figured it out?"

He steps out the door and it shuts behind him.

Shivering, I stare at the walls and the blank grayness is too much. I close my eyes and put my hands on my head. It throbs.

Ian comes back with a blanket, a glass of water, and some kind of medicine.

"If I drink this am I stuck in pixieland with you forever?" I ask as he drapes the blanket around my shoulders, tucking it in.

He laughs. "I wish it were that easy."

"I thought I read that somewhere."

"That's fairies. This is just regular bottled water and an aspirin. Your head hurts, right?"

I nod slowly.

"I'm sorry about that."

"Was that you? Did you drag me here?"

He keeps tucking the blanket around me. "It had to be done. Sorry about the rock, though."

I stand up, throwing off the blanket. The movement was too quick and the world sways. Ian catches me by the elbow and steadies me. I yank my arm away, humiliated and furious. God, why can't I even stand by myself?

I turn my anger on him. "Did you hurt Nick?"

"No, he's a snug little doggy in a nice little doggy net."

I raise my fist. Rage curls inside my chest. I can't control it any more. "If you hurt him—"

"What would you do? Beat me up?" Ian fake shudders. "Oh, I'm scared. No offense, Zara, but you aren't that intimidating."

He moves toward me and smiles. "But I'm not going to hurt

him. We don't need to hurt him, Zara. We already have what we want."

His words sicken me. I swallow the nausea and hold on to the rage.

"And what you want is me?" I deliberately raise my eyebrows, trying to show no fear. "That's a cliché."

"Clichés are clichés for a reason," he says.

"What about Betty?"

He shrugs. "I have no idea where your grandmother is. Look at this place. Do you know what it is? It used to store furniture. It's a concrete room, perfect for holding prisoners, kind of like that Amnesty International crap you're always going on about. Trying to save the world, that's you, Zara. But you never thought about who would save you, did you?"

"I don't need saving."

"No, you don't. You're perfectly safe here." He comes closer and sniffs the air. He's just a foot or so away from me. I try to back up farther, but I'm already against the wall. He smiles but there is sadness in it. "As safe as any of us can be when we aren't in control, when we aren't in power."

"Did you have to mess up Betty's house?" I ask.

He laughs. "That wasn't us. That was the king. He has a temper, you know, kind of like you. It runs in the blood, no matter how hard you try to keep it down, and I think you have quite the temper simmering under the surface, boiling to get out."

"So he's changed tactics. Made you kidnap me."

"No. He has nothing to do with this. This is all me." He pushes his hand through his hair ultra-casual, and then pulls a Swiss Army knife out of his pants pocket. He takes a pick out of it and starts cleaning his nails.

"Nice intimidation tactic," I say. "Very textbook. I'd expect something more original from pixies."

He doesn't respond, but he blinks. His jaw gets all rigid. After a couple seconds, he puts the pick back in place.

"You are so sweet, Zara, and so innocent and likeable. But no one can ever save someone else, you know? We can only save ourselves. You know that, don't you?"

He reaches out and his fingertips graze my cheek, tracing the line of my jaw bone.

I refuse to move. "Did you need to be saved once, Ian?"

His fingers stop. His eyes bore into mine and he whispers, "Maybe."

"You weren't always a pixie. They turned you." I swallow and his eyes flash with the truth. I keep talking. "You aren't the pixie who has been chasing me in the woods. I know that. You feel different somehow."

His fingers move again, slowly. I turn my head, but his fingers keep moving.

"No," he says. "That wasn't me."

I make myself look at him then, his pale skin. His too-deep eyes that aren't human, not really. How come I never noticed that? I was too busy being sad, too busy noticing Nick, too busy being flattered that somebody liked me, I guess.

"Who was it?"

"The king. He wants you. And believe me, you do not want him to have you. It's much better for everyone if you go with us. He's gotten weak and we're having a turf war, really, and you're the key to ending it all." He shakes his head. "Who would know, that someone so short and so sad would be the one we were waiting for. We all want you or hate you."

"Why?"

"It's destiny. You're the one. Zara. Princess. Didn't you ever wonder about what your name means?"

I don't get it. "My mother named me."

"Exactly."

"What do you mean, exactly?"

"You're the continuation of the blood line. Whoever claims you claims the kingdom."

"That's ridiculous."

"No it's not."

He grabs my face with his cold hands. "Do you know what it is to be pixie kissed, Zara?"

I know.

"It turns you," he continues. "It's painful, but if done correctly, the human doesn't die, but she grows. She becomes like us. Some humans, humans like you, already have pixie in your blood. I did."

"Right." It's hard not to be sarcastic. Sarcastic is so much better than scared, anyway. And the thought of having pixie genes terrifies me, God. Is my mom a pixie?

"It makes you more powerful when you turn, and more desirable throughout." Ian's fingers tighten on my chin.

"And you're the one who is supposed to turn me?" I ask, trying not to shudder.

"I had to fight Megan for it." He shrugs. "I didn't think she'd let you survive."

I freeze.

"That's right, Megan's a pixie too, and she has her eyes set on the kingdom. You're the only thing in her way, at least, that's what she thinks."

"And the man in the forest . . . ," I whisper.

"He wants to turn you, of course. He must. He's the one who found you, but it's not all finders keepers all the time, is it?"

I swallow hard. "Is he my father?" He can't be my father. My father is some random guy my mom hooked up with in a "foolish moment." My father is not a pixie because that would mean . . .

Ian laughs. "No one's told you anything, have they? Wolves' cognitive processing is a bit slow. Eagles and tigers aren't that much better."

"But you guys go to school. You . . . how can you be a pixie? Is everyone in this town inhuman?"

"No. There are plenty of humans here. And there are the weres of course, unfortunately. But we hide our pixieness with a glamour. That's just how it is."

"Are there more of you? In other places?"

"Of course. Shhh . . ." His other hand cups the back of my head. I can't move. It's like my body just gave up. I try to lift my hands to push Ian away, but they won't go.

"You are such a jerk."

He leans in closer. His mouth is just an inch, the tiniest inch, away from my mouth.

"I love the way you smell." His sentence touches my skin with his breath, and the wound on my hand tingles and I snap out of it somehow. Somehow I can move again. My hands shove him away hard. His face registers his shock. I bash past him and run for the door, throwing myself against it and yanking at it.

"Megan! Let me out! Megan!"

The door won't budge and Ian is next to me in an instant. He throws me across the room and I smash against the wall.

A sickening sound echoes throughout the space as something in my arm breaks.

The lower part of my arm dangles at a funky angle. It doesn't hurt. Shock does that for a second so the body can try to save itself, try to run and fight. I power myself back up and dive for the opening door. I yank off my bracelet and throw it at him. It hits his chest and burns through his shirt.

Megan opens the door, smiling. "You having a hard time, Ian?"

He ignores her.

I plead with my eyes.

She ignores me.

"Zara," he says, his voice higher. "Don't make this hard. Now you're hurt. That lowers your chances of surviving. You need to survive."

I race by him, but he's fast. Ian is always so fast. I should have known he isn't human. He grabs me around the waist. Another bone in my arm cracks and my knees buckle. The shock is wearing off and pain slashes through my arm and into my shoulder. I try to grab my arm with my good hand, but he holds on so tightly that I can't move.

"Just let me kiss you, Zara," he says in a lovely convincing voice, like he's asking for an order of french fries at a diner.

"Just do it, Ian," Megan orders.

He hugs me tighter. A scream breaks through the room. It's my scream. The bone sticking out of my arm sends warm, wet blood down my arm. Ian's eyes turn wild. He licks my blood. It covers his lips.

"You don't have to say yes," he hisses. "It's just easier that way. It's like when you're at the dentist. The more you fuss, the harder things are, the longer it takes, the more likely you are to get hurt."

"I hate dentists," I say, trying to twist away. My hand, the one that's scraped like a rune, glows. I press it against his face. He screams but doesn't let go.

A growling noise seems to come from somewhere. Maybe me? Ian moves closer. I stare at his blood-covered lips. They are full and cold. I know they're cold.

"No," I say, sobbing from the pain but still trying to wiggle free somehow.

We both fall. The floor smacks against us. Ian's eyes fill with need.

"I need this, Zara," he says. "I need . . . Please, help me, Zara. I need you to . . . I can't stand it, just being regular, just being a minion."

Megan yells, "Ian!"

His lips come closer to mine. I push at him, woozy, dizzy. I've lost too much blood. I can barely keep my eyes open.

"No," I whisper. "Please . . . no."

But his arms are tight and his lips are close and he has this need. And me? I can't do it anymore. Ducking my head down against his chest to avoid his lips, I fall toward darkness.

Nosocomephobia
fear of hospitals

The growls aren't human.

I know that.

Even though I can't open my eyes, can't make my mouth form one dumb word, I know that the growls aren't human or pixie.

"She'll be okay, she'll be okay," a voice says. A girl's voice.

The world makes no sense. Snow covers it. I am beneath the snow. That's it. Right? The snow covers me, heavy, blank, white.

A man's voice: "I'll kill him."

The girl again: "She already did."

Something wet touches my cheeks. A washcloth? A tear?

The man again: "This is my fault, all my fault. I didn't protect her."

Nick?

Betty's voice: "Yes, you did. I have to splint her arm. She's lost so much blood."

Betty! Gram!

Someone touches my arm and the pressure startles me back, out of the snow, back into the concrete room. I scream.

"Zara!"

The girl: "She has a massive lump on her head. And her arm's so broken."

The world fades away again. I hear another voice, my dad's voice.

"Zara, hold on," he urges me. "Hold on."

"Daddy?" someone says. I reach out, looking for something to grab on to, but someone holds my arm down.

"She's hallucinating."

The snow comes down inside me, above me, all around me.

"It's cold," a voice says. "I'm so cold."

The snow falls and falls and falls and I let it bury me. There is nothing else to do. It is so cold.

They won't let me go.

"Zara," one of the voices insists. "Zara, we need to get you out of here. Can you sit up?"

I try to swim through the snow, back up to someplace warm. And I do, but pain hits me, shoots through my arm, pounds in my head. I flutter my eyes and open them, but I can't focus.

"Nick?"

"I'm right here, sweetie."

"My mother calls me sweetie," I croak out. Why is my voice so faint and funny, hoarse yet whisper thin? Where's my mother?

I gasp as someone puts something on my arm. I try to open my eyes again. "I can't see."

"Did he kiss her?" a girl asks.

It's Issie. Issie? Why is Issie here?

"I don't think so, not for long anyway. I came right in," Betty answers. "Nick, did you see him kiss her?"

"I don't think so."

"It hurts," I manage to say. "Please make it stop hurting."

"Okay. Okay, sweetie. It's okay," Nick's voice comes again, close to my ear. I grab his shoulder with my free hand. It's naked. A naked shoulder. "We have to get you out of here, get you to a doctor. Okay?"

I nod. My hand presses against his skin like it wants to burrow in and hide. "You're so warm."

Issie's voice soothes me. "We'll take care of you, Zara. Don't worry."

My eyes start to focus on Nick's face. His eyes—perfect, brown, and human—stare at me, blending into the walls, into my unconsciousness.

"Don't leave me." My hand drops from Nick's shoulder. I can't keep it up.

Cold. Ice. Frozen. Death.

Novercaphobia, fear of your stepmother.

Nucleomituphobia, fear of nuclear weapons.

Nudophobia, fear of nudity.

Numerophobia, fear of numbers.

Nyctohylophobia, fear of dark wooded areas or of forests at night.

Everybody always leaves.

"Don't worry," Issie says. "We won't leave."

Everybody always leaves.

"Don't let Ian . . ."

Gram growls. "You don't have to worry about Ian anymore."

Nick pulls me against him. He is so warm, burning warm, and it hurts to be moved. I scream. Even as he holds me, the cold and the darkness comes, waiting to take me again.

I wake up in the hospital. My arm is hoisted above my head and encased in white plaster.

"Nick?" I whisper.

Gram jumps up and grabs my good hand. Her face cracks into a half smile and there are tears in her eyes. "Zara?"

I blink. The light hurts my head.

"It's bright in here," I try to say.

She lets go of my hand.

Fear cramps my stomach. "Don't go."

"I'm just shutting off the lights," she says, flicking it off. She hustles back and takes my hand again. "You had me some worried, little one."

"Am I okay?" My voice starts to sound a little better.

"You have a nasty break. Two bones in your arm. You have a concussion, a serious one to add to your minor one. You also have bruised ribs."

I would shrug if I could. Instead, I try to smile. "That's all?"

She laughs and squeezes my hand a little bit. Then her face twists into something serious. "Do you remember what happened?"

I lie to my grandmother. "No."

She bites her bottom lip a little and watches me. "Nick said that you—"

I try to sit up, but it's too hard. "Nick? Is he here?"

"I sent him home. He's been here all night. That Issie girl too, and Devyn. They were wiped out. I don't know how many phone calls I had to make to their parents saying they were okay. Finally, they just had to go."

My heart drops.

"They didn't want to leave, especially Nick."

Gram wiggles her eyebrows. I can feel myself blush.

"He's a cute boy, that one," Betty says. She lets go of my hand and smoothes the hair off my forehead. "I've called your mother, who is hysterical, blaming herself for sending you up here. She's trying to find a flight in, but the whole East Coast is one big mess. There's a massive storm front. I've never seen anything like it. It's not even officially winter yet."

She holds a glass of water to my mouth. I swallow. It tastes like metal.

"She doesn't need to come."

"I told her that." She settles the water on the side table. "But maybe she does. I haven't exactly done a good job taking care of you."

"Sure you have."

She chokes a little laugh out. "Right. That's why you're here in the hospital with another concussion and a broken arm."

I avoid her eyes and focus on the light weight of the hospital blanket that covers me. "So, was that you? Growling?"

She nods, squeezes my hand.

"Holy crap," I whisper.

"You keep talking like that you'll end up sounding like me."

I gulp. "Was Daddy?"

"He kept you and your mother safe for a long, long time, Zara." Her voice trembles. "He loved you both so much."

She pulls the blankets up a little higher. "I'm sorry, Zara. Your mom and I, well we didn't know there was more danger.

There hadn't been any danger for over a decade. Even when the Beardsley boy went missing, I hoped that it was a human who took him or that he did run away. It's foolish." She runs a hand across her eyes. "People don't want to see the truth sometimes."

"Not if it's a bad truth," I agree. "I've been denying everything. That there were pixies . . . that there was something supernatural going on . . . how hollow I've been . . . who my father is."

She looks at me and gives the tiniest of nods. "I've made a fine mess of it. I'm getting too old to battle pixies."

"That's not what I hear," I say. I take her hand. There are age spots across her delicate skin, but her fingers are long and powerful. "Why didn't mom come?"

"Even your dad couldn't have kept her safe here."

"Why?"

She runs a hand through her hair. "It's the king's hometown. Her presence here would have driven him crazy no matter how hard he tried to control it. If the king knew she was right here, he'd have to come after her. He wouldn't be able to resist."

"So we were hiding? All that time in Charleston? My whole life? We were hiding?" My head tries to wrap itself around it, but I can't. The world is so different than I thought, so totally, ridiculously different.

She nods. "I'm sorry that Ian got to you, Zara. I know I let you down."

"Where were you? I thought you were hurt when you didn't come back home."

"The truck broke down halfway. Someone sabotaged it. I started hiking back and it was taking forever, so I turned. Then I realized that the pixie had already beat me to the house, so I hid out, waiting. I knew you were safe at home but I also knew you wouldn't stay at home. I figured you'd leave and when you did the pixies would strike. I wasn't quick enough, though. I should've gone after you first instead of getting Nick out of the net."

"No," I say. "That was the right thing. And then you followed us to where Ian and Megan took me."

"It was an easy smell to trace."

I solid the question out. "Did you kill him?"

"If I hadn't, your boyfriend would have."

Ian is dead. She killed him. Probably ripped him apart like tigers do. I shudder.

"He's not my boyfriend."

"Ha. That's a good one. I saw you two tonsil surfing out there."

I could kill her. "I don't even have tonsils!"

"I know that and I bet Nick knows that now, too." She slaps her leg because she's just too funny for words. The door opens and Nick stands there, filling out the frame. He rushes over to my bed and hovers over me but doesn't touch.

"Well, well, well, speak of the devil," she says, snickering a little bit and standing up. "Looks like you've got company, so I'm going to run and get some decent coffee. We both know I just make horse swill."

She kisses my forehead and searches my eyes with hers. I don't know what she expects to see.

Then she turns to Nick. "You going to stay here for a bit?"

He nods.

"You take good care of her. She's the only granddaughter I have, okay?"

He stands a little straighter, the way people do when Betty gives an order.

"I promise."

"Good." She marches out the door, leaving us alone.

The moment he seems sure she's gone, Nick bends over and kisses my cheek. My lips feel abandoned. His other hand touches my cheek.

"I was so worried about you," he says.

"You left."

"Betty made me. I was just hiding in the other room."

I exhale, everything inside of me relaxing. "Really?"

"I swear."

He looks so solid and worried and sweet, very, very sweet. I don't know how I'd manage without him there, with me. My eyes close. They are so heavy.

"I'm scared, Nick."

He squeezes my hand and his face hardens. He fiddles with my blanket, tucks it around me, just like my grandmother had. I am very well tucked.

"I hated what he tried to do to you." Nick chokes a little bit, all emotional. "Turning you into one of them. You could never be one of them."

But aren't I already? If my father is one. It means it's in my blood, but Nick doesn't know that. Nick can't ever know that. I reach out my good hand and touch Nick's cheek. It's all rough, stubbly. "Would you hate me if I was? If I was a pixie?"

His eyes search my eyes. "No."

I don't think either of us know if he's telling the truth.

"What about the other ones?"

He lifts an eyebrow. He has beautiful eyebrows. "The other ones?"

"The pixies, the other pixies?"

Sometimes when cats see a mouse, they torture it. They could kill it easily with one good bite, one swipe of the claw, but instead they play with the mice. They torture them, watch them suffer. The mouse always tries to run away, but always knows there's no hope, that the cat can get them any time, anywhere. I am worried that pixies are like that.

"Issie and Devyn have been out looking. They haven't seen any signs." He pulls a hand through his hair and then uses that same hand to massage the back of his neck. Blue half circles shadow the skin beneath his eyes. He seems so tired.

"So they're gone?" I ask, hopefully. I search his face. "Do you think they're gone?"

"I think they're regrouping. I think it will take them a while, but they'll be back." He sighs and then straightens his back. "We'll be ready for them, in any case. It's okay, Zara. It's over for now."

"Are you sure?"

I open my eyes for just a second to see his nodding, beautiful face hovering just inches above mine. "I'm sure. They can't turn you now, you're too hurt. You have too many drugs in your system. You'd die. You're no good to them dead, not yet, not until after you've turned."

He runs his hands along my shoulders and I shiver, a good shiver.

His voice comes out husky. "I swear I won't let that happen."

I close my eyes again. It's so hard to stay awake, to think. I murmur, "You're nice, aren't you, Nick? You're nice?"

His lips kiss my forehead. "I try."

I call her. Of course I call her. She's my mom.

"Zara!" Her voice is frantic. "I'm all packed. I'm still at the airport, waiting for a flight. Everything keeps getting delayed because of the damn storm. That doesn't matter. What matters is, are you okay? Oh, God, I can't believe you got hurt."

"Did Gram tell you what happened?"

I can hear her suck in her breath. "Yes."

I am silent. I wait. A nurse walks down the hall.

Finally, she says, "I thought it was all over."

The hospital is a boring, plain white; a blank slate. "Tell me why we lived in Charleston. Was it just because we were hiding? Were you only with Daddy because he kept you safe?"

"I owe you a lot of answers, Zara, but I swear to you that I was with Daddy because I love him."

"Yep."

I can almost imagine her twisting at an earring, trying to figure out what to say. "We were hiding. I was hiding."

"From the head pixie guy?"

"Yes."

"The king?"

"Yes."

"And why did he want to get you so badly?" I want to hear her say it. I want her to tell me.

"I double-crossed him, Zara. I did something he wanted but only under certain conditions. Those conditions made him weaker, and . . . and . . . he wanted me to stay. When Daddy died, I . . . I thought he'd come after me, not you. I thought he'd be down here and you'd be safe with Betty up there. I thought—"

"Is he my father? My biological father?"

"How do you know that?"

"Mom?" I press her.

"Yes. Yes, he is your father."

"So I'm part pixie?"

"No. No, you aren't. You're all human because we never kissed, I never turned. Don't you see? I think that's part of the problem, part of why he's so weak. I mean, I'm not a hundred percent positive but I think to be strong he needs to have an actual pixie queen, a soul mate—"

But I don't want to hear any more. I hang up the phone.

"Everything will be okay," I tell myself in the muted light of my hospital room.

Nurses pitter-patter down the hallways. Someone's TV in another room plays an action movie. There are a lot of gunshots and explosions.

I close my eyes and try to sleep, but all my dreams are about my mother reaching out her arms and me turning away.

Gram brings me home the next day. My mother's flight was canceled, along with 223 other flights along the eastern seaboard. She is trying again today. If nothing works she's going to drive the fourteen hundred miles herself.

"She's trying awful hard," Gram says.

"Yep."

The roads and driveway have been plowed and the trip in her truck isn't too bumpy.

The snow covers everything, glistening, pure.

"It looks beautiful," I say as she turns into the drive. "Did my dad like the snow?"

She nods. "He did. But he liked the warmth more, like you. You two are a lot alike. Always liking it warm. Always having your causes."

"I wrote my first Amnesty letters with him."

"I know."

"You really think we're alike, even though we aren't related?" I reach around my body with my left hand to open the door. It jostles my broken right arm and I cringe.

"Blood isn't always the strongest link," she says, hopping out of the truck. "Let me help you with that door."

She puts her arm around my waist and we hobble through the snow together.

"Did you know my biological father?" I ask her.

"I never met him," she says. "I doubt he'd still be alive if I did."

We make it to the porch and through the door and then she settles me on the couch, fussing the entire time. She makes me chicken noodle soup, which for Gram, the non-cooker, is a really big deal.

Nick smashes through the front door, swinging it so wide that it smashes into the wall by the stairway. He cringes. "Oops."

"It's okay," I say. "It's just a wall."

He has an armload of irises and daisies and tulips and he presents them to me. "I didn't know what kind of flowers you like."

"I like all of them."

"Yeah?"

"Yeah."

He tries to hand them to me, but then remembers the cast. "I'll put them in water."

Betty swoops in the room ridiculously fast and she grabs the flowers out of Nick's hands. "I'll take care of them. You lovebirds just sit on the couch and think swooning things at each other."

"Gram!" I try to scold her but she just laughs and heads to the kitchen. "I love her, but she's embarrassing."

Nick nods and pulls me down onto the couch with him. I nestle into his side.

"It's good to have you home again," he whispers.

"Yeah," I whisper back. I can see Gram bustling around in the kitchen, humming and cutting the ends off of flower stems. "It's funny to think of this as home."

"But you do?" he says, and he seems to be smelling my hair.

"Yeah, I do."

His breath touches my hair. I can feel it there, light but solid. I take in a deep breath and then say, "I've been thinking, and I've got a plan."

He sucks in air. His entire chest moves. "A plan?"

I turn to face Nick so I can study his reaction. His face is calm and still. I say, "To find Jay and the Beardsley boy. To capture the pixie king."

"Well," Betty bustles in. Two tulips dangle from her hands. "Let's hear it."

Nick's out patrolling the edge of the woods and after a half hour or so, Issie and Devyn come over.

"We thought you were a goner," Issie blurts, bouncing up and down. "I am so happy you aren't dead."

"Yeah, I'm still here." I nod. "I called my mom from the hospital yesterday. She didn't answer all my questions, but she promised she would when she got here."

"She's coming?" Devyn asks. He settles his chair by the couch. Issie plops next to him on the floor, looking up at us while we talk.

"She tried to get a flight, but they were all delayed and canceled. So she's driving," I say.

"Do you think that's a good idea?" Devyn asks.

"At first I did . . . now I don't."

"Because . . . ," Issie prompts.

"Because I think she's really the one in danger, not me, at least when it comes to the pixie king guy. I think I'm just the bait."

"The bait," Devyn says, deadpan serious like it's all suddenly making sense.

"Think about it. For almost seventeen years my mom hasn't come back here. Why?"

"It's cold," Devyn says.

"It's creepy," Issie adds.

"That's not good enough. Not with my grandmother here," I explain.

Issie looks around "Where is the ol' grandma?"

"Patrolling around outside," I say. "Okay. Wait. What was my point? Okay. My point is that my mom hasn't come back because she's been afraid to come back. She's been hiding from the pixies. But why?"

"Good question," Nick says, coming in the front door.

"Dude." Issie raises her eyebrows. "You don't even knock anymore, do you? How rude is that?"

"It's not rude. Is it rude?" Nick looks at me as Issie starts giggling and chanting *rude dude, rude dude.*

"Kind of, but I'll forgive you. You're interrupting, though." I pat the couch. He sits next to me. "So, my mom lived with my dad, this were guy, and weres are some of the only things that can fight pixies. But then my dad dies. He dies right when he sees the pixie king outside our window. He dies right when we need him the most."

"That sucks," Issie says.

"Issie . . . ," Devyn warns.

"What? It does." She looks at me. "So, your mom sends you here so Betty can protect you."

"Right," I say, plucking at the string around my finger, "or to get me out of the way because she's afraid the pixie king will use me to get to her. Which he has. She didn't think ahead far enough. She sent me here, right where the pixie guy lives, and then she comes after me here, to this place where he's the most powerful."

Devyn scratches his ear. "What I can't figure out is why the pixies are here in the first place. Why here? Why Bedford?"

Gram opens the door and comes into the living room, a big wet stain on the front of her flannel shirt. We all stop talking.

"Why don't you tell us, Gram," I say.

She pulls off her wool hat. "Tell you what?"

"Why there's so many pixies here."

"They've been up here a while. It's remote."

"Because of the iron?" I ask. "Is it because in cities the buildings are made of steel?"

"There's that. The rest of the world didn't care much when cows disappeared, didn't notice when boys disappeared," she says. "Especially before the Internet and satellite news. The rest of the world is not interested in what happens in a tiny Maine town east of nowhere. But times changed. Even the last time, the pixies had to be more careful. The state newspapers got wind of the boys disappearing."

"Why did the pixies care?" Nick asks.

She leans against the banister of the staircase, not really entering the room. "I don't think the pixie king likes taking the boys. But he has to. It's a need. He can't resist."

"So why don't people just kill him?" I want to know.

"First, not everyone knows about him. Not even all the weres around here know. But there'd just be another one to replace him, and that one might not be quite so troubled by his needs." She gives each of us a focused look. "Do you know what I mean?"

Issie shudders and grabs on to Devyn's arm.

She continues, yanking her fingers through her hair, trying to straighten things out. "The pixie king only maintains control through power. When he's weak he loses control. Some pixies like that Ian or Megan try to take over. To do that, they have to find their own queen."

"So why Zara? Why did Ian want her?" Devyn asks. He leans forward, fingers twitching like he wants to take notes.

"I think it's because she has some pixie genes already. We already know that her mother attracts them and maybe—"

"What do you mean some genes?" Nick interrupts.

"Because of who her father is."

I try to get off the couch, but Nick's hand holds me in place. "Her father is the . . ."

Betty's eyes flash. "You didn't tell them?"

My stomach falls into a broken place, acting just like my arm.

"Her biological father is the pixie king," Betty finishes.

Nick is the first one to react. He jumps up, his mouth wide open. He basically shouts in Betty's face. "You always knew this?"

She nods.

His hands clench into fists. He turns on me. "So Zara's part pixie?"

"I don't know how the genes work, Nick," Betty explains. "It's not like we've done a full genetic rundown on her. She seems normal."

"I seem normal?" I mutter.

"But she's prettier than normal," Issie says.

"And she's a fast runner," Devyn adds.

"But not supernaturally fast," Gram explains as Nick stomps around the room. "Nick Colt, would you just calm down? Steam is coming out your ears."

"Zara's part pixie!" he yells. His eyes flash, full of menace. "She can't be part pixie."

"Are you listening to a thing I'm saying?" Gram asks, and her face is far from happy or patient. "Her father is a pixie. That does not mean that she exhibits any pixie tendencies."

"She's a freaking pixie!" Nick yells. He looks at me like he's never seen me before and he doesn't like what he sees at all. "Jesus!"

He storms across the room and slams the door. It sends shock waves through my heart.

"Nick!" Issie yells, leaping up after him.

"He's such a wolf sometimes." Gram shakes her head. "Leave him be."

The tires of the MINI squeal. Something inside me scrunches up and heavies.

"We have to go after him," Devyn says. "He's dangerous when he's like this. Sometimes he turns."

He starts wheeling across the living room floor. Issie starts after him and then runs back to me. She throws her tiny arms around my shoulder, jostling my broken arm. "It's okay, Zara. Even if you were a hundred percent pixie, you'd still be Zara."

Tears spring out of my eyes. My throat closes up.

"He won't be stubborn forever," she says and then lets go of me, running out the door after Devyn.

Gram and I sit there for a while. I'm on the couch. She's sprawled across the big red chair.

"So much for the plan," I say. I lower my voice to a whisper, "How are we going to catch the king without Devyn and Nick?"

I'm supposed to be the bait. He's supposed to think I'm alone. Then when he brings me outside Betty and Nick will attack. They're at an advantage outside. Devyn will be the lookout. Then we'll force him to tell us where Jay is. We know he's going to come for me because he wants to use me for bait: bait to get my mom back.

"You want to bail?" Gram eyes me. I eye her.

"No. You're tough enough to take down a pixie king all by yourself, aren't you?"

"I'm tough enough to take down an entire army of those damn kings. You okay?" she asks.

I shrug and wipe at my eyes with the back of my good hand.

"I wish someone had told me all this a little earlier," I manage. "Like when I was nine or something."

She strides over and sits on the couch with me. "Ah, c'mon. We've only made a couple hundred mistakes. But you're in charge now. I think things'll get better."

She gives me a tiny fake punch on my thigh and then gives in to the grammy in her and hugs me close. She smells like the forest and wood fires. She smells safe. I lean in and cry.

"You think he'll hate me forever?"

"He's a fool if he does."

I sniff. "That doesn't help."

"You should have seen your father when he found out about your mother," she says. "He was out of his mind."

"So why?"

"Why what?"

"Why'd she do it?"

"She was trying to save the boys."

"Huh?"

"Your mom's a little like Nick. She has a hero complex. She just hides it better. Do you know what turned Nick on to the pixies in the first place? Not that he knew exactly what they were."

I don't answer.

"Well, Devyn was out crashing around the woods, running cross-country, when an arrow hit him, right in the spine. He screamed and fell. It hit him in the perfect place to paralyze him. Nick heard him scream and raced to where he was. He carried him to the road, but neither of them had figured out what it was that did that. It wasn't until you got here and saw the king outside the cafeteria that they all started putting it together."

"Oh my God. What did the police do?"

"They figured it was a hunter going after a coyote. They saw Nick's tracks, but pixies don't leave footprints."

"Yep." I swallow hard. "That's so weird. This is all so weird."

"So, anyway, that's what turned him on to the fact that something was happening. All of a sudden he wanted to be this were knight, protecting the world. He's always out patrolling, every lunch break, every study hall, every cross-country practice. The fact that they've taken two more boys . . . It's killing him."

I nod. "But what about my mom?"

"The only thing that stops the pixie king's need is his queen. He's been too long without her. It's flaring up again."

The fire crackles. We both jump. Jumping is not part of the plan.

"So she had sex with him to get him to stop taking the boys."

Betty just squeezes her arm around my shoulders a little tighter. "Yep."

"Oh my God. So I'm basically the child of a rape?"

"She was willing. She consented."

"Because she had to!"

"She chose to save those boys, Zara. She was brave. Maybe stupid, but brave."

"But now it's starting all over again."

"His need has returned."

I think about it. "When is she going to get here?"

"Tonight. Around seven probably."

"And he wants her back because he needs to turn her, so he can be powerful again." It's not a question, it's just me trying to get the truth into my brain, trying to understand it all.

She doesn't answer, just stands up and says, "I'm going to see what we have for supper."

I slowly move my head. "You want help?"

"Nah, you just sit there and let things settle. You've got a lot to think about."

It's time for the plan. I say my lines really slowly, the lines we planned back at the hospital. "I guess you'd better be getting a call soon, huh?"

She stares back at me. We talk like the house is bugged.

Neither of us know about pixie hearing, but we aren't going to chance it.

"You still think I should go in if I get a call?" she says. She lowers her voice. "I'm not sure if we can just leave you here without Nick close by."

What she means is: can we do the plan without Nick?

"Yeah," I say. "You can. I'll be fine. Everything will be fine."

"I'd rather he came." She shuffles over and kisses the top of my head. "It's good to have my granddaughter back."

"It's good to be back," I say, because it is.

So I sit there. I sit and sit and sit, but I do not think at all about our plan or how Nick's sudden departure makes us down one were. I just remember how it felt to have Nick's lips moving against my lips. I just remember how warm he is.

A couple minutes later my grandmother's beeper goes off. She eyes me, man-strides over, and takes my pulse, which is ridiculous. I broke my arm, not my heart. Then she checks my head for fever. I must pass because she straightens up and crosses her arms in front of her chest.

"They've got a big accident on the way to Acadia. Life Flight might have to fly in. They've called me on," she says really slowly. "I think I have to go. That okay with you?"

"Yep." I grab my *Norton Anthology of British Literature.* I have so much homework to catch up on. I've missed two days of school. It's plausible for me to grab it.

She pulls on the coat that hangs from a peg by the front door. "I've called Nick. He should be here in ten minutes."

"He's coming here? He didn't go all wolf and attack some sheep or something?"

She smiles. "He's a hothead, but he's not a fool."

I don't say anything.

"You're blushing," she teases.

"You are not a nice grandmother."

She opens the door. Cold air bursts in and the fire in the woodstove seems to grow taller. "But you still love me?"

"Of course," I say.

"Good. You take it easy. I'll be back soon, but not too soon, if you know what I mean."

Then she mouths the words, "Stay safe."

She winks and is gone.

Grandmothers.

He arrives about five minutes after Betty leaves.

He knocks on the door, which I know Betty left unlocked so I wouldn't have to get off the couch.

I don't invite him in. He just walks on through. Obviously he's been here before. Obviously he is the one who pretended to be my dad.

He's still wearing the black cloak that he had on when I saw him at the airport in Charleston and outside the cafeteria doors. He is tall and pale, like me. His hair shines dark and wavy and well cut. He has deep eyes that are beautiful, like the trunks of big trees.

I freeze.

"Zara."

He lets my name dangle there. Then, as casual as anything, he shuts the door behind him. The cold air stays in the room. I shiver.

"You're cold? I'll put another log on the fire."

He strides across the room, opens the stove door, and puts another log in. Sparks fly up. He catches one in his hand and crushes it, then lets go. He isn't burned.

I find my voice. "What are you?"

He cocks his head at me and wipes his hands together like he is getting rid of dirt. "You don't know?"

"I have no clue." I am almost telling the truth, because I know the basic facts of what he is, but not the essence. I am far, far away from the essence.

I pull myself up straighter on the couch.

"You saw me at the airport, and I called to you in the woods," he says. "And when your surrogate father died I was there."

"At the window."

He nods.

We let this news settle over us for a minute. Surrogate father? Only father is more like it. "Did you kill him?"

"Of course not."

"Really?"

He fiddles with the fire, tossing an ember back and forth between his palms. It would be cool if it wasn't so freaky.

"You're following me," I finally say. "Why?"

"Because I'm trying to reclaim what's mine."

"I'm not yours."

"You are. You always have been. You always will be."

"That's crap."

"Is it? Look inside yourself, Zara. I think you'll find what's true."

"I don't know what's true anymore. But I know you're starting to sound like a bad ripoff of Darth Vader in an old *Star Wars* movie. And I know you're trying to hurt me."

He shakes his head and listens to the air. "Never."

"Which part? The Darth thing or the hurting thing?"

"Both."

I roll my eyes. I look around for a weapon. There's the fireplace poker, but it's pretty far away. There's the lamp, but can I really do any damage one-handed? I just need to get him outside.

He moves closer, voice smooth. "Why don't you come back with me? I won't hurt you."

"Come back where?"

"My house."

"You have a house?"

"Of course I do."

"Is it a magical faerie house with gingerbread walls and a candy roof? Or maybe Tinker Bell is flitting inside, ready to grant me three wishes."

He cracks a smile. "No. It's a big house in the woods. It's surrounded by a glamour. People don't bother us."

"Glamours hide the truth of you."

"You've been researching."

"A little."

"So, come back with me."

"Why? So you can bait my mom into a rescue?"

"Would that be so bad?"

"Yes."

"Zara." He sighs. The wind bellows outside. "How can I make you understand this? I need your mom. If I don't get her, more boys will die."

"That's ridiculous."

"No, it's just how it is."

I think for a second. "If that's true, then why did Ian try to turn me?"

He loses his composure. His face shifts into something worried, something almost human. "Did he kiss you?"

"Almost. Betty killed him first."

He almost smiles. He pulls his hand through his hair. "Betty is fierce."

"Is that why you stay away when she's here?"

"Not even a pixie wants to tangle with a tiger."

He blows on the ember in his hand. It turns to dust.

"You seem like you could handle almost anything," I say.

"This?" He smirks. "Parlor tricks."

We stare at each other.

"Ian tried to turn you because he knew you would be a powerful queen. A queen with my blood would make him into a king. Ian tried to turn you because he thought I would take you as my own."

"That's disgusting." I move my cast arm onto my lap. The weight of it is heavy.

"I agree."

"Are there lots of them? Renegade pixies like Ian and Megan?"

He nods. "Too many now that I'm weak. They can sense it. They come from all over to try to conquer me, take my territory. We aren't the easiest race."

"Obviously."

"You have a choice here, Zara." He moves his lean frame and sits next to me on the couch. He puts his hand over my good one. His is still hot from the fire, almost burning, and it feels good compared to the coldness of Maine, the coldness of me. "We can go back to my house where I will answer your questions and we will wait for your mother there. Or we can wait here for the wolf boy to show up. One of these things is not a good idea."

"Why is that?" I ask, even though I don't want to.

"Because I have this need. And your wolf? He looks appetizing."

Kinetophobia or Kinesophobia

fear of movement or motion

I agree to go. He smiles, triumphant, like he knew he'd win.

"I'm delighted," he says like a real gentleman, like he didn't just threaten Nick. He guides me out of the house. I shrug off his arm and he laughs, amused. "I won't hurt you, Zara."

"Right. You won't hurt me as long as I'm cooperating," I say as he opens the door. Cold air bursts in. He helps me on with my coat. I can only get one arm in because of the cast. I look out at the nothingness of snow and woods. I look for signs of Betty or Nick. "Are we taking the Subaru?"

"No. We'll run."

Running is not part of my plan. Stopping right here is my plan.

"I'm not actually supposed to run," I try to say. "The arm and everything."

"I'm sorry about your arm."

"Really?"

He swoops me up as if I weigh nothing, leans me against his chest, and carries me the way grooms are supposed to carry brides over thresholds. He is cold now, away from the fire. He smells of mushrooms. "Are you afraid of heights?"

He keeps my good arm against him, and doesn't even jostle my cast arm. It's smooth and quick and I don't have time to protest or even to say anything. Then he flies. Literally.

Over his shoulder a dark shape on all fours emerges from the woods and roars.

Betty's missed us. My heart screeches in my chest.

The trees blur as we smooth-smash past them. They become dark shadowy shapes. He zips over the snow. The wind whips my hair back against his chest. Snow falls, covering our faces, covering us as we fly, faster and faster. This speed is what I always wanted when I was running, this unbelievable quickness. It is amazing and beautiful and I can barely describe it, barely experience it, and then we stop.

Betty will never find me. There's no trail.

He sets me down on the rolling ground in a large clearing in the middle of tall pine trees. My breath whooshes out like I'd been holding it.

"Oh, that was amazing," I say before I realize it.

"You're glowing. I thought you hated me."

"I do. But flying? I don't hate flying. I read this book once where—"

"You read?"

"Yeah."

"Good. I like philosophy myself. It's good to have a daughter who reads."

I swallow, shift my weight on my feet. They won't be able to follow us here; we left no tracks. I can't believe we flew. "Can all pixies fly? Because I was totally unprepared for that. I mean, I didn't read that."

"Only ones with royal blood. You can."

"If I turn pixie."

"Of course." He points at the clearing. "Here is my home."

"The clearing?"

"You don't see the house?"

"No."

His face shifts like I've disappointed him. "There is a glamour surrounding it, but because you're my daughter you should be able to see through it."

"Uh-huh." I shiver. Snowflakes land on his hair, whitening it.

"Humans see what they believe is there, not what actually is. It doesn't take much effort to hide ourselves and our natures from them."

"Oh, thanks. Pixie Lesson 112, right?"

"Sarcastic. You aren't at all like your mother. When she's scared she becomes quiet."

I stop biting my lip. "No, I'm not. I'm not like her at all."

He sighs. "Just try to see what's really there, Zara. Then we'll go inside, out of the cold."

"Fine."

I stare at the clearing and it shifts, shimmers almost. A snowflake lands on my eyelash. I close my eyes as it melts. Then I open them again.

"Crud," I mutter.

I can hear the smile in his voice. "You can see it?"

"I don't know how I missed it."

"The glamour."

The house isn't a house. It's a mansion—huge with large-paned windows on each of its three floors. It's clapboard sided and painted a creamy yellow, like old houses on the Battery in Charleston. Its stately straight lines seem to soar up toward the sky. It's not ostentatious, but it's large, screaming of old money and tea in the parlor and croquet in the backyard.

I turn my head to tell him that but my mouth drops open and my tongue seems to bail on being an active participant in the conversation.

"You see me as I am." He smiles.

His teeth are a little pointy.

But it's not his teeth that get me. It's the fact that his eyes are silver with black pupils. It's the fact that his skin shines like blue ice. It's the fact that he's taller than I thought, wider.

"I don't look like you," I say finally.

"No. You look like your mother."

"I have your hair. My mom always said you abandoned us but that's not how it was, was it?"

"No, she abandoned me." His face shifts into sadness. His eyes seem smaller. Then he looks back at me. "Let's get you inside, out of the cold."

I follow him because I don't know what else I should do. I follow him because I want to keep Nick safe and I'm hoping that my plan is still *the plan* somehow, that somehow they'll follow us here and find me and Jay. I follow him because I want to find out what kind of monster my father is. Yes, it's true. My father.

The large mahogany front door opens for us. He leads me inside to the front hall. One step. Another. It smells of wine and beef and mushrooms. Bright light shines off the marble floors. People line up against the upholstered walls. Most of them wear normal people clothes, but some are in prom-dress-type stuff and tuxes. They bow, one after another, an entire room. There must be a hundred of them. But they aren't people. They're pixies without the glamour. Their teeth are pointed like sharks' teeth. Their skin is tinted blue and their legs are long, longer than normal. My knees shake.

"Our court, the dark court," the king announces. "Please rise."

The pixies stand up straight. I do not know what to do. I give a little wave as all their eyes stare at me, silver pixie eyes.

"We'll meet you in the back ballroom," he says, steering me into a side door. I watch the pixies swarm away before he shuts the door.

"Are those all the pixies there are?" I ask.

"No. Just most of the pixies in this region. The ones that belong to me."

"There's more than one region?"

"Of course."

"Right. Of course." I walk to the window and stare out at the snow.

"I'll leave you here to wait for your mother," he says. "I have preparations to make. Feel free to roam around the house, Zara, but I'm afraid you can't leave."

"So I'm a prisoner."

"A guest."

"Guests can leave," I say. I face him. "I want to see Jay Dahlberg."

He flinches.

"I insist," I say.

"He's upstairs. Two flights. Third door to the right. It's not pretty, Zara. But I can't hide what I am. What I need."

I take in the beautiful curtains, the leather couch, the plushness, the orchids everywhere. "None of this is pretty."

Once he's out the door I count to sixty and then I leave too. I walk up the white marble stairs with the dark red Afghani runner. One flight. Another. I pass pixies who glare at me, pixies who sniff the air. Their movements are too fluid for humans, their eyes too fierce. They look at me like prey. Some touch my arms, my hair, whispering, "Princess. Princess." It's all I can do not to tear out of here screaming. Instead, I just keep moving up and up till I'm on the third floor.

I count the doors to try to focus, to calm my heart, and then it's *the* door, the door that Jay Dahlberg should be behind. It's just a regular door, wooden, with a gold, shiny knob that's engraved with rune-like writing. I wonder how many prisoners are captured behind such ordinary doors. Pulling in a big breath, I turn the knob and open the door.

Jay Dahlberg is on top of the sheets of a large bed, twisted on his side. His arms are full of bite marks and he's only wearing boxers and a ripped-up T-shirt.

"Oh, Jay," I whisper and shut the door.

He doesn't stir as I step quietly across the plush carpet, another oriental, hand woven. Figures. He doesn't move as I touch his arm, right above five slashing marks, where they must have taken his blood. His skin freezes against my fingertips. His skin pales beneath the fluorescent light. His back is carved with slashes and bruises.

"Jay?" I say, touching him a little more. "Jay?"

He moans. His eyelids flicker and open. His lips are cracked but still manage to move. "Hey, you're the new . . ."

"Girl. Yeah, I'm the new girl," I say for him. "I'm going to untie you and get you out of here."

His eyes shock wide open. "You can't. The pixies."

"I know all about the pixies," I say, working on the knots that bind his feet. "I do not give a rat's ass about the pixies. I am getting you out of here."

I start on the knots around his hands, but it's hard with my splint on. I finally get them and ease my good arm around his waist. "Can you stand?"

"Sure," he says, but he wobbles the moment his feet touch the ground. "Sorry."

"You can lean on me. It's okay, but there are a lot of stairs," I say. "We'll take it slow."

We are almost to the door when he stops. "New girl . . ."

"Zara."

It is an effort for him to speak. His body trembles away from my hands even though he needs me to hold him up. "He cut me. He licked my blood. And then they all do. It's like . . . it's like they're sucking your soul away. He could . . . he could do that to you."

"It's fine," I say. "I'll be fine. You are going to be fine. No one is going to hurt you again, okay? Not on my watch. Now, let's just get you out of here."

I open the door and listen. Nothing.

"Wait," I whisper. "Did you see any other guys here?"

He works to move his lips. "No."

"A boy? The Beardsley boy?"

"They said he was dead."

Anger knots inside of me, matching the ache of my broken arm. "I am getting you out of here."

We start down the hall. I think of all the stairs. I think of all the pixies. I do not care.

Noctiphobia
fear of the night

It isn't easy, but we make it down the hall, down one flight of stairs.

"Where are the pixies?" Jay whispers. "They'll suck on us. They'll come."

"I don't know. In the back room, I think. It's okay."

But then we hear voices, reaching up the final flight of stairs. The voices come from the front hall. My heart pains in my chest. This is not part of my plan. She shouldn't be here yet. She's supposed to be here later when everything is over.

"Yes, you got what you want, okay? I'm here." A woman's lilting voice says, shaking, trying to be tough, but not quite making it. Why couldn't she have just told me all this before? Why did she have to lie? Because she wanted to keep me safe, I guess.

"My mom," I whisper to Jay.

"Your mom is here? Why is your mom here?" Jay totters against the banister.

"To save me." I pull him closer, trying to keep him upright.

He struggles to understand. "But you're saving me."

"I know, it's okay. Come on."

We make it halfway down the stairs and I can finally see what's going on. My mom is standing in the middle of the front hall, right on a large white square of granite. Her arms are crossed in front of her chest. The king stands on the black square next to her. The pixies are lined up on the walls again, surrounding them.

"It looks like a giant chess board," Jay whispers.

I haul him down another flight of stairs.

"You have no idea how much I've missed you," the king says.

My mother smirks. She does not say anything.

"You've made me wait a long time."

She rolls her eyes. I thought she only rolled her eyes at me. Jay and I make it down another step. Nobody seems to notice.

Finally she says, "Your pixies attacked our daughter."

"They were renegades. They've been dispatched."

"Yes. By Betty."

He does this giant melodramatic sigh. "I have dispatched the others."

"The others?"

"It was quite the conspiracy. You know I lose my power when I don't have a queen with me. So upstarts who are power hungry take advantage."

I'm not going to let him get away with this so I yell from the stairs, "You killed Brian Beardsley. Look at Jay. He's almost dead."

Everyone turns to look at us, including my mom. Her arms drop.

The pixie king throws his arms out to the sides. "You know I can't help it."

"You could just stop!" I yank Jay down another stair, closer to my mother, closer. She looks at me with panicked eyes. I'd like to hug her, even though I'm so mad at her. I'd like her to know that I forgive her, that I understand what she is trying to do. I focus on him, the king.

"It's in our nature," he says.

"Then change your nature. You don't have to torture. You don't have to kill."

"Then I would die. Then another pixie, perhaps one more cruel, one less enamored of human peculiarities will take my place."

"So?"

Both my parents look at me. Jay wobbles. I balance him.

"People die all the time for the greater good. It's called being a martyr. Plus, you were stalking me, calling me, trying to get me lost in the woods. That is a definite no-no in the Good Father Handbook," I explain, taking one more step and finally I'm on the flat floor. The pixies hiss like wild animals. They inch closer to me, sniffing the air, smelling Jay's blood probably, getting hungry, wanting to suck. The king motions for them to move back. They do, but you can tell they don't want to.

"I wanted you to come to me of your own free will," he says to me. "I wanted you to want to know your father."

"Get this straight, getting someone lost and confused is not having them 'come to you of their own free will.' Plus, you pretended to be my stepdad, which is just pure evil."

My mom leaves her white square, coming to put her arm around me. It feels good. "He did what?"

"I was getting desperate," he explains.

"That's lame. That's a lame excuse," I say, as Jay crumples to the floor. I try to catch him, but I'm too small even though he is light. No pixies even try to break his fall. "And now it's time for us to go. I don't suppose you guys have a wheelchair or anything I could put Jay in."

My mother stiffens next to me. "Zara . . ."

I don't want to look at her face, but I do. I almost double over, the hole inside of me is so big, so huge. "Mom?"

"What else can I do, Zara?"

"And you'll just stay here? With him? The torturer?"

She nods, one slow movement of her head. She keeps her hands on my shoulders.

I stomp my foot like a baby. "That's the craziest thing I've ever heard."

"I know you don't always believe it, but you are the most important thing in the world to me, and I must keep you safe." Her eyes sweep over my cast, take in Jay on the floor, and then she kisses my cheek before turning away from me, turning to him. "You'll let them go. You promise. You'll let them go and never bother them again if I stay here right now?"

He nods. "I promise."

"Mom!"

She pulls me to her one last time. "I'm so sorry, Zara. I thought this wasn't inevitable, but it is. What's my freedom compared to—"

"He'll make you a pixie," I insist. "One of them."

She doesn't answer.

I pull away. "You said inevitable. Nothing is inevitable."

Pixies pry me away. They carry me to the door, take me out into the snow, and drop me there. Two more plop Jay Dahlberg beside me.

"You could have at least given him some clothes!" I yell, but they just go back inside and close the door.

Asthenophobia

fear of fainting or weakness

"Hell," Jay mumbles. "Hell. It's cold."

"Do *not* worry," I say, yanking him up with one hand. He barely makes it. "I have a plan."

We hobble toward the boundary of the woods. I take off my jacket, try to get it on him. It's way too short and small, even though he's so skinny now, but it's something.

"What are we going to do?" He shudders.

His feet are blue and naked.

"We are going to get help," I say as we make it to the woods. I whistle and then I yell. "Gram!"

Nothing.

"Nick!"

Above us an eagle circles. It screeches. Two seconds later they storm out of the woods, a massive white tiger and a wolf, a beautiful brown wolf. They are wild and fierce looking. Gram is beautiful but so . . . so . . . I don't know. She's strong. Her muscles are massive, feral, gorgeous. And Nick? Nick is here. He came back to help, like he said he would before he found out about the whole pixie gene thing.

I raise my hand and smile so big my teeth hurt from the cold.

"Holy . . . Holy . . ." Jay staggers back.

"You're hallucinating," I tell him. "Do not stress."

He passes out, which is only to be expected. I half catch him with my good arm, stagger, and place him gently on the ground.

Both Gram and Nick are growling and angry; teeth bared, ready to kill and ready to spring and tear before they are killed. But I know there are too many pixies in there for them to handle. I know that killing is not cool, no matter how awful people or pixies are.

"I have a better idea," I tell them. "You've got to trust me. We're going to go into phase two of my amended plan. It's amended since Mom came early. I guess it's part plan and part rescue mission. I'll tell you at home, okay?"

The first thing we do is wake Jay up, sort of. We balance him on Gram's back. She will drop him off where someone will find him quickly. I take my jacket so there's nothing tracing him back to me. She leaps off into the woods, and Nick and I head back to my house, where we will call Issie, wait for Gram, and then start the plan. Because I think I have one and it sure as hell better work.

Atychiphobia
fear of failure

Phone service is back up and Devyn calls Issie, and then leaves to bring her over. Gram calls Mrs. Nix, the school secretary.

"She's a bear," Betty explains after she hangs up the phone. "I trust her."

I don't even blink.

Nick stalks around the room, angry, not really looking at me.

Finally I grab him by the arm and say, "What?"

"You went with him."

Something inside me bristles. "He threatened you."

"I can take care of myself, Zara." He yanks his arm away and heads into the kitchen, where Gram is studying the silverware.

"It was part of the plan that I go outside with him," I say. "We talked about it at the hospital. You know that. I was the bait. You and Gram would attack. It almost worked perfectly."

"Only because I came back with Devyn. Only because he saw what direction he took you in."

"We had no choice. We had to get Jay."

Betty holds up a fork. "Do you think there's iron in this?"

I blow her off and shout down Nick. "I found out where they were. Did you ever think of that? Now we can go after them, trap them there."

"How do you propose we do that, genius?" He leans against the counter, crossing his arms in front of his chest.

Gram coughs. "No name calling."

"Yeah," I say. "No name calling, dog breath."

Gram tries not to laugh. She holds up her hands. "I'm going to go wait in the living room while you two lovebirds kill each other."

"We can find the house again by retracing our scent trail, right?"

"It won't last long. Not with the snow," he mutters.

"That's why we're doing this now."

He eyes me and something in his shoulders relaxes. "How do I know? How do I know you aren't in on it? Aren't pixied?"

Gram calls in from the other room, "Because she couldn't wear the iron bracelet, dog."

"Hey. Now who's name calling?" I yell, smiling, before I look back at Nick. He's bending over at the waist like he has a stomach cramp. I reach out to almost touch him, but don't. My voice gentles out, "You okay?"

"I feel stupid," he says really slowly. "Of course you wouldn't be able to wear the bracelet if you were a pixie."

"It's okay," I say, but I'm not sure that it is.

A muscle in his cheek twitches as he storms across the

hardwood floor and into the living room. But at the threshold he turns and says, "I don't want you to take chances, not for me, okay?"

I swallow and try to make a joke of it because I don't know if I can keep holding it together any other way. "Okay, Mr. Lovey Dovey."

They come on snowmobiles. Nick piggybacks Devyn in because he hasn't brought his wheelchair.

"I hope I start healing faster," Devyn says as Nick drops him into the white chair by the door.

"Yeah, I'm sick of carrying you," Nick says, but you can tell he's just bluffing.

"You're already freaking the doctors out," Issie says, sitting on the braided carpet. She leans back against his legs. "You're supposed to be completely paralyzed."

"They'll just call it a miracle," Gram says as Mrs. Nix comes in. She opens her arms. The ladies hug. It's kind of cute. Mrs. Nix blushes when she sees us.

"So, I'm a bear," she explains, eyeing us all. "Wait? Is Issie something?"

"Nope," Issie pouts. "All human. All the time."

"The coolest human ever," Devyn says, reaching down and ruffling her hair.

I take charge. "Okay, Betty's explained what's going on, right?"

Everyone nods. Nick perches on the arm of the couch, and Mrs. Nix sits in the other green chair as I pace across the braided rug.

"So, my theory is that the pixies can't cross iron," I say. "My iron bracelet burned Ian. Plus, it says on the Web site that they hate iron, even stick to rural areas just to avoid it."

Issie asks, "Why iron?"

Devyn goes into full geek mode and answers before I can, "Iron is one of the last elements that is created by stellar nucleosynthesis."

I have no idea what he just said.

Neither does anyone else.

"English, Devyn," Nick commands.

Devyn's exasperation shows in the way he pulls his hand through his hair. "It's really heavy. It's really dense. And its nuclei have these ridiculously high levels of binding energy. It's strong, really strong."

"But why don't pixies like it?" I ask.

Devyn shrugs. "Does it matter?"

Mrs. Nix clears her throat. "That's one part of the folklore that has stayed consistent about pixies. It always says that they can be killed with iron, that they avoid it."

"Well," I say. "Let's hope that's true."

"What's your plan?" Nick asks.

"To make them prisoners," I lock eyes with Nick, and then indicate that I'm thinking about the basement. "We have these big metal railroad ties from train tracks. And some wire. Mrs. Nix, you brought some more with you, right?"

"Right," she says.

"We have duct tape and stainless steel forks," I check them off.

"This is a weird idea, Zara," Devyn says. "I mean . . . yeah. Wow. Forks?"

"It is the best I can come up with." I wipe my hands together, try not to think about my mother trapped in there, try not to think about Jay Dahlberg's wounds, and try not to think about the possible moral implications of what we're about to do. "Everybody set?"

Everybody is set.

"Good," I say. "Let's get going."

"You think this will work, Zara?" Issie asks.

We are hiding behind a tree trunk. We've got a massive stash of barbed wire and railroad ties behind us.

I grab her hand and squeeze it. "I hope so."

She squeezes back. "Me too."

"You don't have to help, you know," I whisper.

"Oh, shut up," she says, blowing warm air onto her hands. "Friends help friends fight pixies."

"Right," I say. "Right."

I glance over at the other trees. Betty is behind one. Devyn and Nick are behind another. Devyn's in eagle form, and Mrs. Nix is a bear. Everyone else seems human. The end of some barbed wire dangles from Devyn's beak.

Mrs. Nix lumbers toward the house. She sniffs the air. Her bear paws pad heavily against the earth. She wiggles her ears forward. That's our signal that no pixies are outside.

Nick gives me the thumbs-up. We haven't talked much about me being the daughter of a pixie. We haven't had time. My mom's more important now. But I'm still afraid of what it might mean for us, for me.

Not important now.

I give the second signal and we go. We sprint toward the house, carrying ties and stabbing them into the earth. One after another, we shove them down. Is and I work together because neither of us are super strong and my arm holds me back. Devyn's yellow beak glistens in the twilight. Wire hangs from it. He wheels the barbed wire around, connecting the ties. We have to hurry before the pixies notice that something is happening.

Issie shoves a tie into the snow. "You're sure there's a house there."

"I swear," I say, laying out another tie. My muscles burn from the weight. "I can see it. I promise."

"Sometimes it sucks being human," Issie says. We both lean in, slamming down another tie.

"No, Is. No, it doesn't."

We hauled all of the iron stuff over here in carts hitched behind snowmobiles that belong to Issie's parents and Mrs. Nix. I didn't realize how heavy the ties were then, but they are. It's adrenalin that keeps us moving. Gram dumps some more. Devyn grabs more barbed wire. His giant wings flap through the air. The circle is almost complete. We only need a few more.

Nick rushes past me, his arms full of ties. He cuts across the front lawn. The front door of the house opens. Mrs. Nix roars out a warning.

I throw down another tie.

"Nick!" I yell. He looks up. "They're coming out!"

A pixie rushes toward Nick. His teeth are fanged and deadly. He lunges for Nick. Nick lashes out with the barbed wire. It hits the pixie in the face. Steam rises from a burn mark on the pixie's skin. He stumbles to the ground, hand to his cheek. Nick stands there, waiting.

"Get back, Nick!" Gram yells.

Nick hesitates. His muscles seem to bunch up and shake. He wants to turn wolf. I know it.

"Now!" Gram orders.

He rushes back toward her, leaping over the wire and tires, outside our almost circle.

More pixies leave the house. They are all dressed up for some sort of party. The velvet and satin gowns flap in the wind. The tuxedos all seem perfectly tailored. They should be beautiful, but I know what they are. They are not beautiful, because beauty is about grace and love and hope. They are all about need.

Mrs. Nix takes the last bit of barbed wire out of Devyn's mouth and wraps it around. The circle is complete.

"Change," Gram orders Nick. "Now."

A railroad tie falls over. I rush to grab it. My hands try to push it deeper into the cold hard earth. It wobbles, pulling at the pressure of the wires, destabilizing the whole thing.

"Gram!" I yell. "A little help here."

She runs to my side. We both force the tie down, using all our body weight to stabilize it. The pixies start chanting, some crazy monotonous words that my head doesn't understand, but my body shudders, chilled and terrified.

Nick appears at my side, wolf again. His hackles raise. He growls, teeth showing. The muscles in his back tense.

I press my hand on his side. "No. Stay outside the circle. With me."

The pixies are still funneling out the door, ignoring the injured one by the steps.

My mother appears at the doorway. She's wearing a long white gown that has way too much lace on it. She starts across the snow, one foot in front of the other. She slips along the side of the house, while the rest come forward, one horrible mass of them.

The circle wobbles. It has to hold. I grab the tie, try to steady it.

The wind blows Issie's hair. Her eyes are all terror. She can see it now, obviously. "Zara, back up."

Then the king strides out. The wind lifts his hair. He glares at us, at his pixies. He knows what we've done. He raises his arms. The chanting becomes louder, evolves into war cries, wild and frenzied, but the pixies themselves are still moving slowly, judging us and the situation, waiting for orders, I think.

"Can you see him?" I ask Nick, as Devyn lands on his outstretched arm. The talons rest on a special glove so they won't cut through the skin.

Nick growls.

Gram says, "They've dropped the glamour. I see them."

"Don't change," I say. "Okay?"

She nods.

The pixie king makes eye contact with Gram. In less than a second he is standing in front of her. He is taller than she is. His eyes have gone silver. Only barbed wire and railroad ties separate them.

"Tiger?" His face shakes with anger. "You . . . you did this."

Gram laughs at him. She laughs at the pixie king like he's nothing. "Naw, I didn't think this up. Your daughter did."

He turns toward me. Zip-flashes in front of me. His eyes are all silver and liquid like the iron we've surrounded him with. "You've trapped us."

The white thread that's been around my finger since my dad

died breaks off and flits in the wind. It crosses the iron bars and he catches it in his hand. He pinches the thread between his fingers, stares at it.

Mrs. Nix's bear form swats a pixie man out of the way. She strolls the inner boundary, growling, creating a diversion.

"Your highness!" one of the pixie women says. Her voice panics in the wind.

"Do not approach the bear," he orders. "Only in groups of five. Surround it."

Mrs. Nix stands on her hind legs. Devyn flies to the roof, a wire hanging from his beak. He attaches it to the chimney. A pixie dangles out a second-story window, trying to snatch him. He misses Devyn and roars.

"The queen, your highness!" the same pixie woman yells.

The king breaks his glare for the tiniest fraction of a second and looks to see what is going on off to his side. This is where my mother is. I know he sees her about to cross the wire circle. I know, but he doesn't do anything. That's when I realize how trapped he really is, trapped by his nature and his role, trapped by his need. Still, he's making a choice, a kind choice.

"Your highness!" the pixie repeats. Her blond hair flies wildly in the wind.

He ignores her, just stares straight into my eyes as Issie helps my mother across the barbed wire. Mrs. Nix leaps after her, back to us, back where it's safer.

Nick thumps his tail against the ground. He and Mrs. Nix guard her, using their bodies as an extra layer of protection.

"You trapped my mother," I say. "I had to get her free."

The king stares at me. I stare back. The coldness of him is immense. Nick comes and presses against my side. I stare at my prisoners. I don't know if this is right or not. I don't know if Amnesty International would approve, or if my dad would approve, but it's all I can think to do.

Another pixie leaps forward, arms open, trying to capture my mother. His tuxedo hits the iron wires first. Then he starts to burn. Three other shrieking pixies pull him back. I grab the tie again, trying to stabilize it from the wiggling.

Nick growls.

The king finally, publicly, notices that my mother is out, free, walking next to Issie, coming closer to me.

He roars, "What have you done?"

I don't answer. My heart beats crazy happy just to see her get across the iron. She's not burned. She's still human.

"Zara." His voice is measured. "I need her to maintain control."

"You don't need to be in control. You're all trapped. So there'll be no more stealing boys, no more shooting arrows in the woods, getting people lost. It's all over." The metal is cold on my fingers.

Devyn grabs more wire, starts another flight. A group of pixies leaps for him, screaming, a wild, chaotic mess. They start clawing at each other, lost in fear and hunger, angry. A pixie in a pink dress shrieks when another wearing a black gown lashes at her, slashing through the skin on her arm.

"Zara?" The king tries to be calm and nice. He tries to look human. It doesn't work. "Do you know what this means? Do you know the power that I'll lose? The need? We will fight in here. We will kill each other."

"I know," I say and my voice shakes as I stare at him, this man who is in my blood, but not me. He is not me. Still, I understand his need, his fear. He is stuck in this awful place where there is no moral way to move forward. "I'm so sorry."

And I am.

I let go of the tie. I turn my back.

He rushes at me. The moment he moves my mother screams, lunging forward. She can't help. She's too far away. His hands curl around my arms and he pulls me closer to him. His hands and arms are burned and blistered from going over the iron. He's still strong, though. My broken arm jostles. My teeth clench. The pain is crazy. Snarls come from my right and left.

"Stay back, Mom." I yank a fork out of my pocket and jab it into the king's leg. He screams and loses his grip, toppling backward.

"Get in there," I demand.

He glares at me. Steam comes from his burning skin.

My mother stands next to me. She's holding a bread knife. "She means it."

He stands up and moves back. His face flinches. "You wouldn't."

"I would do anything for my daughter." She says. Her hand doesn't even shake.

"In the house," I order. "All of you. Now."

They turn and move like ants, streaming back into their nest. He is the last one to go inside. He waits.

I offer him this, "If I can think of something else to do, I'll come back. I promise."

His head barely moves. His voice is a whisper in the cold, bitter wind, but I can still hear it. "Are your promises like your mother's?"

"No," I say. "My promises are like mine."

My mother wraps her arm around my waist. She kisses the side of my head. I'm not sure which of us is trembling more. She doesn't say anything as he shuts the door.

"Okay. Fast," I order. We hurry. Nick turns human again, climbs up to the second and third floor, duct-taping knives and forks to the windows, taping wire across the panes. We do the same thing on the lower floors.

"I hope it holds," Issie says, ripping duct tape off and slapping it on some wire, sticking it to the wall.

"We'll come back every day and check," I say, twisting the wire over a window.

A pixie smashes her face against the glass. She shows her teeth, growling. Nick leaps down, jumps toward the window, snarling, protective but still human. I slap a spoon right where her tongue is. Even though there's glass between us, she leaps away.

Gram and Mrs. Nix finish sealing off the door. Bear paws are like hands. I never knew that.

We all step back and step over the wire. The entire place is full of wire and iron and railroad ties, duct tape and silverware. It looks bizarre, like some sort of Disney house warped by an angry filmmaker.

"Good," I say.

"Good." My mom grabs my hand and walks me back to the snowmobile.

The pixies howl in the distance.

"I can't see it anymore," Issie says.

I can.

"You're too far away from it now," Gram says. "The glamour hides it from humans and shifters."

I can still see it.

A pixie screeches from somewhere inside the house. The woods seem to tumble under the weight of the noise.

Nobody says anything, not even when we get back on the sleds and ride away. Sometimes there are no words. Sometimes you just face your fears and you capture them, locking them away.

Days pass. We struggle through them. My mom and I head out on snowmobiles and stare at the house.

"I can't see it," she says.

"That's because you're actually human," I say.

"If the glamour hiding it is still there, he must still be alive." She shuts off the snowmobile and we just stare. "I can't even see the wire."

I can see it all. It must be that pixie side. It looks ridiculous. A beautiful house circled by railroad ties and barbed wire. Forks and knives and spoons duct taped to windows.

Wind blows some loose snow in swirls around us, tiny snow twisters. I close my eyes against the cold.

"You okay, sweetie? Does your arm hurt?" she asks.

"I'm good," I answer and open my eyes. There's no point trying to shut out the house. I can see it in my dreams.

"It's safe, right?" I ask. "They can't get out."

She nods. "They can't get out. It was a smart idea."

She leans off the snowmobile and grabs some snow in her hands. She balls it up and throws it. The snowball splats against the side of the house. She suddenly looks younger, more powerful, more like she did when my dad was still alive.

"That felt good, even if I couldn't see it hit." She smiles. "Want me to make you one?"

It's crazy how we can change, how even your mother—who

you thought was the wimpiest of all wimps—can pull out a hard-ass stance against a supernatural being. Like even you yourself can be tough.

I reach out my hand for her snowball. "Yeah."

Everyone can be brave, right?

I'm into that. I throw the ball. It smashes into the side of the house, splats, and falls. My mom throws her arm around me for a second and we stand there.

The pixie king stood in my grandmother's living room just a week ago. I'm back at school again, but things are different. My arm is in a cast. I can't run anymore so Issie has roped me into planning the annual Harvest Ball that is on Halloween.

My mom and I don't know if we're going to go back to Charleston. We think we might stay. It's not fair to Devyn and Issie, Mrs. Nix, Gram and Nick to be the only ones to check that the pixies are still trapped in the house.

"I'm so sorry about all of this," she tells me, right before she starts the snowmobile. She tells me this every single day.

And I say what I say every single day, "I know."

My mom drops me off at school. She's commandeered Yoko, which is totally unfair.

"Hurry. You're late."

I rush through the doors as the bell rings and try to get to homeroom, but Nick catches me by the arm and pulls me into the gym supply closet. Soccer balls and nets surround us. The air smells like leather sports equipment and mold and Nick. We have to stand close. I look up into his face. There's stubble on his chin, rough edges to the straight lines of him.

"Jay Dahlberg's doing better," he says. His eyes are dark and sad. "He doesn't remember anything. Devyn's parents say it's his brain's way of protecting him."

I swallow. "That's good."

"Everyone thinks Megan has moved away. Nobody knows what happened—that Betty killed her. And they think that Ian was kidnapped by the same guy who got Jay. His family is out of control, going on CNN, Fox News, everything."

I stare at a scoreboard. There is no score, just blank places where the numbers should be. There's no winners, no losers, nothing.

"Zara?" his voice sounds gruffs. "I'm sorry."

"About what?" I shrug like I have no clue.

"When I freaked about your father."

My eyes meet his eyes.

"You were a jerk," I say.

His hands move to my cheeks. "I'm sorry."

I pull away, but I can only go an inch before I bump into lacrosse sticks, not that I really want to go any farther. "Nope. No way. You do not get to kiss me yet."

He pouts.

"Do you admit that my idea of how to trap the pixies using iron was good?" I say using my best lawyer voice.

"I do."

"Do you admit that you are not the only person, or half-person genetically, that can save other sentient beings?"

He crinkles his nose. "I do."

"And do you admit that you have a bad temper, a cute car, and a nice girlfriend?"

I hold my breath.

"I have an amazing girlfriend," he says. And then he kisses

me, which is, you have to admit, the perfect boyfriend thing to do. The kiss is soft and speckling like star promises in a night sky. I stretch into it, wishing that I could hold onto it forever, even though I know that kisses can't last forever—can they?

But it's not kisses ending that really scares me.

No. The only thing that scares me now is me. The Zara I might become. The Zara I don't ever want to be.

Everybody has fears, right? But how many of us have my fear?

Enough, it seems. Because there's a name for it.

Autophobia
fear of oneself

Acknowledgments

Thanks to Doug Jones and Emily Ciciotte for helping me conquer atychiphobia, by showing me that even when there is failure there is love. Oh the corniness!

Thanks to Betty Morse, Lew Barnard, Rena Morse, Bruce Barnard, Debbie Gelinas, and Alison Jones for showing me that I do not need to have syngenesophobia, the fear of relatives.

Thanks to Michelle Nagler, Caroline Abbey, and the crew at Bloomsbury. There is no word for "fear of publishing houses" and if there was one, it wouldn't apply here, because Bloomsbury is just that great.

Thanks to Andrew Karre for taking a chance on me. You are the fearless one.

Thanks to William Rice, Jennifer Osborn, Devyn Burton, Doris Bunker-Rzasa, Bethany Reynolds-Hughes, Dotty Vachon, Gayle Cambridge, Marcy Phippen, Chris Maselli, Emily Wing Smith, the Pirate Whores, the Schmoozers, the Whirligigs, the Hancock County Dems, and my friends on LJ and Fangs, Fur, Fey. Friends make all your fears seem small and you all do that for me constantly.

And finally, thanks to Edward Necarsulmer, my superhero agent and his amazing helpers Abby Shepard and Cate Martin (who has gone the way of good sidekicks). Edward, you take all my fears and make them your own. That's a big burden and you carry it graciously and well. I owe you. A lot.